LONDON

Blood on the Streets

Garry and Roy Robson

London Large: Blood on the Streets

ISBN 978-0-9934338-0-1 Paperback

ISBN 978-0-9934338-1-8 eBook

Published by London Large Publishing

For more copies of this book, please email: info@londonlarge.com

Cover Designed by Spiffing Covers: http://www.spiffingcovers.com/

LONDON LARGE

Blood on the Streets

Prologue

1

The decisions Harry made within the next few seconds would stay with him for the rest of his life - or result in his immediate death. And he knew it. His brain cells fired faster than the guns that cracked and exploded around him with ever-increasing intensity. Clearly, rapidly he assessed and reassessed the options, his alertness born from the survival instinct that burned deep within him.

It was dark, wet and cold enough to freeze the bollocks off a brass monkey. As the biting wind slashed at Harry's face bullets zipped and zinged all around him like millions of angry wasps on a murder hunt. The soldiers of 2 Para had scarcely slept for six nights and had walked for 24 hours without rest before being plunged headlong into the offensive. They were knackered even before the battle started.

Mortar shells were exploding in every part of the compass; the saturated peat was muffling the sounds of detonating grenades and the air carried news of more casualties as the cries and screams of wounded soldiers drifted across the barren landscape. Dying soldiers disappeared like ghosts in the night as they sank into the peat, returning unceremoniously to the dust and ashes from whence they had come.

Harry had been in some tight spots before but this was a whole new ball game.

He found himself cut off from the rest of the men of 2 Para, in a cudweed-filled gully at the foot of Darwin Hill, with just himself and Private Rifleman Ronnie Ruddock in attendance. They had followed their impetuous commanding officer on a crazy, suicidal charge, and in the ensuing chaos had found themselves isolated from the rest of their unit. Harry liked his commander. He was a brave, decisive leader

3

who liked to mix it with his men in the heat of battle. He now lay dead fifty yards in front of them. Harry and Ronnie had watched in horror as fragments from a mortar shell crashed into him and ripped his torso into crimson pieces.

'Down Ronnie,' Harry had commanded in an instant. Luckily, if being stranded in the midst of a well dug-in and murderous enemy can be considered lucky, they had halted their charge before they had been spotted.

From the briefings the soldiers had received before the battle a couple of things were absolutely, blatantly clear. The enemy had more troops and firepower than intelligence had estimated; reconnaissance had missed a string of entrenched mortar positions to the west of their current position and Her Majesty's Royal Air Force were not going to show up and provide air cover. Basically 2 Para were outnumbered, outgunned and on their own.

Harry assessed the options one last time. Option one - fall back. They would be picked off like pheasants on a country shoot. *Fuck that*, he thought. Option two – stay put and await reinforcements. He knew that was unlikely. He could see a group of 2 Para moving stealthily up from the south but to call out to them would reveal their position. They knew nothing of the mortar positions hidden in the curvature of the landscape, and would soon become sitting ducks. Option 3 – return fire from current position. The mortar positions were too well dug-in; opening fire and staying put would invite a barrage of mortar. This option was as good as suicide.

A couple of zillion minor variations flooded his mind before Harry settled on a plan of action. Option four it was then - full frontal assault.

2

Harry's mind was still buzzing like wildfire as the next steps crystallised. If he was going to get out of this mess alive he needed to do three things. Galvanize Ronnie into action, take control of the nearest mortar position and provide cover for the rest of the unit from it, so they could break through enemy lines and take this poxy hill.

He turned to Ronnie, who was quivering with cold, fear and exhaustion in equal measure. The starless sky was casket black as a scar of dim moonlight broke through and exposed Ronnie's desperate features. He looked wasted, capable of doing nothing more than curling up in a ball and dreaming of home. Harry looked deep into those piercing blue eyes that had always made Ronnie such a hit with the ladies, searching to see what was left of the man, examining, probing.

Harry and Ronnie went back a long way. A strong and enduring friendship forged in the mean streets of Bermondsey in south east London - where they had come of age fighting in gangs and standing toe to toe with football firms from all over the country. Harry searched for a memory Ronnie could cling to and recalled the Battle of Stamford Bridge, 12th February 1977. The time when the two of them had stood side by side in the Shed, the part of Stamford Bridge stadium made famous as the haunt of Chelsea's notorious football hooligans of the 1970s.

Harry, Ronnie and a small band of brothers had taken their life into their hands and, outnumbered 100 to 1, infiltrated that part of the stadium where Chelsea's top boys congregated. That was when Harry first saw Ronnie in action, and understood he was a force to be reckoned with. He'd watched as Ronnie, at the tender age of 15, surrounded by a sea of rabid, lager-fuelled nutters, stood tall as the punches rained down on him like a blizzard of arrows pouring out of the grey, dank London sky.

Harry, of course, had jumped into the fray to help him out. They fought like Lions but were well and truly battered. But the glory! For the glory it was a price worth paying. The story became legendary in their patch. When recounting it Harry loved to tell the part where Ronnie, battered and bruised, never went down, and never submitted to the relentless force of superior numbers. Ronnie loved to tell the part where Harry had dived in to help him out. They loved to big each other up.

Harry looked at Ronnie, fatigued and shell shocked beside him in the gully. Despite the cold he was sweating like a stray cat lost in London's Chinatown. But the eyes told him all he needed to know. Ronnie was down, but he still had plenty of bottle left. Harry made his play.

'Ronnie' he screamed, 'how the fuck you feeling mate?'

Ronnie summoned the strength to talk.

'Shitting my fucking self. Looks to me like we're fucking finished this time H.'

'Right my son, liven yourself right up, now. Here's what's going to happen; we're both getting out of here alive. Remember Stamford Bridge, hundred to one? You didn't bottle it then and you are not going to bottle it now. More importantly my life is in your fucking hands, so buck your fucking ideas up, sharpish.'

Harry was using every possible angle his racing brain could come up with. He knew he was Ronnie's hero, and that it was him Ronnie had just followed on this crazy, suicidal charge, not the Lieutenant. An appeal to their friendship was his best bet.

'The odds are in our favour. There are only four of them in the nearest bunker. Two to one against. We can piss over odds like that. And remember when we signed up, what did we fucking say? If we ever see action we won't fight because it's a job, we'll fight for the fucking glory, just like we've always done.'

Not exactly a Churchillian rhetorical flourish, Harry would later reflect, but it did the job. Ronnie started to sort himself out.

'What's the plan then H?' Ronnie said.

'I don't think those boys know where we are - it's too dark and foggy. They're training their guns the other side of the ridge. The mortar position is 150 yards away. We burst out of the gully, reach the bunker and then bob's your fucking uncle, we have it large with 'em. It's them or us.'

Not much of a fucking plan, thought Ronnie.

'There's a group of 2 Para coming in from the south,' continued Harry. 'They'll see us, see we have them covered. They'll push on and take the hill, save our fucking bacon and win the battle. This is it Ronnie, do or fucking die my son.'

'How the fuck do you know they'll follow us,' said Ronnie. Harry had no real idea how option four was going to pan out.

'Because lions eat hamsters, soppy bollocks,' he said.

H was hard-core, thought Ronnie, full on and as gutsy as they come. If anyone had the qualities, the character, the sheer will to live needed to get out of a situation as hopeless as this it was him. Harry had calculated correctly. Ronnie would follow him anywhere.

'Remember Stamford Bridge,' he screamed.

The boys burst out of the gully. The bitter wind pierced their bodies as their destiny stared them full on in the face. In search of life they went hunting for death.

3

The friends hit the peat faster than Usain Bolt out of the blocks, as mortar fire thundered in their ears. Thirty yards out they saw the scattered arms and legs of their lieutenant. At forty yards out a stray bullet ricocheted off the butt of Ronnie's rifle. Ronnie's guts churned. Inside he was a mess, but intuitively he stayed close to Harry, the only hope he had. Harry, however, was in another place, his senses quickened, his alertness heightened. He was buzzing. He was in control.

After seventy yards the bunker came into clearer view. They moved with speed and stealth and remained unseen, unheard, unknown. *Need to drop at least one of the bastards before we make it to the bunker*, thought Harry. Not yet, not yet.

After a hundred yards Harry raised his rifle, with his heart pounding faster than an exocet missile honing in on its target. Fighting off the dull, aching pain in his legs he took aim at the gunner sitting astride the 120mm mortar, and let off two rounds. The first bullet bounced off the deadly rocket launcher. *Ping*. The second hit the mortar operative in the windpipe. He gargled, fell back, and gasped for the intake of air his bursting lungs would never again experience.

The gunner's mate and the two riflemen bunkered in their foxhole dived for cover as the two angels of death charged relentlessly onward. Ronnie and Harry didn't know it but their luck was in. The bunker boys were conscripts, newly trained and poorly led. Fatally, they hesitated. At a hundred and ten yards out the spooked soldiers had fumbled their rifles into the shooting position. In total they managed to let off just three rounds between them. Two went wide and as the third grazed Harry's earlobe he knew they would make the bunker.

At another time, in another age, Harry would have the deepest sympathy for them. But not here, not now. Harry was choosing to live.

The cacophony of fire from the raging battlefield meant Ronnie and Harry could barely hear each other. But barely was enough.

'Ready son?'

'Ready.'

'Go left,' barked Harry.

The friends launched themselves into the trench with speed and ruthlessness; professional training and instinct took over.

Ronnie thrust his bayonet towards the head of the gunner's mate, who parried and fell back, knocking his head on the mortar, dropping his guard as the pain kicked in. Ronnie seized on the opening. His bayonet pierced the throat of his enemy. A poppy-red deluge sprayed from the wound and Ronnie smelled and tasted the blood of another human being, as his demented face was bathed in a fountain of crimson.

He turned, spitting red and gasping for air. The second of the three soldiers already lay dead. Harry was merciless as he repeatedly smashed the butt of his rifle into the crushed face of the third. As the soldier fell to the dirt, grasping his shattered features, Ronnie completed the rout with a bullet through his midriff. The action was over in less than ten seconds.

The two soldiers took charge of the mortar and opened fire on the other enemy positions dug in along the bend of the hill.

'You're right H, lions do eat fucking hamsters' said Ronnie as the soldiers of 2 Para descended on and overran the remaining mortar positions. Ronnie stared into the distance, relief flooding his body at the realisation he was still alive. The light of the sun was peaking over the horizon. *Every dark night ends in light*, he thought.

But some dark nights have a sting in the tail. The breaking dawn alerted Ronnie to a small movement. Just north of their position a rifle glistened in the emerging sunlight. Ronnie looked on in horror as the situation clarified. Harry was in the direct line of an impending sniper's bullet.

9

No time. No time to warn. No time to think. Ronnie threw himself into the path of his hero and the silent bullet pierced his stomach.

Part 1

1

St. James' Park. A beautiful place for a violent death. Tara and Jemima turned right off the Mall and strolled uneasily into the park, along the narrow footpaths and past the elegant shrubs and flowers to arrive at the picturesque lake that dominates the Queen's Gardens.

It seemed so peaceful, a tranquil oasis at the centre of one the world's great global cities. Today, however, something a little different would be on the menu. Today it would be the setting for a spectacular and colourful pageant the likes of which it had not seen in hundreds of years.

It was a crisp, cold autumn morning as they arrived at a bench opposite Duck Island, in the centre of the lake. The ducks sat huddled together in the middle of their private dwellings, bored and motionless like tourists waiting for the final scene of a three hour Shakespeare play.

Multitudes of international visitors, wrapped warmly in their autumnal coats, were doing what tourists do. Smart phones, tablets and digital cameras snapped and chirped away, recording their slice of olde-worlde history, which would immediately become part of their own personal histories on the cloud, or whatever was the latest term to describe that nebulous mountain of information that people now shared their lives through.

Tara had rung her sister early, the desperation in her voice palpable as she asked for the meeting that would turn out to be the last conversation they would ever have.

The sisters were rich, filthy rich members of the British upper classes - proper posh totty. Tara was the sassier and cleverer of the two, and the sense of superiority of the expensively educated elite rested easily on her shoulders. Her marriage to a wealthy city trader had driven a wedge between her and the rest of her family. They didn't mind the wealth.

The problem was she had fallen in love with an outsider, a self-made millionaire who lacked the blue blood of the aristocracy. Put simply he was from wrong side of town - from south of the river.

'Tara, how delightful. What's it been, two months?' Jemima said when she recognised her sister's voice on the phone.

'I need to talk to you. Privately,' replied Tara.

'My diary's frightfully busy. How about next...'

'No. Now. Today. Let's meet in St James's Park. Please. I need to see you.'

Tara had often played in St James's park as a child and always felt safe and secure in its pleasant, manicured grounds. She now lived in one of the wealthy shires that encircled the capital, and journeyed by train to the terminus at Charing Cross. She took the walk past Trafalgar Square and down The Mall to Buckingham Palace, where Jemima was waiting for her by the imposing metal gates that guarded that great symbol of power and privilege.

'So what's the problem?' Asked Jemima, as they sat down on a bench. She was a sunny, glass-half-full kind of girl who liked her sister and regretted how Tara's marriage had driven them apart. From the distraught tone of their earlier conversation she'd clearly understood that her sister was into something way over her head - like a baby seal cornered by a phalanx of club-wielding fisherman.

'I've stumbled across something awful. I barely know where to begin,' said Tara.

'Well, just start at the beginning and keep going.'

'Oh, Jemima.'

Tears started to roll down her face as she grasped her sister's hand. 'I have such a thing to tell you.'

The rows of silent ducks were still passing their time in carefree oblivion, their stomachs stuffed to the rafters with stale bread.

Two seconds to show time.

14

2

Elemes Aliyev was known for his discreet working methods, at least among the very few people who knew him at all. He moved unnoticed through the world, like a shadow gliding through the air. He had followed Tara, unseen, from her lavishly decorated eight-bedroom home, set in fifteen acres of beautiful garden in Royal Tunbridge Wells.

He boarded the nine thirty train and sat unobtrusively amongst the public. Glancing casually to his left and right he checked out every passenger before nonchalantly picking up a discarded copy of The Guardian. The morning rush hour was over so the train was full of day trippers and exhausted and bored looking wage slaves running late for work.

They hardly noticed him. Discreet. Invisible. Unknown. Just what his employers wanted and had always paid through the nose for.

But this was the man who was about to turn the world upside down. By the end of the day he would be one of the most famous dead people on the planet. Not quite Michael Jackson famous, but not that far behind.

He watched a bead of sweat run down his victim's cheek, sensed her nervousness and relaxed into his paper. What fun he would be having later.

He was in truth a clinical executioner; he'd had plenty of opportunities to complete his mission on the walk to the train station. But something had changed in him just lately. Something profound, something big - a St. Paul-on the-road-to-Damascus kind of change.

The deaths of the last few people he had been paid to kill had all looked like accidents, with the occasional suicide thrown in for good measure. But instead of just doing the day job and collecting the readies he had stalked his victims, watching their habits and foibles and thinking about who they were, what they were like, wondering about the impact of his activities on their loved ones.

It wasn't that he was any less of a blood curdling, psychopathic pleasure killer, but that he had come to get more of a kick out of his activities if he took his time.

But this wasn't the only change. After a lonely life at the margins he had started to crave recognition. He had hung around in the shadows for so long. Why should his art be hidden away in the back streets of Central Asia when he could display his skills in plain view on the streets of London? This once shadowy hitman was no longer immune to the all-pervading celebrity mania of his time: he wanted recognition, of a kind.

When he saw Tara meet up with her sister at the gates of Buckingham Palace his eyes sparkled with delight. Now he had the flavour. Big time. Two for the price of one. Two beautiful English ladies. Buckingham Palace. This was his moment. This was his time.

All ideas of subtlety, of making the whole thing look like an innocent mishap as per instructions, had vanished from his mind as he followed the sisters into the park. He circled the other side of the lake, like a cat, oblivious to the world, before it pounces and rips the bollocks off the pretty Robin at the end of your garden. He prowled past Duck Island and reached the top of the lake.

Tara and Jemima sat down on a bench.

He stalked past the top curve of the lake. His head was in another place. He felt as alive as he had ever felt.

Tara held her sister's hand and began to cry.

He was now closing in on them, on the same side of the lake - the home straight. Still unnoticed, he hid in plain sight, blending into the surroundings like a preying mantis.

3

Aliyev slid stealthily past the throngs of tourists queuing at the overpriced burger stall. The whiff of sizzling beef shot through his nostrils and his blood lust went into overdrive. He strode purposefully towards his victims. In his mind's eye only two people now existed.

He heard Tara muttering something about a big secret as he loomed large over them.

'Hello Tara' he said with a friendly smile, 'Do you want to let me into your little secret?'

Tara looked into his cold, murderous eyes. A chill ran down her spine. Her flesh crawled. Her hair stood on end. She was in no doubt of his intent. But surely not here, in the open, in St James' Park for God's sake? Surely they wouldn't be that stupid. Surely?

She was wrong.

The blade appeared as if from nowhere. The polished steel glistened in the autumn sunlight as it entered the left side of her skull and passed effortlessly through the temple bone and into the cerebrum. Death was instantaneous. The knife sliced upward in a smooth circular motion to split her skull in two, and the flaccid grey matter that holds all our dreams and hopes, our very selves, spilled to the floor.

Aliyev had never been one to waste time. When the moment was at hand efficiency and ruthlessness were his watchwords. No messing about. But this time it had to be different. This time he wanted to put on a show, as he yanked what remained of Tara's head across the back of the bench and slit her throat with the skill and precision of an expert butcher. The knife went swiftly through her Adam's apple as a crimson tide gushed forth.

He glanced around to take in the reactions of his audience. Tourists stared in disbelief, rooted to the spot, unable to comprehend the horror they were witnessing. The ducks quacked loudly and flapped their wings in excitement, as if they had just seen the final scene of some magnificent drama. But this was only Act One. Now he really had the flavour - he was gagging for it.

With terrible intent he moved back twenty yards - which was roughly the range at which he had practised his knife throwing skills thousands of times before, in his previous life in the unregulated circuses of Central Asia. Jemima stared, paralysed by horror, as the steel flew through the air at astonishing speed towards its ordained destination.

The knife plunged into her skull just above the eyes. Another bullseye.

Aliyev stood triumphantly admiring his artwork. Two dead bodies oozing crimson lay entwined on a bench in the Queen's own park. What a day's work. He turned to see the effect on his public as a loud voice screamed from behind him.

'Hands up! ... Hands up now.'

Jack Thornton and Mike Richards were plain clothes members of the Queen's protection unit who secretly patrolled the area outside the Palace. A couple of battle hardened cops who had seen plenty of action in their time. They'd been doing this job three years without incident.

It was better than a desk job: nice bit of fresh air, good money, no hassle. But not today. Today they would have to bite on something that would not be so easy to chew.

'Jesus Christ! Jesus fucking Christ - what the fuck is happening you sick bastard?,' screamed Jack.

Aliyev looked round, unfazed, at the sight of two plain clothes coppers pointing their pistols directly at him, the broad smile still beaming, the eyes still sparkling with delight.

He had learned three golden rules during his life of murdering for fun and profit: move fast, always strike first, be ruthless.

Diving towards the lake, in a single motion he twisted and retrieved his handgun from the inside pocket of his jacket. The first shot of the day in St James' Park smashed through Jack Thornton's skull; the policeman went down like a sack of spuds.

The second shot of the day smashed through Aliyev's rib cage. So did the third, fourth and fifth. The sixth blew a hole in his skull. He was turned into a leaky sieve as holes opened up all over him in rapid succession, ripping through his flesh, shattering his bones, mashing up his internal organs. He was dead before he hit the ground.

Mike Richards surveyed, stunned and disbelieving, the four scattered bodies. The lush green grounds of Her Majesty's Gardens were turning red.

'Fucking hell,' he said.

4

The light pierced H's eyes. Like a corkscrew. Like the corkscrew he had in his hand when he'd slumped onto his bed three or four hours earlier.

Detective Inspector Harry Hawkins, known as 'H' to his dwindling number of friends and multitudes of enemies alike, was stirring in his pit. His head didn't hurt - it never really hurt anymore, as such - but he was bone-tired and his mouth felt like the inside of a Turkish wrestler's jockstrap; he was not a happy bunny. More light flooded the room. Someone had opened the curtains and let in another day. Another day he didn't need.

'Fuck me, Liv, is that really necessary?'

'Your driver will be here in twenty minutes. Breakfast on the table in ten. Liven yourself up, big man.'

H slouched towards the bathroom for his morning routine. The long, sore two minutes relieving himself at the porcelain bowl: check. The quick rinse of the jockstrap and sluice of cold water across the face: check. The shock of seeing the shattered, lined, reddened, eye-pouched mask in the mirror where his face used to be - were there any traces at all left now of the handsome young warrior? - check. The comb-over of the thinning, blasted, straw-like thatch: check.

H was on the move.

Sitting down at the table and craning to kiss his Olivia he became aware, with something like joy, that it must be a Monday morning. The heart-attack-on-a-plate announced it. He was only allowed this once a week now: eggs, sausages, bacon, liver, fried tomatoes, chips and beans, two thick buttered slices, piping hot tea with two sugars. As breakfasts go, this was the absolute dog's bollocks.

Settling to his task and digging in, H reflected fuzzily for a second or two on his good fortune. Olivia. What had he done to deserve a woman like this, at his time of life, with his track record, with his issues? She was his rock, his compass. Unflappable, normal, beautiful Olivia, daughter of the suburbs. He doubted now whether he could face up to the murderous chaos that London was becoming without her.

'More tea, H?'

'Yes please, doll. And put the radio on will you? Might as well see what's happening in the world.'

'H, you don't want to know what's happening in the world, trust me. Eat your breakfast.'

H gave her the look. There was no arguing with the look. Olivia switched the radio on.

'...the gangland war that has pushed London's murder rate to record levels. Just who is in charge of London's streets? Give us a call now with your view of the crisis, on...'

H gave a low, bottomless groan and pushed his plate away. Olivia switched the radio off. She was not one to say 'I told you so.'

'What do you have on today then H?'

'Going to Bermondsey this morning - I need to talk to Confident John. There's bound to be more tit-for-tat bollocks between these Russians and Albanians. Hardly a day goes by now without something. If we don't get on top of this soon...And then the office this afternoon. Some sort of meeting, or "workshop". Complete fucking waste of time. Amisha will know what it is.'

Ping! Olivia checked H's phone. He was not one to pay much attention to it himself.

'Your driver says two minutes.'

5

Amisha Bhanushali hit the bell just as Olivia reached the door and pulled her gaze, as if with some effort, away from her phone. Her outstretched hand was ignored. Another morning ritual.

'H, your driver's here,' Olivia shouted over her shoulder. She always and only referred to Amisha as 'driver.' The high-flying daughter of ambitious Indian immigrants from Gujarat, she strode confidently into the flat. Beautiful, poised and 'posh,' educated at Cambridge and 28, she had been H's partner now for almost a year.

She was the new sort of copper, but she triggered the old sort of jealousy in Olivia.

Amisha entered and headed for the kitchen. 'Morning guv,' she said.

'Morning Ames. Have we got time for a coffee? What's happening?'

'Good or bad news first?'

'Bad.'

'Well, the media's still up in arms. London-as-Syria is a common theme. Law and order in meltdown. That sort of thing. Where are the police, what is to be done? They're calling for someone's head. And you're mentioned by name here and there. My guess is you'll be trending on Twitter by this afternoon.'

H let out his second groan of the morning, like a shattered old dog waiting to be put out of his misery. The 'T' word. Nothing wound him up, or got him down, like this mindless digital mob rule. He didn't know how Twitter worked, but he knew two things: he was clearly accumulating more and more enemies, and he couldn't name or put faces to them. Give him a cornered villain brandishing a crow bar any day. Any fucking day.

'Why? What now?'

Joey Jupiter is all over you again. He's recirculating the 'slag' clip. And this time it's had a lot more views.'

'You mean more people have watched it?'

'Yep. Over 200,000 on Youtube. You'll be famous soon at this rate.'

Six weeks before H had been blissfully unaware of this 'celebrity blogger,' as Amisha called him. Now the 'jumped up, soppy little two-bob wanker,' as H called him, had become his nemesis. And for what?

A few years before, on a bender with a few of his old muckers from the Falklands, someone had filmed H, in full flow, on the subject of his ex-wife. H thought it was just pictures being taken. Next thing he knew he was on Youtube, ranting good humouredly but out of context about 'harridans' and 'slags' and 'ducking stools.' All a bit drunkenly embarrassing, but soon forgotten.

Until six weeks ago, when the clip turned up on Joey Jupiter's blog. 'Is this,' wrote Jupiter, 'really the sort of man we want "protecting" Londoners in the 21st century? How can this dinosaur be expected to treat the female half of the population with any respect?'

And so it began. For the last month H couldn't scratch his arse in public without Jupiter, and his quarter of a million 'followers,' getting on his back. And now, with these Eastern Europeans running riot and turning the streets of the metropolis red with each other's blood, it seemed like Jupiter and his minions were on H-watch twenty four hours a day, blogging-tweeting-texting-messaging for all they were worth about his shortcomings - as a man, and as a detective.

'I'll rip his bollocks off for him if he ever gets round me,' said H.

'I don't doubt it for a second, guv. Will you be saying that at the press conference this afternoon? Shall I feed it through to the PR people?' Amisha asked.

'Turn it in Ames, I'm not in the mood. Finish your coffee.'

Two minutes later they were in the car, H behind the wheel, and heading north out of Eltham towards Bermondsey and their meeting with Confident John Viney. It seemed, for a while, like it was going to be another 'normal' day of fear, loathing, blood, guts and Eastern European corpses.

6

'I don't know why Olivia always calls me your driver. You haven't let me behind the wheel in six months,' Amisha said in mock exasperation.

'I don't need to be driven around just yet, thanks, nor wheeled around in a buggy nor spoon-fed porridge nor have my arse wiped because I've shat my nappy. There's still a little bit of lead left in this old pencil, don't worry about that. Focus on your screens. What's happening? Any good news from Joey Jupiter?' As much as he hated him it was difficult for H to ignore Joey and company.

But Amisha had already tuned out of the conversation, her face now rapt and trancelike in the backlit glow of her phone and tablet, her eyes scanning the never ending streams of information. It seemed to make her happy. It seemed to make them all happy, as far as H could tell. 'Good, that'll keep her quiet' he thought, as he gunned the car towards Bermondsey.

Bermondsey. Last of the old-school London manors, bastion of the world that H - and a good proportion of the villains it was his lot to badger - had come out of. Or so it was always said. Truth was, his old stomping ground was changing, and changing fast. Like everywhere else. A lot of the old faces had melted away. Confident John, though, had stayed put, supporting the few pubs that were left, running his book and keeping his ear close to the ground. He wasn't exactly a grass, but he and H went back a long, long way, and if anyone knew what the Albanian firm which had taken up residence in the area were up to it would be him.

This thing between them and the Russians had driven H closer to the edge than he'd ever been. For years it had been a fairly predictable struggle for control of Soho - drugs, people and sex trafficking, the usual things. But these last couple of weeks the dogs of war had well and truly been let slip, and the bodies had been piling up like they hadn't since...nobody knew when.

These fucking psychopaths and their endless fucking vendettas.

Close to a dozen murders in less than a month, and a queasy panic beginning to grip the city.

H had drawn the short straw on this one and found himself in charge of the investigation. A proper shit sandwich, with all the trimmings. But now he was determined to do a last bit of proper coppering before they put him out to pasture. Get these bastards sorted out...

'Guv,' said Amisha, 'you'd better hold onto your hat. Something big's kicking off...Christ on a bike...the Internet's just exploded!'

'What, what is it?'

'Some sort of bloodbath...in St. James' Park.'

'St. James' Park? For fuck's sake! Quick, turn the radio on.'

How quaint, he's still living in the old world.

'They won't have it yet. It's only just happened. Social media's driving this one. Some tourists have stumbled across a bloodbath. It's a Twitterstorm, #slaughterinthequeenspark. Jesus - look at this! There's bodies everywhere. Guv...you've got to see this.'

H's head was spinning and he found himself short of breath. This was all he needed. The beeping and pinging of Amisha's gadgets was driving him nuts. A bloodbath? Bodies everywhere? In the Queen's own park? Just after breakfast time? Fuck!...we're losing it. Is nothing sacred anymore?

He'd have to hit the ground running on this one, or someone would be having his guts for garters.

Ping! His own phone piped up. He swung the wheel and headed towards Westminster Bridge before he answered it. Confident John would have to wait.

7

H cranked up the siren and put his foot down before taking the call from his guvnor, Chief Inspector Hilary Stone. A smooth operator if ever there was one. It wasn't that long ago that he'd been her boss; before, inevitably, she was promoted above him. It was the first time in his not-so-glittering career that he'd had a female boss. He was still coming to terms with it.

He had a grudging respect for her ability to work a room of superiors and high flyers like a newly elected politician on overdrive. Always neatly dressed, an ability to make other people think they were important and an easy eloquence allowed her to climb the greasy pole in a way H never could, not that he could ever have been bothered.

When they'd first met H had made a play for her during a drunken night out, after cracking a major murder case. Never one to grasp the intricacies of female sexual messaging, he had been sternly rebuffed. Sometime later, over a liquid lunch, Hilary confided that she also preferred the ladies, or, as H put it, 'batted for the other side.' With sexual tension off the agenda their professional relationship kind of worked OK.

'H, what in God's name is going on in the West End? My PA has just shown me a murder scene exploding all over the internet. In St. James's Park. It's not even been called in yet.'

Hilary had always been good under pressure, thought H. Until now.

He often had cause to feel grateful for how good she was at making sure he could get on with the job in his own way, the way she kept the top brass off his back. But since London had started going to hell in a handcart, and with the unsolved murder rate spiralling by the day he'd noticed the cracks appearing in her well-manicured persona. She was starting to feel the pace.

In all the years he'd known her she hadn't sworn and this was the first time he had even heard the 'G' word.

'Already seen it. On my way.'

Something approaching relief came over her. It wasn't his patch, and he had other things to do, but she wanted him there early. He was the best copper on the force at reading a murder scene. She knew his record. No one else was even close to his clear-up rate - even if his methods were considered by some to be unorthodox and outdated.

'H, find out what's happening. Find out who could have done this. St. James Park, broad daylight, tourists everywhere. Please, for God's sake. Get this one sorted.'

Blimey, thought Harry. A second use of the 'G' word and a 'please.' Upstairs must be close to hanging her out to dry.

'I'm on it,' he said.

He ended the call. The beautiful geek to his left had slipped into a parallel universe. Multiple tabs were opening on her tablet and her phone was pinging with a whole host of airborne updates as her co-ordinated eyes and hands moved faster than the wings of a hummingbird on speed.

'I've never seen anything spread this fast. A million hits and it's only been on Twitter for twenty minutes. That's more than the Pope's Christmas message. I'm telling you guv, this is going to go worldwide.'

Different clips and videos were appearing from multiple sources; the tourists of London town had been well and truly entertained. Amisha was piecing the multiple pics and clips together like an electronic jigsaw, trying to work out the timeline of events.

'There's a clip showing this guy firing multiple rounds,' she said, 'looks like he's killed three or four people, including two women slumped on a bench, who are appearing in more and more pictures. Everyone at the scene is taking pictures of them and posting them on Twitter.'

Amisha flashed a picture of the gunman.

'Mike Richards.' said H. 'Solid lad. Worked with him a few years back, at Carter Street nick before it was closed down. He's now part of the Queen's Protection Unit.'

'Ok,' said Amisha. Realising her mistake, she returned to the puzzle, instantly merging with the machines as she assimilated the images and video clips flooding in.

She barely noticed H's expert gear shifts as he veered in and out of the London traffic as fast as a fat kid in a sweet shop. He knew every inch of this town, every rat run and dark alleyway. He kept to the back streets to keep clear of the grinding London traffic, and decided to stay south of the river until he reached Westminster Bridge. The concrete jungle estates of South London passed by in a blur of architectural ugliness. He skirted the Elephant and Castle roundabout and zipped past an estate where a gang of hoodies, huddled under a pissed-stenched stairwell, were crowded around a phone; they were displaying more alertness than he would normally expect. He knew exactly what was animating them.

'Three million hits,' said Amisha, 'the Twitter spike is already fifteen times above the previous record in this timeframe. We're witnessing internet history in the making.'

What the fuck is she on?

H swung the car past the last roundabout before Westminster Bridge, blistering hot wheels smoking and screeching like a banshee on a bender, and put the pedal to the metal. Beneath the bridge a sewage boat chugged past on its way to a sewage dump near Pitsea in Essex, but the shit on board was as nothing compared to the shit that was about to hit the fan when he entered St. James' Park.

'One minute away,' he shouted 'tell me what the fuck's happening, and tell me now.'

8

H and Amisha sped on. Past The Houses of Parliament (*bunch of fucking nonces*), right down Whitehall and past Downing Street, home of the Prime Minister.

Amisha said, 'six million hits. India, Russia, America - millions upon millions.'

'Oh for fuck's sake,' said H. 'I don't give a fuck about Twitter hits or early birds in America. What are all these fucking pictures telling you?'

'Right guv, I think I have it. Two women walk into St. James' Park, one blonde one brunette. There's a blurred picture of them in the background of someone's selfie before the killing starts. From their clothes, or what I can see of them, I'd say late forties or early fifties. They look, shall we say, well bred. I'd speculate they're not the type of women you might usually associate with gangsters.'

In the selfie they are in the process of sitting down so they must have just got to the benches. It's now 10.20 and based on the Twitter comments I'd say this was 20 minutes ago. They are now both dead - here's a pic of what they look like.'

She quickly flashed the picture of the unrecognisable dead bodies of Tara and Jemima, slumped over the bench.

'Fuck me. Then what?' Said H.

'I think they were killed within a few minutes of sitting down. There's a clip of some crazed nutter throwing a knife into the skull of the brunette. The clip reveals the blonde already dead, so assume the same guy killed her first. Weird thing is after the second killing the psycho is bowing like a busker at a street show.'

Amisha showed the clip of Aliyev shaping up like a professional street entertainer as H turned left off of Trafalgar Square and headed down The Mall. Alerted by the

Twitterstorm, flocks of tourists were descending on St James' Park and H had to slow down to navigate the growing crowd.

'Know him?,' Amisha asked.

H had performed surveillance on most of the murderous villains now frequenting London's underworld. He'd looked at enough mug shots in the last few months to last him a lifetime. But this was a new face.

'Never seen the sick bastard before. Look at his fucking boat race. Looks as happy as a nonce who's been given the keys to a nursery. What's next?'

'Your man Mike then turns up with what looks like another plain clothes officer. The psycho busker shoots the other officer. There's a picture of his slumped body. I'm guessing he's dead but that's not certain, and there is no clear shot of his face. Mike then takes out the psycho.'

Amisha showed him another few clips as H pulled to a halt as close as he was now likely to get to the murder scene, given the throngs of people heading in the same direction. He watched with satisfaction as Mike filled the murderer with enough lead to contain a nuclear reaction.

At least that's one less murderous bastard on the streets.

Amisha was about to see H at his best, in his element; taking control of and reading a murder scene. When murder or violence was in the air H went into overdrive. He was made for moments like this. The switch had flipped and H was in the zone.

'Right, let's get this crime scene under control before it gets completely fucked up.'

9

H hit the ground running - almost literally. Amisha had never seen anything like it. His door was open and he was halfway out of it before he switched off the ignition.

This is getting to him.

He headed for the scene, barrelling and barking through the rain like a turbo-charged Mussolini. But there was nothing comic-operatic about his next moves - he was all Anglo Saxon bluntness and deadly earnest.

'Get these people back! Straighten the tape! What is this, open day at Buckingham fucking Palace? Get that lot with the cameras further back. There's dead people here…Jesus wept!'

'Ames,' he continued, barking back at her, 'I need to get to work. Get this sorted out; we've got the Keystone Cops in charge here. Straighten this lot out, for fuck's sake, get this park cleared now.'

'Right you are guv,' said Amisha.

But H had already moved on. Putting the fear of God into all and sundry was one thing. What he needed to do now was merge with the scene, put his senses and his copper's intuition to work. He calmed himself and focused in.

He did not like what he saw.

On the ground, in front of the bench containing the broken bodies of the two women, was the body of the copper, face down, blood still oozing from his head. The texture and colour of the grass around the head reminded him of a cake Olivia had made him a few days before. H moved in, low and slow, and squatted beside the body. He craned his head to try and get a look at the face. The muscles in his stomach and throat responded to what he saw before his conscious awareness did. Clunk. Ugh.

Jesus, fuck…it's Jack Thornton. Jack T. This bastard's killed Jack. Here? On a day like this?

32

H's senses were reeling. The smell of blood was in his nostrils and working its way towards his mouth. The muscles in his face were quivering and he couldn't control them. He stayed put, down low and quiet, and tried to regulate his breathing. Time passed. He didn't know how much.

Another fallen comrade.

'Everything's under control guv, the park is almost cleared...guv?' Amisha's voice snapped him out of it.

'Are you alright down there? Is there anything I can do?'

No response.

'Guv, you need to see this.'

H reared up, inhaling hard and brushing down his trousers. 'See what?'

Amisha pointed towards the body of the assassin. With gestures of hand and arm she motioned him towards the mortal remains of what would now be, for a time at least, the world's most famous murderer.

Aliyev was lying on his back, splayed out like a six year old boy playing war games. The forehead had collapsed inward and what was left of his brain had splattered upwards, out of the head, into a flume of what looked like vomit.

'Now that's what I call putting one in the nut,' said H to no one in particular. 'Good man, Mike. Good man. He always was.'

But it was the lower part of the face that Amisha wanted him to see. The frozen rictus. Of joy. Of warped glee. Of pleasure at having done what he'd done. This was straight out of some insane-circus clown-on-a-killing-spree nightmare.

'This one looks like a proper nutter, guv.'

But H was already looking back, over his shoulder. Worse was coming, and he knew it: it was time to have a look at the women. No way around it. H hated doing this more than anything. Dead men didn't bother him much on the whole; he'd seen scores of them in his time. Many had died in the line of duty and a good proportion of the rest had deserved what they'd got. Good riddance to bad rubbish. But women...all the gender workshops and cultural sensitivity courses he'd been forced to attend over the last few years couldn't prevent his guts churning when it came to this. Swallowing hard, and with his eyes beginning to smart, he moved back towards the bench.

10

'Well bred. Mature.' That had been Amisha's social assessment of the women in question on the basis of the images that flickered on her screens. While they were women. Now they were a tangled mess of flesh and blood, thrown together and washed up onto the bench as if by a massive crimson wave.

At twenty yards out from the bench, H was steadying himself for the worst. He noted, despite the mess, that Amisha had been right: what could still be made out of clothes, shoes and bags looked high-end and designer. These were not the kind of pumped up and bejewelled molls so loved of his new found Slavic and Balkan acquaintances.

Ten yards out, all of his senses were kicking in again. He struggled to retain what composure he'd managed to put together while standing over Agani.

What was happening to him? Was he finally losing it? At five yards out the mess in front of him began to resolve itself. But while he was still unable to make out human facial features, it looked and stank like a bad night at the abattoir.

Amisha would have to be kept away from this.

She's not ready.

H came to a halt, straightened himself up and focused in. He snapped on a fresh pair of gloves. He was going to have to have a poke about in this. One of the women's heads had been all but hacked off and was just about hanging by a combination of backrest and tendon over the back of the bench. And then it happened. Abruptly, without warning, for the first time in years. Just when he didn't need them the Falklands flashbacks returned; torn bodies, blood, guts and splatter all around him, stinking mud, senses reeling. He was not sure now exactly where he was. His heart was trying to burst out of its cage; his ears were throbbing and his eyes were stinging.

His experience kicked in. *Sort yourself out H.* He moved in, again crouching down low.

Look at the other woman first. At least her head's still in one fucking piece.

He put his fingers under her chin and raised her head, gently. Very gently. He felt the knife before he saw it, as it brushed his thigh on the way up. Fuck. With effort he brought her face level with his. The forehead was a dog's dinner, but the knife had done little damage to the face. It was the face of a beautiful woman, strangely calm. H began to choke and struggled to fight back a wave of anguish and pity the like of which he'd not felt since the aftermath of Goose Green, when things had first started to go wobbly. He had a strange feeling he knew her, but his famous speed of thought under pressure was, for once, letting him down. A wedding, a funeral, a photograph of a summer's day half a lifetime ago?

He let the head down as slowly as he'd raised it and set himself back on his haunches.

So pretty. What could she have done to deserve this? What is going on in this fucking city?

He rocked on his haunches; images from old documentaries about mental hospitals flashed across his mind. He was feeling heavy gravity. His body was telling him to lie down. To get down on the ground. To stay there until…

Amisha's voice again snapped him out of it. He stood up and saw that she was bearing down on him fast, about twenty yards out, jabbering big decibels into one of her gadgets. He sent her two hand signals in quick succession: stop; turn around and go back. These he accompanied with the look: no buts.

Now for the lady in waiting.

He moved gingerly around to the back of the bench, taking in the vista of the park, the stalled traffic on the Mall, the throngs of Londoners and tourists flocking to the gates of the park to take a closer look at the reality of what they'd seen in

36

cyber space. He stood for a moment and closed his eyes. Calming himself, he was trying to visualize his approach to the body. Positioned as she was, he'd have to back up, perhaps sit on, the top of the backrest in order to get a proper look at whatever was left above the neck.

H opened his eyes and positioned himself. He looked. And he saw. He saw a face that he knew, and knew well. He couldn't put a name to it, but it was a face from deep in his past that didn't need to be named. His mind stopped, and the world began to spin around him; his body convulsed and he emptied the contents of his stomach onto the blood-soaked grass.

He slumped to the ground. He had seen a face, or what was left of a face. And now it came to him. The face belonged to Tara Ruddock. *Had* belonged to Tara Ruddock. But where was she now, Tara herself, lovely Tara - surely not here, amid these butchered remnants?

And where was he?

In St James' Park, in broad daylight, slumped against a park bench, eyes closed. He heard sounds, but they seemed far away - not part of his world.

'Guv?' he heard. He said nothing. He thought nothing.

11

Amisha had studied long and hard to get where she was. Her parents demanded it, and she'd driven herself with zeal. But who knew that psychology module she'd suffered through as an undergraduate would turn out to be so important?

H had been under pressure, enormous pressure. That was for sure. But she knew him well enough to think it was unlikely that he'd lost it and gone to bits completely. He had not passed over into psychosis; he was probably in a dissociative state, which, in laymen's terms, meant he really wasn't handling the situation very well. He'd had to put the shutters up for a while. She might be able to bring him out of himself. That was her hunch, and her hope.

The first slap across the face he didn't respond to. The second one was harder. A big open-handed bitch slap. He stirred a little and opened his eyes.

'Guv!, Guv!...it's me, Amisha. Look at me. Are you with me H?'

H looked like he was trying to pull it together. To focus.

'Tara...it's Tara. Tara Ruddock,' he mumbled. He was slurring his words. Amisha prayed he hadn't stroked out.

'What's Tara? Who's Tara? Speak to me H,' she said.

'Tara. Ronnie's Tara. Lovely Tara. Tara Ruddock. Tara Fortescue-Smythe. Tara...'

'H!,' said Amisha, shaking his shoulders, 'look at me. Focus. Let's get back to Tara later. Do you know where you are? Do you know my name?'

No answer.

'You've got to snap out of this guv,' Amisha shouted, 'you've got to take hold of things. We can't let people see you like this. Big crowd here now. There's media people here, cameras, the lot. This thing's gone viral, big man.'

The colour returned to H's face. He sat upright, and his eyes met Amisha's for the first time.

'Are you getting this, guv? Are you getting what I'm telling you?,' she asked.

'I need a sharpener, Ames. There's a flask in the motor. Glove compartment.'

Amisha sped off. H got to his feet. He felt a little steadier now. He saw for the first time the phone lying beside what was left of Tara's head. He trousered it without thinking. No way was he going to let the phone's contents go public before he'd had a look. He owed that to Tara. And Ronnie.

Amisha returned two minutes later, breathless, to find H standing, a little woozily, and surveying the scene. She handed him the flask. He took a long slug. And then another. And another. He straightened up and swept back his thatch with both hands. The bright morning was changing as clouds began to congregate.

'Sorry about that Ames. Had to sit down for a bit. Bring me up to speed.'

Amisha decided to start him off on details, to get him focused, and save the worst for last.

'Well, the forensics people are here. They want to get started and I can't hold them off. The scene is secure but there's a lot of people milling about, rubberneckers mostly but a good few professionals now. TV, radio and plenty of freelancers. They're all screaming for a statement, in between snapping and filming and uploading, and…we've got to try and get some control of this guv. Oh, and your mate Joey Jupiter just arrived. Will you say a few words to them?'

'No I fucking will not.'

Amisha was exasperated: 'Guv, you've got to put on a show here. Provide some presence, reassurance…something. This incident is now well and truly viral. It's worldwide. God knows what kinds of spin'll be put on it. We've got to try and control the message, guv. Or the likes of Joey Jupiter will crucify you.'

'Amisha, if you put Joey Jupiter in front of me now I'll ram his rinky-fucking-dink phone so far up his fucking arse he'll have to lasso it out with dental floss.'

Phew, thank God. He's back. The guvnor is back.

'Steady on guv. No need for that. You want to give them more ammo to throw at you? Try and think big picture. Please, for all our sakes.'

Amisha's phone rang. H found it in his hand. It was Hilary.

'Where on God's earth have you been H? What the hell is going on down there? This whole thing's exploding, whatever it is. What are you doing?'

'Guv, I…'

'Shut it, H. Listen. Go now and talk to the media. Face the cameras. Calm and steady messaging, the usual things. Is that clear?'

'Guv, the thing is…'

'Detective Inspector Hawkins, you will go, now, and you will follow my orders, or you will never set foot in this office again. Unless it is to come and clear your desk and empty your locker. The choice is yours.' Click.

Shit, she's in Mary Poppins mode.

He steadied himself on his feet. Amisha touched his arm and motioned him towards the throng. He'd already made out the greaser hair, the massive comedy beard, the huge belt buckle, the pointy shoes…Joey Jupiter and his pals were waiting, like a pack of braying hyenas ready to tuck in to their wounded prey.

12

The big TV company cameras - BBC, ITV, Channel 4, Sky, CNN and the rest - were still setting up on the Mall, two hundred yards from the crime scene. Behind the newly installed perimeter fence barring access to the park itself their anchors were jockeying for position, along with hundreds of phone and tablet wielding observers. Stationed at the front of this heaving mob, nearest to the park, were Joey Jupiter and his entourage.

H and Amisha were closing in on the melee slowly, the big man himself feeling and looking weak, dizzy and unsteady on his feet.

'I'm not up for this, Ames,' said H. 'My mind's a blank. Tara… Tara's dead. Nothing's making sense.'

'Steady, guv. You can do it. Calm and steady, as per your instructions. Keep it simple. Just the usual clichés. Don't get drawn into anything.'

'Oi, Oi,' H heard Jupiter shout, 'looks like Detective Inspector Hawkins has had a few already.'

A gale of gleeful, cynical, smartarsed laughter. The massed ranks of gadgets clicking, pinging, zinging, popping and flashing in the gloom as the darkening clouds scudded overhead. A roar of questions and comments, none of them decipherable. Somebody produced a box for H to stand on. Amisha stationed herself behind him, ready to break his fall should he collapse backwards.

Jupiter forced his way to the front of the frenzied mob and held with both hands onto a crash barrier, unbudgeable as the storm broke around him. This was his time. He could smell H's blood. He went in for the kill.

'Detective Inspector Hawkins, can you tell us what has happened here?' he shouted. 'Is this connected to the wave of killings your force, and you in particular, appear to be unable to control? Who is running London's streets? What reassurance can you give us that you are the man for the job? Are you really fit for purpose Detective Inspector?'

More laughter. More cheers. More jeers. H swayed a little on his box. He was looking at the Union Jack fluttering above Buckingham Palace. It merged in his mind with another, grubbier version of itself, tattered and torn in a field eight thousand miles and thirty two years away. He thought of Ronnie, and he thought of Tara. He could not, would not, meet the gaze of the mob. His eyes began to fill with tears, and his legs began to shake again.

'OK guv, let's just pop you down,' he heard Amisha say. He felt her hand on his arm, and beneath his elbow as she eased him down onto the grass.

A minute later he became aware that they were in the back of a car. Amisha was beside him. She was gawping into a tablet, whispering under her breath, 'Fuck...Fuck... Fuck.'

H came to himself. 'What is it, Ames?' She turned the device so that H could see it. Jupiter had wasted no time. Beneath a picture of a ravaged, distorted version of himself in the grip of a thousand yard stare, he read:

HAS 'H' LOST THE PLOT?

LONDON'S 'TOP COPPER' IN ST JAMES' PARK MELTDOWN

'#harryoutofhisdepth is already trending on Twitter,' Amisha said.

13

Ronnie Ruddock walked into his luxurious five star hotel in uptown New York and punched the UP button. *What a few days*, he thought, as he rode the lift to the penthouse suite with its dramatic views across the New York skyline. He really was on top of the world. From barrow boy on the back streets of South London to The Times rich list.

He popped the cork from the champagne already waiting for him and supped straight from the bottle. He downed the contents, took out a bottle of beer from the mini bar and cracked it open with his teeth. Thirty years of high flying hadn't changed him that much.

It was just after midnight as he stood admiring the bright lights of New York. The vibrant cityscape stretched out before him, teeming with life and pregnant with possibility. He thought of its sublime beauty, the majestic shapes and the individual ambition that had gone into making them. The people on the streets were rushing around like so many manic bees in search of their nectar, looking for action, looking for love, looking for the world's greatest salami on rye. This really was the city that never slept. And he'd made it here - in fact this Englishman in New York had made it every fucking where.

He'd just pulled off one of the biggest fracking deals yet concluded in America. He nonchalantly tossed the signed copy of the contract onto his bed.

He did his best to put the events of the day out of his head but his mind was still racing. He'd been working on this deal for months and to finally put pen to paper had filled him with immense satisfaction. After another couple of beers he started to relax, the elixir of alcohol kicking in, calming his mind as he relinquished the trials and tribulations of the day.

He thought about his wife and kids back home in England. He had been working on this deal for months and had barely had time to talk to them as he burned the midnight oil, poring over every minuscule detail. This was one deal he was not going to lose. Relations with his wife had become a little strained. But now there was some time to heal, to get to know them all again. His tough upbringing had taught him the importance of family sticking together - he was fiercely loyal. He'd make it up to them now. A nice holiday somewhere tropical.

It was 2 am in New York when he decided to call it a night and hit the sack; he was out before his head hit the pillow. It wasn't dreams of business deals and wealth that made him sleep so soundly, but the thought of the holiday he would soon be having with the folks back home.

Brrrr, brrrr

Ronnie was relaxing on a beach in the Bahamas; the kind of beach that in travel agent speak would be described as idyllic, offering a fleeting glimpse of paradise amongst the sea of troubles that come our way in this unforgiving life. He was lying on a sun lounger, without a care in the world, sipping cocktails next to his wife; her mind buried in the latest bestselling Romantic novel.

Brrrr, brrrr

The ringing of the hotel phone in his bedroom was starting to impose itself on his subconscious. It merged into his dream, re-imagined as a bird of paradise singing a sweet overture to the world from one of the palm trees that lined the beach, like a host of celestial angels looking over him, protecting him.

Brrrr, brrrr

The noise was forcing its way brutally into his conscious mind now, more like a pneumatic drill boring into his skull than a bird of paradise. The beach faded into the background as he reluctantly came to terms with the knowledge it was a dream. Only a dream. For a moment he tried to stay there, but it was too late. Ronnie opened his eyes.

Brrrr, Brrrr

He looked at the clock on his bedside table. 6.30 a.m. in good old New York. The deal was all tied up and he had left instructions not to be disturbed.

Who the fuck can that be?

Ronnie reached sleepily for the phone.

'Who is it?'

'Ron, it's H.'

In all the years he had known him, H had never once called him while he was away on business. And in all the years he had known him H had never once sounded so, so...

The adrenalin exploded through his body like a catalyst thrown into a bunch of chemicals. He sat upright, the muscles in his back constricted with tension and expectation. He was having a fight-or-flight moment. But there was nowhere to run, no-one to fight.

'H, what's happened?'

H didn't know what to say. When he'd picked up the phone in Scotland Yard he knew he wouldn't know what to say, but he also knew he had to do it. The news couldn't come from anyone else. He loved Ronnie too much to duck it. His throat tightened. His breathing became sporadic. Short, sharp breaths.

'H, what is it mate?'

H realised all the compassion, sympathy and kindness in the world were not going to make one jot of difference, so he blurted out the three most difficult words he had ever had to say in his life, in the only way he knew how: straight and direct.

'Ron...Tara's dead.'

14

'Cut off heads and dump bodies in Thames.' Vladimir Agapov's instructions to his minions were usually short and to the point. He wasn't a man to waste words.

He took a black comb from the inside pocket of his single-breasted, dark blue bespoke jacket and swept it through his slick black locks, whilst smiling at the two bloodstained Albanian captors on the floor before him.

'You kill us our brothers will come. For you, your mother, your father. Everyone you know will die.'

Agapov knew they spoke the truth, but the war for control of the huge riches available in London's underworld was well underway. The time for mercy was long gone; kill these two or set them free, the Albanians had arrived. The game was on.

Vladimir straightened the jacket that had been crumpled during the beating he had just administered, and admired his thick smooth hair, good looks and muscular body in the full length mirror fixed to the wall. Yes, he knew the Albanians were coming, whatever he did. He rethought his instructions.

'Cut off heads. We will deliver to friends in Bermondsey. Dump headless bodies in Thames for eels to feed.'

He walked, all spritely, up the stairs of the basement and emerged into the bright plush surroundings of his London headquarters, situated in a dead-end alley just off Peter Street in Soho.

Soho, one of the most expensive parts of one of the most expensive cities in the world. Where high life millionaires sat in cafes with low life drug dealers, where tourists from every country on earth descended for the daily round of entertainment. Right at the heart of the capital, where the life was, where the action was, where the money was, the unofficial corporate headquarters of the London sex trade. Agapov loved it.

The private members club owned by his organisation was unknown to most people, accessible by a well policed door. The alleyway was rarely visited by anyone other than early morning refuse collectors and, of course, the wealthy members of this most discreet of clubs. Admission was strictly by invitation only.

Agapov walked into the small bar at the end of the central corridor. A surly group of Russian mobsters sat sipping vodka and laughing with a posse of prostitutes who had arrived early, preparing themselves for the afternoon shift with a few glasses of vodka.

Many types of prostitutes worked for Agapov's organisation. Some plied their trade on the streets at night, some were virtual slaves confined to quarters in grubby, dead end hotels. The clientele of the main establishment required something a bit more high class. These girls were independent, glamorous and educated. At around a thousand quid a pop, he made sure they all knew their claret from their Beaujolais.

Agapov gave the nod to one of his henchmen, who felt the reassuring rush of heat pass through his body as he downed his vodka and slammed the glass down on the marble table. He raised himself from the plush leather sofa and walked across the room, brushing past one of the many pricey exotic sculptures that adorned it.

'Viktor, what time will package arrive for tonight's private party?,' asked Agapov.

Viktor checked his phone: 'Package will arrive in 15 minutes, boss.'

Vladimir spent the next 15 minutes doing the rounds. He checked into the many bedrooms and private function rooms connected to the corridors of the labyrinthine building. All seemed calm and in good order. At the rear of the building, hidden from prying eyes, were the two holding cells where he kept their most exotic contraband, reserved for the extra-special clients.

Viktor reappeared and said, 'Boss, package has arrived.'

Agapov made his way to the back door that led out to the alleyway, which was just wide enough to allow for a medium sized van.

A large, burly man pulled up and jumped out of the front seat. The deep scars hacked out of his cheeks spoke of a life lived on the edge. His deep set, sunken glass eye didn't quite fit, and his one good eye bulged out of its socket. His "don't look at me, don't fuck with me" persona was living proof that humans are scarier than monsters.

Even Agapov was wary of him. They nodded to each other in recognition and then the burly man opened the rear doors of the van and signalled to its contents to get out.

'Fresh merchandise,' he said, as the two young boys clambered from the rear. The drugs they had been doped with did nothing to hide the sadness and despair in their eyes.

Vladimir guessed they were seven or eight years of age before he called them over. He checked out their teeth and hair as if they were show ponies at a country fair.

He said 'Pretty boys. Clients will like. Has doctor checked them?'

'Yes,' said the burly man, 'mint condition.'

'Perfect.'

Agapov nodded goodbye to the burly man and led the two boys through to the padded rooms at the rear.

'Inside.'

The boys followed instructions as if in a dream, now no more than shadows on a cloudy day, pale imitations of what they once were. A henchman locked the doors behind them.

Good business tonight.

15

Basim Dragusha pulled out the drawer of his desk. He sat in a makeshift office in a caravan in the centre of what was known as an official travellers' site, smack bang in the middle of Bermondsey. It seemed an inauspicious place to choose as headquarters for the UK operation of the latest international gangster firm to arrive in London, but it suited Dragusha just fine. It was the perfect base to do business from. His men could come and go unnoticed, and none of the travellers who shared the site - marginal and widely despised as they were - would dare say a word to the authorities.

It wasn't exactly Soho, but that would come in time.

He took a bottle of rakia out of the draw and handed it to his old friend Fatos.

'Here' he said, 'drink.' Fatos Gazjet opened the bottle and took a long slug. He set the bottle down and pressed the damp cloth he was holding firmly to his face. 'Is only flesh wound. Will heal,' he said.

Fatos had been tasked with collecting a shipment of cocaine from Holland, arriving at the port of Harwich, sixty-odd miles north east of London. In the process of what seemed like a routine pick up he had lost three men. One was dead. The other two, as far as he knew, were alive and probably not so well in the hands of the group of lethal killers who had bushwhacked them.

'What happened?' asked Dragusha.

Fatos took another slug and kept the bottle in his right hand. His body was shaking and he was in need of medical attention. He winced slightly as he pressed the wet dishcloth once more onto the wound.

'They already in wait for us. We pick up package from boat as usual. As soon as we left boat Qendrim got bullet through head. Six men surround us. They tossed Qendrim into sea and

49

took Shkodran and Shpend with them. Then cut my face. They give me message for you.'

'What was message?

'They said "tell Dragusha get fuck out of London, or everyone dies". Simples.'

Dragusha stood unfazed and implacable as he processed the news. He rubbed the sides of his thick black moustache and contemplated the situation.

'Shkodran and Shpend are good men. Will say nothing of our plans. By now will probably be dead.'

Dragusha snatched the rakia from Fatos and took a hit. He was angry and disappointed. Angry and disappointed that Fatos had allowed himself to be followed and taken out so easily. Angrier still that he had lost three good men. But he knew how to hold his anger in check and when to use it to devastating effect. He didn't care if revenge was a dish served cold, warm or piping hot, just as long as it was served as a generous portion. His vengeance, when it came, would be something to behold; but now was a time for thinking.

His thoughts were interrupted by a knock on the door. He opened it and surveyed the wider scene before paying attention to the small man who had interrupted him.

The caravan site was shaped like a triangle, surrounded by three major roads. A kind of nowhere place passed by and ignored by the heavy and relentless London traffic that swarmed around it day after day. It had been there now for almost twenty years. The older inhabitants had remained insulated from the surrounding community in a state of ever-present suspicion of the outside world. The outside world had dubbed it 'The Island' and kept its distance, in a similar state of suspicion of its inhabitants. Although some of the children now attended local schools they never, ever brought outsiders back. This secrecy suited Dragusha right down to the ground. A tailor-made community into which the police rarely ventured, a tiny isolated hamlet at the heart of the city: zone 1, ten minutes from the Tower of London.

A group of his enforcers mingled with the travellers, standing in constant guard. He was safe here; it would take a small army to get through to him.

His attention turned to the visitor. A small man with thick milk bottle glasses and a black leather case looked up at him. Dragusha beckoned the doctor in. The Doctor wasn't a real doctor with seven years training and a certificate. In fact he had hardly ever seen the inside of a hospital. But they called him The Doctor anyway: he was the closest thing they had to one.

The Doctor entered to attend to his latest patient. He rinsed through a fresh cloth, cleaned Fatos' face wounds and took out a needle from inside his case. He went about his work meticulously, sewing the wounds with considerable care and skill. Fatos didn't flinch as the stitches were pulled slowly through the tears in his flesh, and the two sides of the open gash reacquainted themselves.

The Doctor enjoyed his work, which was just as well, as lately he'd had plenty of it. 'All done,' he said as he tied and then cut the end of the thread with a pair of scissors. He handed over a small mirror so Fatos could admire the handiwork. The scar on the left side of his face started just under the eye, snaked its way down past his nose and mouth, and came to a halt just by the edge of his jaw bone. He nodded to The Doctor in appreciation of a job well done.

Dragusha handed The Doctor a wedge of twenties, ushered him out of the caravan and returned to Fatos.

'So they want us to get fuck out of London. Who they think they are dealing with? I wonder what next move will be?'

16

He didn't have to wonder for very long. The next move came on top straight away. Dragusha and Fatos threw themselves to the floor of the caravan as the sound of automatic rifle fire peppered everything on the site. The Russians had arrived, and they were not here to party.

Bullets were flying everywhere. It seemed to the populace of this most clandestine of camps like they'd been dropped onto the set of a 1930s B movie, in which a carload of gangsters pulls up and opens fire in a battle for control of the alcohol trade in uptown Chicago. But this was no Hollywood production. This was for real; this was modern London in the here and now and the battle was not for alcohol but for control of drugs, prostitution and the modern slave trade.

Dragusha reached for the handgun in his drawer and peeped over the window above his kitchen sink. As he did so two packages were thrown into the site amidst all the mayhem. He watched as his men dived for cover, fearing the imminent explosion that would blow everything to smithereens. But, as the black van that had transported the bringers of mayhem sped off, an explosion never came.

The calm that comes after the storm enveloped the camp. The screaming stopped. For a moment all was still and silent, as a collective holding of breath united the camp in silence, in expectation of another round of gunfire. But the onslaught was over. The Russians had come to send a message, not to finish the job.

Dragusha left his caravan and looked around to assess the damage.

He picked up the first of the packages. It was still warm and moist as he opened it to reveal the contents. The lifeless eyes of Shpend had been left open and now peered out at him, the crazed stare reflecting the awful moment of terror before death had come to him.

He threw his glance to the other package with a full understanding of its contents.

Both dead. My brothers.

A desolate mother emerged from one of the shoddier caravans with the lifeless form of her young daughter in her arms. Her weeping and wailing reverberated around the camp, the pain and the torment they expressed drawing the crowd together. Dragusha, ever alive to unfolding events, tossed down the heads and took his opportunity.

'Look, look my brothers, my sisters. We try to live our lives in peace. We just want to be left alone to live our lives. We do nothing to harm anyone. And how we get repaid? They attack us. They come to our home. They murder our sons and daughters. Where are police to protect us? No police. Now we protect ourselves, in way of our ancestors.'

As the crowd came together and encircled the grieving mother with her child Dragusha acted quickly. He returned to his caravan and gave his weapon to Fatos.

'Leave site now. Take men and all weapons with you. Police will be here in five minutes. I will call.'

Dragusha was a patient man, always ready to play the long game. At heart he was a strategist who understood the rules of urban warfare and the importance of propaganda - the disintegration of Yugoslavia and the experience of Kosovo had taught him hard lessons. His eyes remained on the bigger prize. He picked up the bottle of rakia, took another slug and relaxed into the narrow sofa, there to reflect calmly on the situation.

His enemies had raised the bar. They were well entrenched in a number of locations across the capital and their small army of gunmen and contacts in high places made them formidable foes. But they had made a tactical error with the scary heads routine that he could exploit both with the British media and the bosses back home, who would be prepared for additional investment in search of the retribution they would be duty bound to pursue. That was the easy part, but it would not get him to where he wanted to be. He knew the Russians had more men, more guns, more of everything. He knew, in the long run, he couldn't defeat them, drive them out of London and take the major prize.

But he wanted in. He wanted a slice of the action that London offered, and everything that went with it. The wealth, the power. He wanted to go large - London large. And that, for now at least, meant plenty. He understood that superior force would only ever negotiate when faced with a force it knew it could not defeat. His enemies, it was clear to him, had become over-confident. Where all those around him saw chaos and mayhem he saw an opportunity.

A wry smile took hold of his face as he heard the sound of multiple sirens getting ever closer. It was a sound he liked. It reassured him things were in motion, and that he was at the centre of events, where he liked to be, where he needed to be. As hordes of police cars encircled the camp and cordoned off the surrounding area he called Fatos: 'Contact all leaders for conference call tomorrow. We make plans. We make them pay.'

17

'Guv,' said Amisha as the car moved on, back to New Scotland Yard for the debrief, 'I feel that Chief Inspector Stone is not going to be a very happy bunny. To say the least. Have you thought about what you're going to say to her?'

'The truth, I suppose,' said H.

'And that is?'

'I've lost my way, Ames. Even before I saw who had been killed I was wobbling. It's just…all got to me. I saw Tara…and then this Jupiter fucker trying to wind me up. I'd just seen the butchered remains of my best friend's wife, and…'

'That's it, guv. We'll just say you were overwhelmed by grief. Even the famous 'H' is human after all. This could even go in your favour.'

'I doubt that, Ames. I doubt that very much.'

The car pulled up; Amisha led H into the lobby through a babbling swarm of journos and happy snappers. She felt like a mother leading her wayward son to the headmaster's office for a major bollocking.

H was lost and disoriented but there was something he had to do. It couldn't wait, and only he could do it.

'Give me five minutes,' he said, as he disappeared to the gents. His hand shook as he searched for the name on his phone and pressed the call icon.

When he returned she saw the tears in his eyes and understood immediately who he had been speaking to. Despite the impending storm, the mayhem and the meltdown he had found the courage and presence of mind to make what must have been the hardest phone call of his life.

Where does character like that come from?

On the way up to the seventh floor in the lift she straightened his tie and brushed his jacket down. She looked him in the eye, and saw with relief that someone was home.

'Ready?'

'As I'll ever be,' said H.

Fuck this for a game of soldiers.

They emerged into a scene of barely controlled chaos. A blur of frenzied activity, of comings and goings, of gadgets buzzing and pinging, of barked commands.

Not much different from that load of bollocks in the park then.

'Not one word, H?' One voice was emerging, loud and clear, from the squall - and silencing it.

'Not one word? Do you have any way at all of explaining what just happened in the park? In the full glare of the global media? With four butchered, mangled bodies still warm and oozing their blood into the ground just out of camera shot? At a time when we are being accused of losing control of the city, and with panic beginning to grip - I mean really grip - the streets? You cannot find one single word of reassurance, of authority, of... '

Amisha had been right; Hilary Stone had already binned H's old arsehole, and was now furiously tearing him a new one in front of colleagues new and old, some of whom he had known for thirty years.

The room fell silent.

'Not like you to be lost for words, Detective Inspector Hawkins. My office. Now.'

It was to be the inner sanctum, then. Stone, H and Amisha in procession, with Graham Miller-Marchant - known variously around the office as 'the drone,' 'the little manbot' and, in H's formulation, 'that utter, utter wanker' - following on.

Stone closed the door behind them. She seemed to have regained something of her composure.

'Talk me through it H. Please, just talk me through it.'

'Um...I lost the plot maam,' said H.

'You lost the plot,' said Stone.

'You. Lost. The. Plot' she repeated, seeming to savour the words. 'And this is what, an explanation? A justification? For failing entirely to discharge your normal duties in the most basic manner?'

H said nothing.

'H,' Stone continued, 'work with me here, please. I need to understand what just happened. We've got you shambling around the park looking like you've just fallen out of an all-nighter at Ronnie Scott's, a crime scene that looks like a chimp's tea party gone wrong and an encounter with the media about which...I'm lost for words. Much like you were.'

H stared into space.

'Maam,' said Amisha, 'perhaps I can shed a little light on the matter.'

'I wish someone would,' said Stone.

'Detective Inspector Hawkins was acting under considerable duress this morning, maam. Two of the victims in the park were known to him; one a former colleague, one an old and close personal friend. I would suggest that this was not a normal crime scene, nor a normal morning's work. I think Inspector Hawkins was, for a time, in shock. Or in a temporary dissociative state, to be more precise.'

'Interesting. Am I correct in understanding that you are now, Ms. Bhanushali, an accredited police psychologist?' Said Miller-Marchant.

At this H stirred. He straightened up and began to move towards Miller-Marchant; his fists were clenched and his jaw was working. Miller-Marchant backed up, until the door of the office left him with nowhere to go.

The speed and ferocity of H's next movement astonished Stone and Amisha alike. How could that bulk be moved with such speed, such precision?

H's hands were around Miller-Marchant's throat, and were forcing him down, down...

'H!,' cried Assistant Commissioner Stone, 'Inspector Hawkins!'

18

While he waited out the five-minute silence imposed by Hilary Stone following the release of his grip on the throat of Miller-Marchant, H mused on his contempt for this man, this opposite of himself. The two had never liked one another. That much was obvious to anyone who'd had to endure two minutes in a room with them.

But it went deeper than that.

H was sitting - he knew this because Olivia had spent years telling him, and even Amisha was now beginning to pipe up - on a seething mass of anger, resentment and frustration 'of volcanic proportions.' Olivia had even tried, back in the days before she really grasped what kind of man he was, to get him into some sort of counselling.

But Harry Hawkins didn't need counselling; he understood very well where his rage came from.

From seeing good friends and comrades blown to pieces in a bleak, windswept shithole. From risking life and limb in the service of his country and getting little thanks for it on his return.

From being the Met's Golden Boy, with an unequalled homicide clear up rate, to yesterday's man in twenty years. Because he wouldn't play by the new rules. But he hadn't changed, the world around him had.

He understood bad men, wanted to prevent them from making good people suffer, and he had an old school moral compass: capture-convict-punish, and punish hard. Force must be met with force. An eye for an eye and a tooth for a tooth. Leopards do not change their spots. Somebody has to wield uncompromising authority, or things will fall apart and the law of the jungle will prevail. That was what he'd learned coming up on the streets of South London.

H remained what the first couple of decades of his life had made him: independent, self-directed and nobody's yes-man. *You can take the boy out of Bermondsey...*As far as he could tell the constant parade of young graduate coppers too scared of villains to be of any actual use on the street was destroying the police force.

His career had bottomed - or ceilinged - out. He was kept on because nobody could deal with villains like he could, and his clear up rate was off the charts, but he was not and would never be part of the new regime. His path up the greasy pole was well and truly blocked. And it was blocked by men like Graham Miller-Marchant.

H loathed Miller-Marchant's smarmy Oxbridge tones and double-barrelled name; he loathed his sharp suit, pointy shoes and immaculate hair; he loathed his phones, his tablets and his Powerpoint presentations; he loathed his team meetings and workshops, conducted in a babbled code that no normal person over forty could understand; he loathed his fast-track rise and his oily 'yes maam' routine; he loathed his ignorance of the street and real people and his habit of bringing in sushi for lunch every other fucking day; he loathed, when it came to it, everything about him.

H snapped out of his reverie and looked across the room at the object of his loathing, still slumped in a heap against the door.

'It's not him you hate, really, guv,' the increasingly bold Amisha had ventured to tell him recently in the car, 'you're projecting your own bad emotions and issues onto him. That's what it's called: projection.'

'Yes, well I'll project him out of a fucking window one day soon if he keeps on... He's doing my nut.'

And here they were, now, in this becalmed room. Himself, Amisha sitting quietly, Miller-Marchant still regulating his breath and trying not to meet H's eye and Hilary Stone, glowering at all and sundry like a school governess from a 1930s film.

'OK, Ladies and gentlemen, are we ready to resume?,' she said, 'There is, you may all remember, the small matter of London burning down around our ears to contend with.'

'I suggest we…'

Bang! The door flew open, no knock. An underling surged in, wildly excited and breathless.

'Excuse me, maam,' he shouted, almost out of control, 'but you need to see this. Something's happened south of the river. Something big.'

19

This time they were not getting it second hand from social media. They had an officer on the ground, streaming images from his experimental lapel camera to the incident room in which they were now huddled. Images of what looked like more bad news.

The call had come in about ten minutes before. Shots fired in Bermondsey, in and around the illegal caravan site known locally as 'The Island.' Not much was clear at the moment, except that shots had been fired into the caravans, apparently from automatic weapons, and that the wire fence around the site had largely caved in.

'Get an armed response unit down there, now,' barked Stone at the room.

'Constable, hang back outside the fence and set up a perimeter, wait until the armed guys arrive. Are there any witnesses?'

'Yes maam. We've got three people saying a black van drove up and smashed through the fence. Whoever was inside threw something out and sprayed the whole place with bullets as they backed out and drove away. They were shouting something, but the eye witnesses didn't recognise the language.'

'That'll be Russian or Albanian I should think, maam,' said H.

But she did not reply. She was sitting now, and holding her head in her hands. H pulled a chair up close to hers.

'Hilary, you alright? he said.

'What now, H? More dead bodies, another bloodbath? When's it going to end? How are we going to stop it?'

These were rhetorical questions, H understood. Her focus was all on the screen, waiting for confirmation that the armed response unit had arrived and for someone to start to tell her what the hell was going on down there. Down there, south of the river.

'Always trouble down there in your patch H,' she said. 'I need you to be straight with me. Are you up to this? I can't send Miller-Marchant down there; they'll have him for breakfast. I'll put him on the St James' thing. We need to find out if they're connected. I want my best man down there. Are you up to it?'

'Only one way to find out,' said H, pulling on his coat.

He motioned to Amisha to follow him.

'Where we off to, guv? Bermondsey?,' she asked.

'Yep, by way of the boozer. This can wait five minutes; whoever's been shot down there's not going anywhere. I could strangle a pint.'

They hit the street and headed for the car. As they were crossing the road Amisha's gadgets exploded, pinging and zinging for all they were worth. She handed her phone for the second time that day to H. It was Hilary again, shouting, and sounding like she was on the verge of losing control.

Welcome to my world.

'H…it's…heads down there. Severed heads wrapped in blankets. They're finding severed heads in blankets.'

20

The kid's lapel camera had not done it justice - seen up close, The Island was an absolute mess. Some of the caravans had practically been demolished, shot to pieces and left hanging in bits, their interiors on display. Like something straight out of a war zone. H had not seen a place so shot up since he'd left the army. Not in his twenty years of coppering in the metropolis.

Fuck me, what sort of weapons are these bastards using?

All was quiet now. The scene was secure, and they knew the tally: two dead and half a dozen injured, most of them inside the caravans. And to top it all off, two heads, each in its own wrapping. On their way now to forensics. Eye witnesses, from both on and off the site, were being gathered at the local nick. Interpreters had been called for to help with the former, but H knew that would lead nowhere: they would all play mute.

'Well, there's not much we can do here for the minute, Ames. Let's go and see if Confident John can help us start to pick the bones out of this fucking mess.'

'Guv, you've never really told me why you insist on calling him "Confident John" all the time,' Amisha asked in the car. 'That's not what it says on his birth certificate, is it?'

'Because that's his name Ames. Has been for years. When I was a kid there were a lot of Johns about round here. As we got older we had to find ways of distinguishing them. So we had John the Plumber, John the Mechanic, Postman John, Sex-Case John, John the Scaffold Murderer, and Confident John. Actually he was called Shy Nervous John for a long time, but then in his thirties he fell in love with a bird and changed. Became more confident.'

They found the man himself plotted up at the bar in the Crown and Anchor, studying the racing form in his paper. His usual pitch, this time of the day.

'What's happening, John?,' said H, patting him on the back.

'Hello H. Long time no see. I wondered how long it'd take you to get down here. What you drinking?'

'I'll have a large scotch. She'll have orange juice,' said H, motioning to Amisha with a nod of his head. 'We'll be over at the corner table.'

Settling down into her chair, Amisha realised how she'd come to love these sessions. It was like being an anthropologist, getting to know some exotic tribe. These guys had their own history, their own way of behaving, their own way of understanding the world, their own language. It was the language she really liked, and she'd noticed lately that it was beginning to rub off on her.

'Mark my card for me, John. What the fuck is going on here? What was that turnout at The Island all about?' asked H.

'Give me a chance, mate, it's only just happened. Obviously someone's had a pop at the Albanians on the site. You've got two choices, basically. It's either the Russians, part of the bigger thing that's been going on, or another Albanian firm. One of their vendettas.'

'Which would you put your money on?'

'Neither H, at this stage. The thing is, these Balkan Mafioso always keep schtum. You never get a dickie bird out of them. Not that they speak a lot of English. They keep themselves to themselves. They're violent, ruthless. And they're tooled-up to fuck. This is all way past sawn-off shotguns, mate.'

H sighed, heavily. 'Tell me something I don't know, John.'

'What you don't know, H, is that this bollocks is only just getting started. Whatever that was about this afternoon, they'll have to meet fire with fire. If it was the Russians we'll wind up in the middle of a full scale war. If it was another Albanian firm it'll be part of a vendetta, which is almost as good as a war. Those fucking things never end. The fun and games we've had so far are going to look like a fucking vicar's tea party by the time this lot have finished.'

H fell silent. The enormity of what he was going to have to keep on dealing with was beginning to crush him again. He was under heavy gravity, as he had been earlier in the park, and felt like getting his head down then and there.

'Time to head home, guv? It's been a long day,' said Amisha.

Good girl.

'Yeah, get me out of here Ames. Thanks John. Keep 'em peeled.'

'Will do, H.'

It was almost dark outside now. And raining. And their car was gone.

21

As Amisha pulled out her phone to call for cabs, H hung his head and let out one of his deep, long, slow groans.

'How much worse is today going to get?' he said, as if to himself.

I can't take much more of this. I've had enough.

'Come on, guv, it's only a car. We've got others. Your cab will be here in a jiff. We've got bigger fish to fry. If Confident, No-Longer-Shy-And-Nervous John is right we're going to have a full-scale war on our hands before much longer.'

'I'm not worried about the car, Ames. Whatever little fuckwit has had that away can keep it. It's the phone. We've lost the fucking phone. I left in in the glove compartment. The phone.'

'It's not like you to worry about phones, guv. I thought you hated them? I've listened to more of your rants about "fucking phones:" this and "fucking tablets that" than I've had hot dinners.' Amisha, clearly, was beginning to go native with the lingo.

He's going to pieces. Little things are starting to fry his brain.

'Listen to me, Ames. It was Tara's phone. I picked up Tara's phone. This morning. In the park.'

Silence. Amisha was taking her time to process this one. It was a blinder, even by H's standards.

She cleared her throat and took a breath.

'So, guv, let me see if I'm getting this right. You're telling me that you have removed a vital item of evidence from a crime scene - the scene of a murder - and have kept it in your possession?'

'Ames, listen. Tara Ruddock is…was… the wife of the very best friend I've ever had. A man who was prepared to lay down his life to save mine. A man I grew up with, round here, and have known all my life. He's about the only person in this world I trust. Really trust. What was I supposed to do? I wasn't thinking straight this morning Ames, you know that. But I'd do it again. Whatever it was that Tara got herself into…is something that I don't want the world and his wife to know before I do. I need to protect them…him. Loyalty, Ames. It's called loyalty.'

Another pause.

'I see,' said Amisha. 'And what is to be my part in all this?'

'No part. Go to Hilary and put her in the picture. I've dragged you into some old-school bollocks here, Ames, and I'm sorry. Protect your career. You're going to be a top notch copper one day. Go to Hilary, get yourself clear of this. I'm tired…I'm going home.'

Two cabs pulled up at the top of the street and the pair moved towards them.

'Have a good night's rest, guv, we'll sort this out in the morning,' she said.

'Go to Hilary, Ames. Set the record straight. Do the right thing.'

'Fuck Hilary,' Amisha said. 'We've got to get that fucking phone back. God alone knows what it might be able to tell us.'

22

They walked towards their cabs. The rain fell in sheets. Amisha didn't know it yet but her attempt to calm H's inner demons was about to be blown off course as his fragile composure came under renewed fire when he heard the ringtone, the ringtone that told him his ex-wife was on the other end of the line. It was a sound out of time, a ringtone he wasn't sure he would ever hear again.

Time slowed into small chunks, like a film moving at one frame per second, as H considered the name emblazoned across the screen of his mobile. The last time he'd upgraded his phone he thought about removing her number but he'd kept it in case she ever needed to talk to him about one of the kids. It had been a long time since they had last talked, or rather screamed at each other outside the court after completion of the final divorce proceedings.

'Fuck you and fuck your prick of a boyfriend,' had been the last words he'd said to her.

Julie and H had met at school. As a young girl Julie loved to read stories of princesses trapped in towers, of chivalry and knights in shining armour. When they had first met it seemed as if she had found the man she had been looking for since she'd heard her first fairytale. He was strong, full of life and ambition, and his wry sense of humour made her laugh. They had met young, married young, as in a true love story that never ends.

H had done his best to put Julie out of his mind - but every now and again his subconscious forced her back to the foreground of it. He still regularly recalled the moment they first met. The young, striking blond with the winning smile and bubbly personality, laughing with carefree abandon at his childish jokes and youthful pranks. So beautiful, so genuine, so perfect. How he had once loved her.

What does she fucking want?

Amisha noticed his facial expressions distort with a peculiar mixture of anger and puzzlement, and the muscles in his back constrict and contort, whilst he considered whether to accept or decline the call. He pressed the accept icon.

'What's wrong?' he said.

It was painful for Julie to hear his voice again. She knew he knew this wasn't a social call so dispensed with the social niceties.

'Little Ronnie's in trouble.'

When one of the proudest moments of his life had arrived there was only ever one name he was going to give to his first-born son. He'd dubbed him Little Ronnie to distinguish him from the other Ronnie, and it had been a tag that Ronnie Hawkins had to live with. As a boy he'd enjoyed it, loved it to bits in fact. Being named after the great Ronnie Ruddock, as his father always referred to his friend, had been an honour, and he always listened attentively when his father told him about Ronnie's meteoric rise to riches. But he'd enjoyed much more the few occasions, after H had had a few too many down the local boozer, when his father opened up and told him some tales from the old days. He'd loved the stories of Ronnie and his dad growing up in Bermondsey, the skirmishes and brawls they had got into, the tight spots they had, more with luck than judgement, managed to worm their way out of. How they had finally 'grown up' when they made their pact to join the army and fight for Queen and Country.

'Better to believe in something' H had schooled him, 'than waste your life rucking on the streets of London.' Once or twice Little Ronnie had asked his father about his time in the Falklands, but on each occasion he had got the look. H never spoke to him about his days in the army.

Little Ronnie himself had been a good kid. Not the brightest kid on the block, for sure, but he'd always had a good attitude and worked hard to make his father proud. Until the divorce. The divorce had ruined everything. H had only seen Ronnie a couple of times in the last few years. Neither time had gone very well.

'What kind of trouble?'

Julie gave it to him straight:

'Serious trouble, he's been arrested for smuggling heroin into the country.'

Amisha couldn't hear the words and watched on helplessly as H convulsed and his face drained of blood.

If his son had been involved in a few youthful skirmishes, no problem. After all H had not exactly been a paragon of virtue in his early years. But heroin smuggling was different. H had witnessed first-hand lives destroyed, talent wasted, families ripped to shreds under the influence of hard drugs. He hated them and he hated the people who dealt them. In H's world view the heroin trade was evil: no ifs, no buts, and no shades of grey. He'd put so many dealers away during his spell in narcotics that he'd lost count. H hated the bastards. He was known for it.

But Ronnie was his son, and for H blood was thicker than a euphoria inducing drug.

'Where is he?'

'Being held at Peckham police station. I'm here now.'

'On my way,' said H.

Peckham nick had been re-built in 1990s; it was south London's Fort Apache: the four feet thick concrete walls were reinforced with steel and built to withstand rioting and terrorist attack.

H jumped into the cab and ordered Amisha in beside him.

'Where are we going guv?' She asked.

'Peckham nick,' said H.

23

H burst into the police station, flashed his police badge at the constable on the entry desk and demanded to see Ronnie Hawkins immediately.

Police Constable Tony Jarrow was a new recruit, unsure of the limits of his authority, unaware of who H was and unsure of how he should deal with the force of nature that had just confronted him.

'I'm not authorised to allow...'

'Don't fuck about with me son, I'm not in the mood. Now go and get duty sergeant in charge before I ...'

The door immediately behind the reception desk opened and Sergeant Bobby Venables walked out. He was a solid man, who respected the authority of the force and the power of his superiors, who believed in the chain of command and stuck to protocols. He was never going to be a spectacular success and in H's eyes he was a plodder, but like all organisations the force needed its share of plodders and as far as H was concerned he was ok.

'Bobby, what the fuck is happening with my boy?'

It might not be strictly protocol to allow a Detective Inspector direct access to his newly arrested son but, as a plodder, Bobby understood when the unwritten protocols of the police should prevail. And he knew what H was capable of.

'H. We've been expecting you. This way,' he said.

H followed Venables into the heart of the police station. It was now late and most of the lights were out. Only a few officers were at work, poring over their computers in the corner of the poorly lit open plan office. The moon shone through the rain and the windows, its light side throwing a soft radiance onto the numerous paper files still used by the Metropolitan Police, as if trying to reveal the details of the myriad secrets within them. But it was H's dark side that was in ascendance as he followed his guide down a stairway to the subterranean cells and interview rooms on the lower floors.

'Bobby, who's in charge of the case? It's no random pick up if they've got him banged up in Peckham. How long has the case been running? How long has my boy been in the frame? Why didn't anyone fucking tell me about this?'

Venables just had time to tell him that all he knew was that Inspector Marshall was in overall control before they entered a seating area outside a series of interview rooms. Julie and her husband Justin Evergreen sat holding hands.

Justin's and H's eyes met and Justin hurriedly averted his gaze.

Prick.

H looked at Julie and Julie looked at H.

A few more wrinkles had appeared on her face since last they met. Slowly, ever so slowly, her beauty was fading. But the contours of those luscious lips, the bright green eyes and the beautifully soft long blonde hair were still intact. H's heart rate quickened.

The worry frowns had deepened considerably on his forehead, a new scar had appeared below his left ear and the thatch of hair on his head now looked faintly ridiculous. But she sensed the same old H still lived inside, the same aura that had enveloped him in the last years of their marriage still hung on him, followed him like a dark cloud, ever ready to pour its contents and unleash its remorseless thunder and lightning onto the world.

It was not long after the Falklands, she recalled, that the flashbacks and changes really kicked in. She thought it was temporary, at first, but then it gradually got worse.

She remembered the defining moment. He had arranged a weekend trip to Manchester to meet up with some of his old 2 Para muckers. He'd arrived eager and fully prepared for a nice two-day bender but had instead found Bobby Swan, their host, swinging from a rope in his front room. When he returned the change was complete. She knew she had lost him. The anger, the drinking, the inability to compromise all increased. She tried to love him, to comfort him, but he had pushed her away. She blamed him for killing their love.

Partly in desperation, and because she needed more from life, she had enrolled in an adult education centre to study sociology at evening classes. Justin could hardly believe his luck when the gorgeous blonde walked into his class, looking sad and insecure, like a child at her first day in school.

For her, Justin was everything H was not, and that was exactly what she needed. Talking to a man who was open about his feelings was a new experience; there were not many of those in the south London she knew. She didn't love Justin, not in the way she had loved H. She knew she never would. But she liked him, she liked him just fine and that was enough. That was the best she could hope for, as she stoically pulled her life back together.

The only time H and Justin had previously met was at the divorce hearing and only Ronnie's presence had prevented a bloodbath.

'How could she leave me for that prick, that complete and utter prick,' H had said to Ronnie after the hearing. Many other people who knew them wondered why it had taken her so long.

For a moment an awkward silence reigned as the three protagonists stood rooted to their respective spots in the triangle of love and loathing. Amisha, who had been following H as unobtrusively as she could, did not need to lean too heavily on her detective's instincts to realise H was in the presence of his ex-wife. He had mentioned her once or twice but mostly avoided talking about her. As he mostly avoided talking about any part of his personal life.

'Where is he?' Said H.

Julie said, 'Not sure, Inspector Marshall won't allow us access.'

As if on cue Marshall entered the waiting area. He was another of the university recruits, fast tracked into his position, a highly motivated moderniser determined to make a successful career. H looked him up and down; he did not much like what he saw. Shoes shiny enough to see his face in, tie knotted and arranged to perfection. A good crop of neatly cut black hair sat atop a soft-featured, pleasant face.

Looks like a fucking newsreader.

'Chief Inspector Hawkins, can I point out it is highly irregular for you to be here and ...'

'Room number?'

'Your son is in interview room four but I'm afraid I cannot allow...'

H shoved Marshall out of the way and barrelled on to see his boy.

'Same old H,' Julie whispered to Justin.

24

Little Ronnie was hunched over the white table that adorned the otherwise bare surroundings when H entered the room.

Ronnie turned to see who had entered the cell. Father and son looked at one another. H tried unsuccessfully to hide the disappointment in his face. Ronnie tried desperately to subdue the sense of guilt, the shame and the anger that surrounded and trapped him.

'So what the fuck is this all this about?' Said H.

Little Ronnie looked his father in the eye for a brief moment. His shame was vying for supremacy with the anger for the man who had let him down, the so called hero who had disappeared when he needed him.

'What's it to you?'

'Ronnie son, this is serious. This is heroin. You could go down for years.'

'As if you could give a fuck.'

'What do you mean? Do you understand the depth of trouble you're in? I'm... your father.'

The anger in Ronnie's heart was turning to contempt; bitterness framed his response.

'So where the fuck you been all these years?'

Ronnie's words were razors, slicing through H's heart, the heart in his body and the heart of his belief system in the strength and unity of family - a belief system that had collapsed around him like a deck of cards in a gale. They hurt far more than any beating he had taken in the line of duty.

They left him momentarily speechless. He didn't want to get into a blame game about the breakup of his marriage.

'The past is the past. It's complicated.'

'Too complicated to ring. Too complicated to pick up a fucking phone and press call. What the fuck happened to you Dad?'

H simply wasn't equipped to deal with this line of conversation.

'But son, why heroin? Of all the things in this fucking world to get into. Heroin smuggling. Please tell me it was a plant; something, anything we can use to get you out of here.'

Ronnie had never spoken to his father as he was doing now. In fact he'd never sworn at him before. He was finding it liberating.

'No dad. I smuggled it in. I did it. I'm totally bang to fucking rights. Just fuck off and deal with it.'

He saw the pain in his father's eyes. It was a victory of sorts, the first time in his life he'd come out on top in an argument with the big man. He savoured the moment, for a second, but as victories go this one was about as hollow as they come. As H walked out of the room a solitary tear fell from Ronnie's eye.

It had been a long day. For everyone.

25

When the cab pulled up Olivia went out to meet it and, without saying anything, eased H out of the back and into the house. She led him upstairs and put him, like a boy who's been out to play for too long on a hot summer's day and can no longer keep his eyes open, into a hot bath, and went downstairs to get his scotch.

She'd seen the footage from the park, and had spent the rest of the day wondering how bad it was. H had put up the shutters before - she knew better than anyone how taciturn and moody he could become - but this looked different. Like he couldn't face what reality was throwing at him and had gone somewhere else. And in front of all those people, all around the world…

When she got back to the bathroom the big man was dozing. Good. Let him rest - but not too much. She stripped off and got in opposite him, with the taps at her back, and gave him a little stroke where he liked it. She knew she'd have to ease out the tension before she'd get any sense out of him. He groaned as she finished him off, and opened his eyes.

'Ready for your scotch, Mr Bear?' She said.

'Yes please doll. I'm gagging.'

He gulped from the tumbler like there was no tomorrow, asked for a refill, and gulped again.

Like some great animal finally reaching its watering hole. How I love him.

'Better?'

'Much.'

'Busy day, by the looks of it. How are you?'

'Fucked. Can't remember the last time I was so tired.'

'Talk to me H. I know you're tired, but…do I need to be worried? I saw you on the telly this morning, in the park. It didn't look good. Are you just overworked, or…'

78

H stared at her, and then into the water, for what seemed an age. In the old days he'd have toughed this one out and given her the strong and silent routine. But she'd worked on him for years now, opened him up, and these days he found it harder to keep things from her than to keep them in. It wasn't true that Ronnie was the only person in the world he trusted.

'Liv…remember when I told you what I was like when I got back from the Falklands? How I used to get panicky, and really angry, and really tired, and feel like crying, and not want to go out, and sometimes struggle to figure out what was happening around me?'

'Of course.'

'Well…I felt a bit like that in the park. I just lost it when I realised it was Tara Ruddock. Her head was nearly hacked off, there was blood everywhere…but it was Tara. I just couldn't…How's Ronnie going to handle it? What's he going to do? What…'

For the third time in a day Harry Hawkins was lost for words. Instead, to Olivia's astonishment, he began to cry. And cry. And cry, like a baby, like a blubbering, vulnerable small thing with no one to protect it. She held him. He shook, and wailed, and cried until his face was raw.

When he was finished she emptied the bath, took him out, wrapped him in his bathrobe and led him to bed, tucking him in and kissing him on the forehead.

Little man you've had a busy day.

'Sleep tight, Mr Bear. Let's see how things look in the morning.'

26

Graham Miller-Marchant rose at 5.30, went for his morning run around Wandsworth Common and the streets around Northcote Road, showered, dressed and was at his breakfast bench for 7.00. He prepared his pot of decaff and opened his phone. There'd been a lot of activity while he'd been out. Multiple signs were directing him to the stir caused by Joey Jupiter's latest blog piece, so he went there before checking the mainstream media coverage of the previous day's events.

Beneath a Youtube clip - which appeared to be a mash up of the already infamous 'slags' fragment and a silent H giving his thousand yard stare above the heads of the assembled media in St James' Park, with 'The Laughing Policeman' as the soundtrack - Graham read the following:

PANTOMIME IN THE PARK – THE PLOT THICKENS

News has reached us that Harry 'H' Hawkins – 'London's Top Copper' – covered himself in glory in more ways than one yesterday. After his sterling work in the park, sleuthing for all he was worth despite clearly being the worse for wear, and giving his best impression of a startled meerkat at our impromptu press conference, the great seems to have assaulted a colleague back at the Yard.

Is the pressure getting to 'H'? Or is it all part of his elaborate masterplan to return the rule of law to the capital's increasingly chaotic and blood-spattered streets? This blog, at least, would like to know more about his methods and overall strategy, but unfortunately his superiors appear to have decided that he is not the man to lead the investigation into the sickening murders of the daughters of Sir Basil Fortescue-Smythe and one of Her Majesty's 'special' policemen.

Not that Graham Miller-Marchant, who is to head up the investigation, inspires much more confidence than the 'big man.' Known at the Yard, we understand, as *Little Manbot*, he is said to be more desk jockey than action man. But let's hang fire for a while on this one, folks: he can't be worse than 'H,' can he? The estimable Sir Basil can, at least, look forward to a job done thoroughly, and rest assured that all of the stops will be pulled out for this one – as they always are for people of his kind.

Graham was mortified; the mist cleared, and he could now see that, rather than being given a chance to shine he was in a lose-lose situation. No database on earth, it seemed, had ever heard of, seen or so much as suspected the existence of Aliyev. It was as if he were a ghost. As yet there was no lead, nor suggestion of a lead of any sort on yesterday's killings.

This was going to be a tough investigation, what Hawkins would call an *absolute bastard*. He would have to engage with the upper echelons of the British establishment, and face the brunt of their withering contempt for people like him; he would have to scour the earth for traces of the killer himself, as well as look for dirt in the secret lives of two daughters of the aristocracy; and he would be, at all times, under the scathingly watchful eye of Joey Jupiter and his ilk, who would portray him either as an ineffectual, dithering clown - 'Little Manbot Miller-Marchant' - or as part of a conspiracy to serve the interests and protect the privacy of the most powerful people in the country.

So this is what Hawkins has been putting up with.

His phone rang. It was Hilary Stone.

'Hello Graham, how are we this morning? Had a good night's rest? Ready to go?'

'Yes maam, I most certainly am. Just getting ready to leave.'

'Good. We really need a result on this one Graham. We don't have much time before the media starts to hang, draw and quarter us. I don't want this ship sinking any lower.'

'Understood. Leave it to me maam.'

'Fuck,' he said to himself after hanging up, 'fuck, fuck, fuck, fuck.'

Part 2

27

It was the day of the funeral, and it could not have been bleaker. The wind was howling and the slate grey sky bore down on H like a lead weight as he waited outside Ronnie's riverside flat in his car. They were driving down to Tara's ancestral home in Wiltshire, not far from Chippenham. Sir Basil had arranged a small service in the family chapel. Family and close friends only.

It had only been six days since the sisters had been butchered. There was no need for an autopsy, the whole world knew the cause of death, and Sir Basil had been insistent on an early funeral. At Hilary's insistence H had taken a few days off to come to terms with the momentous events of that day. Despite his protests Hilary had insisted he go nowhere near the Tara case, which was in the not-so-capable hands of Graham Miller-Marchant.

'H, if I get a sniff of you getting involved in the St James' Park murders you're finished. Have I made myself absolutely clear?' She'd said as she packed him off.

'OK guv,' H had said meekly.

For now.

H stayed in contact with Amisha as she concentrated on the carnage in Bermondsey. She had worked relentlessly, piecing together every known reference to the two firms involved. Never one to waste a moment, he had a paper copy of Amisha's latest files on his lap that so he could work on them whenever he got a moment. She had learned that it was pointless advising him everything was now online, if only he would learn how to use the latest Police IT system; a system that contained every detail of the investigation; a system that could run multiple fast paced data matches in an effort to find links and clues amid the mountains of information it contained.

'Guv, the system even runs various "what if" scenarios based on configurable algorithmic parameters that can be entered via numerous online user interfaces,' she had told him when they had first become partners. Both the language and approach to working with H didn't survive first contact.

'What if, what if, what fucking if. If my grandmother had wheels, she'd be a fucking bus,' he'd replied.

When he rang her from his rest bed to ask for the printouts she knew it was pointless to tell him to log on from home. And anyway, even before giving her the chance to go into her spiel he had pre-empted her.

'What if, what if I buy you a nice cup of tea and a doughnut will you get the printouts for me?'

She laughed out loud as she agreed to meet him for lunch, the wry humour signifying to her that he was starting to refocus on the case. Truth was, the investigation team were starting to gather some sound evidence and develop a detailed knowledge of the new eastern European firm on the block. But they needed H. They needed H to get in amongst it, to get amongst the dirt and dig around in it the way only H knew how.

As he sat waiting for Ronnie he opened the file and took out its contents. Amisha had put the pictures of the top two protagonists at the front. He studied the pictures of Basim Dragusha and Vladimir Agapov and read the basic notes. As far as they could tell Dragusha had arrived in London about six months before. Not long after, the violence had escalated. H didn't believe in coincidences.

Dragusha had taken up residence on The Island, which was now under 24 hour surveillance. He was ruthless, yes, but also smart and ambitious. He was no thug sent by his masters to manage low level gangster business. He was here to get a firm foothold, no doubt about it. H flicked through an assortment of photographs of Dragusha's more recently arrived strength, read what information Amisha and the team had amassed on them and committed it all to memory.

He then turned to Agapov, who had been a player in London for some time and was already well known to H. Him and his small army had taken control of significant parts of the London underworld and, in particular, cornered the market in people trafficking. For H this was truly the vilest of all gangland activities, a modern slave trade at the heart of the capital. He was determined to bust the thing wide open.

I'll give these bastards what they deserve.

Various parts of Agapov's organisation had been under surveillance for months. No arrests had been made so far. H had wanted to move on their setup in Peter Street and take Agapov out of the picture, but Hilary insisted on playing the long game. She had an inkling there were bigger fish to fry so H was told to wait it out and gather evidence.

He then turned to the pictures of the two headless bodies that had been washed up in the Thames, in Deptford; bodies that fitted perfectly with the two heads the Russians had tossed into the mix in Bermondsey. It had taken a while but both men had been formally identified as being known associates of Dragusha.

Ouch! Must be some serious revenge being planned. Surprised it hasn't happened already.

H read through the rest of the notes. It seemed Amisha had been very thorough in gathering evidence and perhaps soon some major police assault and arrests would be prepared, hopefully before it all kicked off again. He wanted to get back to work, to make sure he was involved in whatever was being planned.

Good girl Ames, good work.

He turned to the second file on his lap. Amisha had taken a big personal risk in doing what he asked but the update on the Tara case sat before him. He opened the file and started reading. His mood worsened. It was clear that there had been no progress. No progress whatsoever. Nish. Nada. Nic.

There was no information on the identity of the nutter in the park. No connection to the gangland war ravaging London's streets. In all his years of coppering H had never known anything like it. A murderer is taken out at the scene of the crime and six days later not a single thing about him or his motives is known. Had it really been just a random act of violence? An indiscriminate killing by a lone wolf, a solitary, highly trained killer who had sprung organically from the St James's Park undergrowth?

Not fucking likely.

Sir Basil, drowning in grief, was all but unapproachable. And despite the grand public shows of support from Old Shitbreath's friends, they appeared to be treating the hapless Miller-Marchant with utter contempt. He seemed incapable of penetrating their clique in order to garner even elementary facts about Tara's personal life. Anything that might provide the most basic of clues seemed beyond him. Rather surprisingly H felt a ripple of sympathy for Little Manbot. H knew these people, with their private clubs and associations, their old school ties, their walls of silence.

He knew these people alright; and he knew he didn't like them. He hated them.

28

H's anger was about to burst out of his chest when Ronnie appeared from his flat. He suppressed it, knowing that today, of all days, he had to keep it together.

'Ready son?' H said as Ronnie clambered in.

Ronnie said nothing, just exhaled massively and shook his head. No. Not ready. Not ready for this.

They drove down in near silence. Ronnie could not have looked so forlorn and lost, H thought, since Goose Green.

Poor fucker. He's in bits. Don't feel all that clever myself.

The miles rolled on - Ronnie mute, H in the kind of agitated state he couldn't put a name to - until eighty or so of them had passed. The old house came into view. H pulled up next to the high Cotswold Stone wall. Ronnie, in the passenger seat, was staring ahead and gulping hard. H touched him on the shoulder; out they got. Through the gate and into the grounds, and there was the clan, and its hangers on, in full array.

'Stay close H,' said Ronnie.

'Count on it, son.'

Ronnie led the way in, moving slowly and nodding to people as he went. He stationed himself just outside the chapel, on the opposite side of the door to the rest. He did not look at them. But H did. He saw a fair bit of private muttering as they entered and plenty of side-of-the-mouth stuff going on among the cliques. H found himself back in the zone, itching and twitching.

What is it with these people?

They were summoned inside; Tara and Jemima were already there.

Sir Basil - looking haggard, hunched and a hundred years old, and dressed, indeed, in some sort of Edwardian funeral getup - delivered the eulogy. He extolled his daughters' virtues, their beauty, their achievements, and tried to say something about the family's sense of loss. He was having a hard time bearing up, an impossible time, and H felt a pang of sympathy for him. The sight of the two coffins, side by side at the front of the chapel, was overwhelming everybody. This was too much to take in.

Ronnie sat still throughout, staring at the ground, sobbing quietly. H, from time to time, put his arm around Ronnie's silently heaving shoulders, and had to bite down hard to prevent himself from losing it.

Outside, the gloom had deepened; the sky had moved from slate grey to near black. H and Ronnie could see it as they processed down the aisle, hard by Sir Basil and Jemima's husband Oliver (a gormless lump, as Ronnie had him, who was 'something in the city'). Only nods were exchanged. Along with these two, they would be last out.

People had arranged themselves around the garden in a semi-circle, waiting for the coffins to emerge. The wind howled and the sky threatened rain. H was struck by the extent to which Ronnie was keeping his distance from Tara's family. He was polite to condolence-bearers when they approached him, but made no effort to go beyond himself and engage other people. To Sir Basil he had not said a single word.

'How's it going Ron?'

'I can't have a lot more of this H. I want to do the off at the earliest available, alright?'

'Yep, no argument from me on that score son. Ready when you are.'

The coffins came, and H saw Ronnie set his feet far apart and dig them in. To stop his legs from buckling. This, H understood, was to be an orgy of old-school, stiff upper lipped Englishness. No wailing or moaning or gnashing of teeth for these paragons of rectitude. H respected them for it. Better that way.

It was only as the coffins were loaded into the hearse that a few little moans and sobs could be heard. But Ronnie stood firm as they pulled away, and out of sight. Out of sight forever.

He exhaled. 'Get me the fuck out of here, H.'

'On our way son,' said H, taking him by the arm.

They moved towards the gate with as much speed as propriety would allow. They heard whispering and muttering behind them, but they did not look back.

29

It had been a boneshaker of a ride across Eastern Europe, through Germany and the Netherlands, followed by the small fishing boat to an inlet on the Suffolk coast, and thereafter the ride south-westward.

The two battered transit vans pulled up to their clandestine location, a private garage just off of Camberwell Green, in the early hours of the morning. If anyone had been around to see its fatal cargo they would have marvelled at how much you can fit into a couple of vans. If the twenty silent men of serious intent were not enough, the heavy crates that followed them seemed to defy the physics of available space.

One by one Dragusha greeted the new arrivals with a hug, making sure he paid individual attention to every one of them, looking each of them in the eye. His fierce eyes were discernible in the half light of the single faint bulb that illuminated the garage, and his stare held each of them in turn, like mice frozen under the fierce gaze of a marauding cat. He knew most of the men, and trusted them. But the bosses had sent some new recruits. In the battle to come he needed to know the men he stood with would hold firm under fire and assure them, without words, that the consequences of letting him down were worse than anything the Russians could serve them up with. The boxes were cracked open to reveal an arsenal of automatic rifles, handguns and some hand grenades thrown in for good measure. Dragusha rallied the troops and dished out the weaponry.

'Welcome to London. You travel many miles, and must be tired. I understand. But we have problems that must be dealt with quickly. Take rest but soon we move. Take strength and courage from knowing we will soon avenge our brothers.'

He rolled out a blown up map of the location the small army had come to obliterate - a certain private members club in Peter Street - and went through the plan, if a plan it could be called. Paraphrased, in its essentials it was pretty much 'rock up, kick the doors in and annihilate everything that moves.'

'Make no mistake. No one leaves club alive.'

When it comes to putting your life on the line most men, if given a choice, will sooner run for cover than face a bullet. But Dragusha was a rare creature - he was excited by danger and the thought of the ensuing battle filled him with rampant expectation. His will to succeed, to persevere in the face of the odds stacked against him would not be cowed by a couple of severed heads thrown into a shithole of a caravan site on the wrong side of London.

The men ate sandwiches and sipped on water. One of Dragusha's rules was no alcohol before a slaughter – it took the edge off too much and led to a sloppy and inefficient kind of courage. He was happy for his men to drink, but rakia and vodka were for after the battle. Celebrate the victory and lament the dead. And dead there would be - no question about that.

They clambered back into the vans. Dragusha rode shotgun in the lead vehicle. As they pulled out into the back streets of south east London an eerie silence saturated the world. It was the time of night by which most people had locked themselves into the relative safety of their homes, the time of night when the city is transformed into a different place, where different characters populate the streets.

This was a desperate area - one half of the populace were unemployed and the other half were under-employed, scraping a living below the radar. Dull concrete flanked them on both sides; boarded windows and vandalised doors offered an insight into a world where burglary and petty crime were a standard part of everyday existence.

The convoy emerged into Camberwell New Road and then left towards the Elephant and Castle. A group of foxes that had migrated deep into the heart of the city criss-crossed the deserted roads with impunity, feeding on the scraps that even the tenants of the decimated concrete jungles had seen fit to discard.

The van snaked its way past Camberwell and into the Walworth Road. Dragusha looked on with indifference at two lost souls huddled by a shop window - frozen, vanished, undead - and listened with indifference as a far off scream broke the silence. He had seen and heard much worse in his time, back in the old country. A rare walker crossed in front of them accompanied by three Pitbull Terriers, the attack dog of choice of the denizens of this shattered dump - best not to go out without your bodyguards this time of night.

The convoy rolled on, right at the Elephant roundabout and then left towards Westminster. Halfway there. You could cut the tension inside the vans with a knife. The ever-present curls of cigarette smoke hung thick and impenetrable, making the atmosphere as claustrophobic as a coffin.

Dragusha broke the silence.

'London is shithole, yeah? But shithole with money.'

The men laughed. The tension eased a little.

Even after six months in the city he could barely differentiate one south east London concrete housing estate from another. But as they approached Westminster Bridge the city started to come to life. This was 24 hour London, the London the tourist board sold to the globe, the London of iconic landmarks seen on websites and picture postcards everywhere. Landmarks that were known all over the world passed by them, half-noticed by the rows of sombre men sat in the rear of the vans. Westminster Bridge, The Houses of Parliament, Trafalgar Square, that monument to a deadly battle several lifetimes ago, remembered now just as an innocent fable, distant and unreal. But the battle about to erupt on London's streets would be in the present, in the now, and, in its own way, as bloody and as deadly as anything that happened in a far off time on a far off sea.

The vans pulled up outside their destination, in a no parking zone.

'Put Balaclavas on,' ordered Dragusha, 'cameras everywhere here.'

Pete Abbot, driver of one of the famous London black taxis that swarmed around this part of London 24 hours a day, found himself trapped behind the vans and growled with impatience.

'Oi, what you doing, you can't park there…sort yourselves out.'

But Pete looked on in transfixed disbelief as twenty men armed with automatic rifles calmly exited the vans. He had been working the streets of London for twenty years. But this was a first, an absolute stonker of a first. Being a clever man he quickly realised that the gentlemen with the guns were not very concerned about parking illegally and, if he kept his trap shut from this moment on they might hopefully not be too concerned about him mouthing off his thoughts on the quality of their parking choices.

'Fuck me,' he said as he rolled up his window, 'these boys ain't here to party.'

30

The music was too loud for H, and too squawky, so they got a table at the back of the room. They'd been coming to Ronnie Scott's for years now, for their annual reunion. Since their paths had diverged - Ronnie's into the aristocracy and the world of high, global finance, H's deeper into the same tough streets they'd come up on - they always made a point of meeting here at least once a year, partly to catch up, partly to relive their youth.

The room was hot, crowded and smelled of wine, perfume and Italian food. The music pulsed and clattered. Ronnie liked his jazz, had done since he was a kid and used to come here, amongst other hotspots, to hear the funked-up jazz/disco stuff they all loved 'back in the day' - a phrase he did not use in H's company. H himself was not so keen on the improvised, difficult stuff, preferring to hear a crooner working with the standards.

Like his father before him, and as he still hoped his own son might one day become, H was a Sinatra man. Through and through. End of.

Since the funeral they'd made their, through Soho's rainswept streets, around the old watering holes. Or those of them that had not yet been turned into high-end apartments or frothy-coffee outlets. Both of them were, by now, the worse for wear. Both were hurting, and hurting bad.

They'd boozed and talked long and hard, and were now almost talked out. How much grief, pain, anger, and confusion can a man get through in one sitting? They settled into their chairs and Ronnie ordered a bottle of wine that would have put a good-sized dent in H's weekly wages. H tried to move the conversation on a bit, to get on a more normal footing, and assailed Ronnie with some of his professional woes.

'I'll wring the soppy little cunt's neck one of these days. He ain't half the copper I am, Ron. Not a quarter. But he's moving upwards like a rat up a drainpipe. Ten minutes out of university and he's already at my level. He's got plenty of qualifications, and he can Powerpoint you to death, but he couldn't fight his way of a paper fucking bag. That's what they're all like now…it's a nightmare. All of a sudden, I'm the dinosaur. They don't want people like us no more Ron.'

'Stop feeling sorry for yourself H, you are a stroppy old bastard. In ain't 1985 any more mate. You've got to try and move with the times a bit.'

'Move with the times? Move with the fucking times?'

H was gearing up for another rant. Ronnie slowed him down.

'Anyway, all I care about is the investigation. Why is this Miller-Marchant wanker in charge of it? I understand why they haven't put you on it, but is he really the best man for the job?'

'Well,' said H, 'he's what there is now. If it wasn't him it'd be someone like him. But he is out of his depth; Lord Snooty and his pals are running rings round him. I don't know how you've put up with that shower of shit all these years. Something's not right with that lot mate, I'm telling you. Old Shitbreath's got some wrong 'uns round him. They're up to something.'

'You say that, H, but that's just what they're like. I think…'

H interrupted him.

'Listen, Ron, it's not just that I'm too close to the case, it's that…I went off my head in the park the other day. When I saw Tara, I…'

'I know H - I know.'

'My guvnor thinks I'm mentally unstable. She's got me running round after all these fucking gangsters…but she thinks I'm going off my head.'

'You've been off your fucking head for years, mate,' said Ronnie, kicking back in his chair, smiling broadly and raising his glass. 'Here's to you, H.'

H was choked. He felt tears welling up in his eyes. He was losing control of his emotions again.

'I'll get them, Ron. I swear to God I'll get them. Whoever did that to Tara is going to wish they'd never been fucking born. I promise you that.'

The band was between sets now, they noticed, and the place was relatively quiet. Just the hubbub of conversation and clinking glasses.

And then all hell broke loose. Burst after burst of fire from automatic weapons. They both knew the sound well, and for a second the volume and intensity of it took them back to that day in 1982.

'Fuck me!' said Ronnie.

Most of the other patrons were now beneath their tables, hunkering down instinctively. But H was concentrating.

'Sounds like it's coming from Wardour Street, somewhere there.'

A two minute run from where they were sitting, in Frith Street.

'What the fuck's going on, H?'

'I've got a fair idea mate. Stay here...I mean it Ron. *Stay here.*'

H hit Frith Street like a man possessed and barrelled, along the glistening pavement, towards Wardour Street.

I've had just about enough of these cunts.

98

31

H was gasping for air as he trundled into Peter Street. The run from Ronnie Scott's had winded him severely; he was in worse shape than he'd realised. And clearly also becoming more stupid - what was he doing running at full tilt towards bad men equipped like a militia, by the sound of it, without so much as a water pistol in his hand?

What the fuck am I doing?

Such were his thoughts as he staggered towards what looked, as far as he could tell by the fleeing, screaming crowd, like the site of the action. But the madness was only just beginning.

The crowd thinned suddenly and melted away, and in a chaos of driving rain and wailing alarms H made out a gang of heavily armed men piling into two vans. One man was doing all the barking and pointing, and H focused in on him. He recognised the face beneath the balaclava, by the eyes; it had been all over the surveillance footage and photos of The Island in Bermondsey since the shoot-up and head tossing. Basim Dragusha. Amisha and a few of the others who'd been analysing the surveillance data had him down as the No. 1 man on the firm. He certainly looked like a handful now, calling the shots and getting his men the hell out of there. He jumped into the front of the lead van, turned and met H's eye as it pulled away. H would remember the look in those eyes long after; it was mocking, malicious, savage...and happy. Exultantly happy.

Gotcha, you bastard. I'm going to bring your world down around your ears.

H stood, unsteady on his feet, and caught his breath. Before long the initial joy of putting a name to a face gave way to reflection, as he calmed himself. Evil bastards had glared at him before. But this one was special. This nutter was clearly capable of taking violent chaos to a whole new level, in London terms. This wasn't old school gangsters with sawn-off shotguns having a pop at the odd bank - it was warfare, Yugoslavia-style warfare. Did he and his firm have what it took to stop it? Did they have the resources and the will, the fight, the balls? Would they have to call the army in?

An image flashed across his mind: Joey Jupiter, as exultant as Dragusha, stabbing gleefully with his two thumbs at the tiny keypad of a little plastic phone...

Backup arrived: a couple of squad cars and an armed response unit. Ambulance and fire engine sirens could be heard in the distance. The epicentre of the chaos proved to be exactly where H had expected it to be: the Russians' night club. It was now a blown-out hole in the wall, reminding H of those old photos of wrecked buildings during the Blitz, and the bomb sites he grew up playing on, still there in the 1970s while he was learning the ropes in Bermondsey.

Broken glass and chunks of shattered masonry everywhere, alarms still wailing, smoke and dust filling the air and...the smell. The smell of blood, an abattoir's worth of blood, and burning flesh.

He had been here before. He turned on his feet and, without consulting anyone, headed towards the club. His senses were working overtime, his whole body was zinging. But alongside this was a sense of dread, which sharpened as he got closer. He gulped hard and took a breath. Phrases he'd picked up as a boy, and hadn't used in years, were coming back to him:

Black Hole of Calcutta
Charnel House

32

H moved through the entry-level reception area - all was shattered fragments; it was hard to make much out apart from the remnants of coats strewn across the floor by what must have been the cloakroom - and what was left of the staircase. He picked his way up the steps carefully; there was not much left to hang on to.

Fuck me, these nutters have been chucking grenades about like sweets at a kids' party.

The place had taken a massive hit; he was looking at major structural damage. He made it to the top of the staircase and surveyed the scene, and retched. Small fires were still burning, or smouldering, some of them in what had been until recently human beings. Dark redness everywhere, visible in staccato bursts from a flickering lamp: from the plush of the curtains, to the bits and pieces of flesh and intestine strewn everywhere, to the bloodsoaked carpet. The air was thick with acrid smoke and the butcher shop smell he'd caught outside.

Paramedics - *won't be much for them to do here* -, fellow officers and fire fighters followed him up and began their grim work. He moved across the dancefloor, treading gingerly, careful not to look too closely at everything he moved around, and headed for the rooms at the back. He knew there had to be an inner sanctum, where Agapov and his crew would hole up, do their business, have their charlie- and vodka-fuelled orgies.

Bingo. A reinforced steel door blown off its hinges, bodies and body parts clustered around the threshold, all the signs of a surprise attack with very, very heavy tools. H imagined the scene. Agapov and his boys would have stood no chance. One minute it would have been 'hey, Maxim, you want another line?' and 'hey bitch, you come here, now, you eat big Russian sausage' and the next, BLAM! Uncle Basim and his hillbilly army are at the door with a special-delivery Balkan apocalypse.

101

H continued his musings. How many people had been killed here tonight? That would be for entire teams of highly trained experts to determine in the coming days and weeks. Clearly, a lot of women will have been killed, and about that he felt sad. H would lose not a wink of sleep, though, over these cruel thugs being dispatched to meet their maker. They had all been gathered in now, by whomever is responsible for the souls of ruthless gangsters, and H was of a mind to think Dragusha and his little firm had done him a favour.

God knows what the payback for this will be...but at least this bunch of horrible bastards is off my plate.

He suddenly became aware of movement in an adjacent room. He heard a door close and someone running down stairs. A back door escape route. H tried two or three doors before he found one that opened. 'Outside! Quick!,' he bawled, 'someone's legging it!' He rushed to the window and saw, in profile, a man limping slightly but running at speed and turning the corner into Berwick Street. It was Vladimir Agapov.

33

'It's good to talk.' That's what the TV adverts for British Telecom used to say back in the eighties.

H was having none of it; not then, and not now. He didn't like the advert, and he'd watched the Oprah Winfrey show a total of once, under duress. Not his sort of thing.

He might open up to Olivia from time to time if something was really bothering him, but his motto had always been more like 'it's good to drink.' He belonged to the old school, and felt no need to talk things out or develop in any way his 'emotional intelligence,' whatever that might be. Like many men of his generation, and even more so his father's, his touchstone was the great Bert Trautmann: breaking his neck with seventeen minutes to go was no excuse for him to bail out of the 1956 FA cup final. Bert had done what he was there to do.

And now they roll around on the floor clutching their hairbands if someone so much as gives them a dirty look.

What H wanted, standing in Peter Street amid the shattered glass and wailing sirens with the stench of blood in his nostrils and the image of a pile of ruined corpses still fading from his eyes, was not counselling - if he had a quid for every time Hilary had offered him that he'd be a rich man by now - but a good session.

He pulled out his phone and hit Confident John's number. Who else was there, now? Only Ronnie, once in a blue moon. John, clearly already the worse for wear, or disturbed from a deep sleep, or both, answered.

'Hello John, you about? I could strangle a light ale,' said H.
'H? What time is it?'
'About half past two, I think.'
'I'm in bed mate.'
'Get up then - I'll be there in twenty minutes.'

He called a cab from Wardour Street and sat down on the curb outside what had once been The Marquee Club; he recalled halcyon nights here watching, as a boy, Eddie and the Hot Rods. Were they still alive? What might they be doing, tonight, in this wrecked, fallen, senseless world? Ping! went the phone. Olivia. He didn't answer.

Not now. I can't, not now.

H stared into space, trying, again - how many times had he been forced to do this lately, he wondered - to gather his thoughts, remember to breathe properly and process the world of bullshit and horror he seemed doomed to wade through.

Ping! The phone, again. Amisha. H held the device at a distance, as if he'd never seen it before, and was overcome by a wave of nauseous panic. It seemed to be rising up from his guts and clawing at this throat, at his mouth. Without thinking he launched the phone into the air, it landed in the middle of the road and broke up into tiny plastic shards.

A car had pulled up a little further down the street. He didn't see it, and Hilary Stone didn't see him as she got out of it and hurried down towards Peter Street, babbling loudly, her phone glued to her ear.

H's cab arrived. He hauled himself up, utterly exhausted now, and leaned into the driver: 'Bermondsey please mate. Silwood Street. Sharpish.'

34

'Still nothing?,' said Hilary.

'No maam. His phone's gone dead. I've called practically everyone he knows, or at least I know that he knows, and nobody has seen him since he left Peter Street last night,' Amisha replied.

Hilary wheeled her chair back from her desk, sat back with her hands linked behind her head, and exhaled loudly.

'The old bastard's really done it this time. He's off duty, wanders alone into what will probably go down as the worst murder scene we've ever had in London, and disappears from the face of the earth for fourteen hours, or however long it turns out to be. This is all too much, even for him. He's lost it; I fear he's really lost it now. His days as a copper are numbered. We've got to find him before…'

'I'm on it maam. I've just been making calls until now. I think I'd be better off having a "mooch about", as he calls it, see if I can lay eyes on him in one of his old haunts. Permission to get out there, maam?'

'Granted. Don't come back empty handed.'

But Amisha had been economical with the truth. When she'd spoken to Olivia earlier in the day she'd been told that H was probably 'on the missing list.' She was given to understand that this had happened before, and that H would surface when he was ready.

'When he really needs time to himself he takes it, and there's nothing anyone can do about it. He hasn't done it for a while. He used to do it more, he's been better the last few years. So that would be my guess… I hope to God I'm right,' Olivia had said.

Amisha was intrigued, and more than a little reassured: 'But what does he do, where does he go?'

'He finds one of his old mates and they go on a bender. They drink themselves into a coma. And then they drink some more, sometimes for days. It's not that uncommon where he comes from. He calls it having a "good drink", but it's more than that. I think these guys have some sort of death wish - they push it as far as they can. He gets himself into a terrible state, and these days it takes a lot out of him. I'm afraid one of these jaunts will finish him off. A lot of the people he knows use cocaine as well I think. I'm talking about the older guys down there, not the kids. I'm not sure if H does or not. He says not.'

'And all this would take place where?,' asked Amisha.

'Somewhere on his old stamping ground usually. They have their places. There or Soho. I'd start with Confident John if I were you. Find him, Amisha. Please.'

35

Julie let out a heavy sigh and dropped her phone onto the kitchen table for what seemed the fifteenth time. And it was still only 11 am. She hadn't lived through a morning this long, this endlessly long, since H was out in the Falklands.

'Jesus, where is he? Why is he never available when you really need to talk to him?' Justin, sitting opposite her at the table, chewed his sun-dried tomato and kept his own counsel.

It wasn't like she needed to talk to H very often; he'd withdrawn a long way back from her and the kids after Justin had come onto the scene on a permanent basis.

Julie often thought about H's final outburst after she'd put him in the picture once and for all, what seemed like half a lifetime ago:

'Jules, don't talk to me about that soppy little yoghurt-knitting, sandal wearing, sociologist ponce. I don't want to see him and I don't want to hear about him. What is Little Ron going to learn about being a man from that fucking little old Mary Anne?'

'OK H, stick around then, and he can learn how to be a violent, chaotic pisshead like his real dad. Now there's a role model for him. Justin's worth ten of you, you fucking slob. Piss off.'

And now Little Ron was on remand - as confused and unsettled a young man as you could wish to meet. His hearing had been brought forward and by this time tomorrow he would have been up before the beak, and would know more about his likely fate. Julie herself was in utter turmoil, had hardly slept or eaten since his arrest. Little Ron was putting on a brave face; but he was Harry Hawkins' boy, and they were tearing him to pieces in there. His father's enemies, sworn enemies, were legion. Only H could deal with this situation;

she was out of her depth, and Justin knew nothing of the world Little Ron was now struggling to survive in.

She picked up the phone again, without thinking. Nothing. No maximum-call-charge message from a well-spoken robot, no voicemail. Nothing.

'It was always like this. When the kids were little and they were ill, and I really needed help, I could never find him. Always on the missing list, always working, always drinking, never in the house…'

'Well, Jules,' ventured Justin, 'men from that background, that culture…'

Julie had had enough. 'What "culture"?,' she shouted, 'what bloody "culture"? Why are you defending the bastard? All his "culture" ever taught him to do was fight, and work like a maniac, and drink. They're all the same. They talk about family, and honour, and values…and they're never there when you really need them. It's all talk. They're all the bloody same, whether they're coppers, or villains, or something in between. All cut from the same damn cloth. Don't talk to me about their "culture". Pig-headed dinosaurs is all they are.'

Justin said nothing, and took her hands in his. She calmed down.

'Cup of tea, my love?'

She nodded yes. 'If the selfish bastard doesn't surface today, or show up tomorrow, I'll never talk to him again. Not for as long as I live.'

36

Nothing had been heard from H, so Julie, Justin and Little Ronnie's brief Michael Church were the full strength of the boy's support at the hearing. The Old Bailey could still do the business: Julie and Justin, on coming into view of it, had been awed, pacified and made anxious by its imposing majesty.

'Hanging them high and pressing them down since 1734. Good old British justice,' said Justin, through gritted teeth, as they mounted the stairs.

They got into their seats early, Julie ruminating sadly about the past, the breakup of her family and the miserable prospects for her son; Justin thinking about his old research in radical criminology and keeping to himself his bristling contempt for the 'site of power' in which he was now, for a moment, trapped; the lawyer gloomily reviewing his notes. Church had been saying all the positive things on the way up, but was now wearing the face of a man who had been joined during a relaxing session in his hot tub by a giant Richard the Third of unknown origin.

The court was sparsely populated by…whom exactly?, Julie wondered. None of the others present were known to her. Was it some sort of grim, low key spectator sport for those with nothing better to do?

There was a stir in the unseen lower regions of the building and suddenly Little Ronnie was brought up into the defendant's box. Julie shrieked involuntarily and began to cry. The boy was cut and bruised about the face, and looked emaciated and confused. His mother's heart bled; she felt some kind of uncontrollable hysteria growing inside her.

Justin moved to comfort her, placing both his arms around her and drawing her into himself. 'Shh, shh my love,' he said, but was himself shocked and appalled by what he saw next.

The judge had entered, his pinched scowl preceding him. Sir Peregrine Blunt was announced to the assembled company and sat himself down with some ceremony.

'No, not this old bastard,' he whispered to himself, 'this reactionary old brute. Not good. Not good at all.'

Is this not the one we were expecting?,' asked Julie.

'No, this is Old Blunt. He's one of the old hang 'em and flog 'em brigade. As merciless as the day is long. Horrible old pervert.'

'Why pervert?' asked Julie, reeling now, as bad news was followed by worse.

'Oh, just a figure of speech, my love. But they're all perverts, nasty little leftovers of the old public school establishment. All those beatings and whatnot warped them. Look at his face. I can't believe they're still getting away with it. We won't get much out of this old bastard, I'm afraid.'

The room settled. Church cleared his throat and began his shpiel. To Julie he sounded like a detuned radio, buzzing in and out of her ears. She was on the verge of panic, and her old friend vertigo was making an unannounced guest appearance. She heard '…boy with an unblemished record,' '…no previous convictions…,' '…appeal for clemency…,' and finally 'bail.'

The Judge halted him with a raised hand.

'Have you quite finished Mr Church?'

'Brace yourself, my love,' Justin whispered as gently as he could into Julie's ear.

'I have, My Lord.'

Brace yourself.

'Then I must inform you that I have no intention of granting bail in this case. Your client is charged with an extremely serious offence and in my view presents a clear flight risk. He will not be granted bail, nor moved down to a lower court. He will face the full weight of Her Majesty's law, here, at the Bailey, in due course. Take him down.'

Little Ronnie was led down. He would not catch his mother's eye. Julie collapsed to the floor. As he comforted her, Justin fished her phone from her bag and punched in H's number. Nothing.

37

H's arms hurt so much it felt like the fire was working its way down from the top of his biceps to the rest of his body. But he refused to cave in to the pain and grimly continued with the chin-ups on the exercise bar in his bedroom for a further minute before collapsing to the floor, gasping for the oxygen he needed to re-stabilise his heart rate.

He'd woken up an hour earlier and downed three pints of water to slacken the raging thirst of a body dehydrated to an extent that only a three day bender could induce. But his body could only deal with so much water. He opened his sock draw and grabbed the bottle of scotch he kept tucked away in the corner, and took a couple of swigs. He felt the soothing effect of the alcohol rush and his muscles relaxed.

Hair of the dog, nothing like it.

Hiding his sharpeners was no more than habit. He knew Olivia knew where his bottles were, and he knew that she knew that he knew. But old habits die hard.

Olivia entered the room. She'd phoned Amisha the previous night when H had turned up, bedraggled and wasted. She'd taken one look at him and winced when she thought about the amount of alcohol coursing through his bloodstream, but left him alone as he stumbled up the stairs and crashed into bed. She didn't reproach or harangue him. She had simply put a cover on him and kissed him gently.

'I'm surprised you can still do chin-ups after what you've put your body through the last three days.'

'Don't start Liv.'

Olivia had heard the tales of how super-fit he had been in his army days and in the early days of his police career. She had seen pictures of the once legendary six-pack and the powerful biceps. Wouldn't it be wonderful, she mused, if he could look like that again? But he didn't. In fact he looked like

10lbs of shit in a 5lb bag as he admired his paunch in the full length wardrobe mirror. A soft, uncontrollable giggle forced itself from Olivia's mouth.

'What?' he said.

'Nothing, get ready. Your driver says ten minutes' she said, as she left the room.

H went through the rest of his morning routine. As usual it was that bit at the end, the sweeping of the thatch of thin grey hair across the crown of his head, that caused him the most anguish. But thoughts of fitting a rug or having a weave never entered his mind. Celebrity-style hair surgery was not for Harry Hawkins.

Then the ring on the doorbell. Since H's disappearance Olivia and Amisha had spoken a couple times. Their old enmity was fading.

'Hi Olivia. How's the patient? Will he be ready for work?'

'He'll be ready. I'm pretty sure he's had enough alcohol to stun an elephant, but his powers of recovery are still mindboggling.'

Amisha entered the living room; H was gulping hard from a cup of coffee.

'Nice to see you looking so spritely guv, how are you feeling?'

'Hello Ames. I'm fine, what's happening?'

'Well guv, do you want the good news or the bad news?'

'Bad.'

'If you switch the TV on just now you'll find your friend Joey being interviewed.'

H prayed silently that one day he'd meet and get the chance to deal one-on-one with this little wanker; but, nonetheless, he was finding him impossible to ignore, like a bad groin rash he just had to scratch. He picked up the remote and hit the ON button.

'What on earth has happened in this world when ignorant, two-bob ponces like Jupiter can air their fucking propaganda on TV?'

Amisha said, 'He's a social media superstar who now has over a million followers on twitter. We can't ignore him.'

As the TV flickered into life H saw that Jupiter was already waxing lyrical.

'So what should be done?' asked the chirpy, dolled-up presenter with a tone of reverence and admiration for the 'superstar' who sat before her, wrongly assuming that this epitome of social media emptiness possessed a detailed knowledge of gangland London and the policing methods needed to combat it.

'Well, it's very clear that The Met have lost control of London's streets and that their methods and tactics are outdated. We need to…'

H hit the OFF button, looking about as happy as a small dog revolving in a microwave.

'Ames, you said you had some good news.'

'Yes guv, I'll get you up to speed en route. We have to be at the Yard for a full debrief after lunch, but we have a little detour first.'

H kissed Olivia on the cheek, finished up his coffee and looked forward to the 'good news.'

38

H jumped in and banged the car door shut.

'So, what have you been up to Ames. Where we off to?'

'Head for Camberwell Green, I've followed up on some tip-offs from some pals of Confident John. I've got a warrant to search some premises there.' She flashed him the address. The lock-ups behind the back of Camberwell New Road. He knew them well. Lot of history there. H lit up the car and put his foot down.

'So fill me in Ames.'

Amisha had been busy. Very busy. During H's bender she had made a few trips to Bermondsey, getting to know some of the other colourful characters Confident John hung out with, getting close to him, seeing what she could see. This was one of H's maxims.

Have a little mooch about. See what you can see.

Eventually she had been put in touch with Pete 'Pitbull' Patterson. She'd met him in a pub in the Walworth Road. She recounted to H how she was filled with trepidation as she entered it. The sunlight barely pierced the grimy windows. A heavy, old-school fug hung over the place. It seemed that the smoking ban hadn't reached this part of town. The few customers the pub still managed to pull in sat in isolated pockets in its murky corners. It felt like the waiting room at the end of the world.

Pitbull sat in the far corner downing a pint of lager. Three little monsters sat obediently at his feet. Confident John's friends were right; it would be obvious to her who Pitbull was when she entered the pub. Apart from the dogs his thickset neck, busted nose and sunken eyes told the story of an old-school street fighter who had been bashed up one time too many.

She sauntered over, doing her best to look like she belonged in the place but in reality as out of place as the Dalai Lama in a Texan whorehouse. John had not warned her to dress down; in these parts, the only smart people were plainclothes coppers.

'Pitbull?'

'Yeah.'

'I'm Ames. Confident John said I'd find ya in 'ere.' She was dropping her T's and H's faster than a privately educated, champagne socialist politician visiting a cement factory on the run up to an election.

'Can I get you a beer?' She knew social obligations had to come before the verbal. She bought Pitbull a pint and got herself a glass of disgusting and undrinkable white wine. Fortunately she never intended to drink it, but thought it was the standard for a young lady in this part of town.

'Alright fella, Confident John informs me you might have some info I'd be interested in?' She winced with regret when she used the word 'informs'; she knew it was a mistake but she thought she'd got away with it.

'Yeah, he called me. Listen, I ain't no grass. I don't want any comeback. This conversation never fucking happened. Got it?'

'Yeah, got it.'

'Well, the night of the Soho Massacre, I saw them.'

'Saw what?'

'The vans. They came down here, along Walworth Rd. On their way to the West End.'

'How can you be sure?'

'Well, it was two in the morning. I don't sleep well so I was out walking the boys.' He patted each of the three dogs in turn.

'Two transit vans were coming down from Camberwell. They were the only traffic on the street so I clocked 'em. They were the ones in the papers, no doubt about it.'

116

'Why didn't you come...'

'Listen love. No comebacks. You understand. If you hadn't found me I wouldn't have come forward. John asked me to talk to you so I'm here. Get this sorted. It's gone too far.'

'One more question,' said Amisha. 'Have you ever seen this man?' She passed a picture of Dragusha across the shattered oak table.

Pitbull held his best poker stare and considered the implications of his next move. No doubt this was the man in the lead vehicle. He'd made eye contact. It was the kind of face you don't forget in a hurry. Still, he was already in deep so he played his hand.

'Don't ever come back to me. I'll deny ever having met you, but yeah, he was in the passenger seat of the leading van. Those eyes, that face, no fucking doubt about it sweetheart.'

As she recounted the story H started to view Amisha in a new light. A 28 year old Cambridge educated Indian girl in and out of the boozers of Bermondsey and Walworth, working his patch while he'd been out on the razzle. He'd always known she was clever and she'd been very useful translating the mysteries of the world of social media. But now she was revealing a whole new side of herself, stepping up to the plate while her partner was out of the game.

Good girl. She's worth ten of that prick Miller-Marchant.

'Fucking hell Ames, you're starting to have the makings of a half decent copper.'

She smiled, and continued her story.

'That was yesterday. I pulled every CCTV camera from Walworth and Camberwell and traced the vans back to their starting point. The search warrant came through but we decided to monitor the premises through the night. Nobody has come or gone. Right here and then second left,' she said.

H pulled up outside the garage. A posse of Police Constables and officers from the armed response unit were already in attendance.

117

'Do we know anything about the owners Ames?'

'That's the thing guv, they boarded up and left over a year ago. Emigrated to Australia. As far as the records show the place has been left empty since then.'

39

Police Constable Frank Jones had heard H was on the way so came prepared, handing him a decent cup of builder's tea from the local greasy spoon on arrival: strong, two sugars.

'Thanks Frank.'

H sipped gratefully as another PC, a young and eager new recruit by the name of Duwain McGregor, took out the bolt cutters and cut through the padlock that secured the garage door. H sipped on his tea and released a sigh of pleasure. Old brains do love a cuppa.

H bent down, lifted the aluminium rollover garage door and stood at the entrance to the lockup. His breathing was relaxed and gently rhythmic as he felt inside, flicked on the light and surveyed the scene.

The place smelled musty and stale. Mouldy sandwiches turned blue with fungus were left on a table in one corner. Two rats loitered in the shadows, unperturbed by the new arrivals as they munched away on crumbs from the feast. In the other corner some wooden crates were stacked in a pile.

But smack bang in the middle of the garage was the *piece de resistance*. The main prize. The two transit vans had made their way back to their starting point, the false number plates matching those of the two vans witnessed at the massacre in Soho. What secrets would they reveal wondered H, as he downed his tea and flicked on a pair of gloves.

Forensics were on the way and H wanted them all over the place, like flies around a turd on a hot summer's day. But he wanted to check everything himself first.

He made his way over to the sandwiches. They were wrapped in some old newspapers. He carefully started to peel away the sandwich wrapping. He'd expected the paper to be a tabloid, maybe The Sun or The Daily Mirror, but the font size and sheet size showed it to be a broadsheet.

'Ames, looks like one of our murderers is a Times reader, that's a turn-up for the books.'

Amisha looked on and noticed H go wobbly as he held up the page to the light and surveyed its contents.

'What is it guv?'

'Fucking hell, it's Tara's obituary,' he said as he handed the paper to her, 'what the fuck are stale sandwiches in a lock up in Camberwell frequented by a band of murderous thugs doing wrapped up in a copy of Tara's obituary?'

'Don't read too much into it guv. News of Tara's murder has been in every paper for the last ten days.'

But H didn't believe in coincidences. The picture of Tara had shocked him but he was holding it together. Amisha noticed that rather than rendering him helpless, as the sight of Tara's body had done in St James' Park, it was actually livening him up, spurring him on.

In unison the detectives moved over to the crates.

Used to transport the arsenal of weaponry these bastards took to the party in Soho, H surmised correctly as he lifted the lid on the boxes. Useful as evidence when they nicked the bastards but probably not much would be revealed to forensics.

Now for the vans. H tried the back lock of the first of them and found it to be open. He looked inside. The van had been cleaned recently, that much was clear. He stepped back and made his way to the driver's seat at the front. He was about to try the lock when he noticed a piece of paper from the corner of his eye, protruding from the front wheel. He bent down to pick it up. It was a cut-out from another newspaper. He wasn't sure which one; it didn't really matter.

'Fucking hell this just doesn't make sense. No fucking sense at all. A lockup in Camberwell used to plan the biggest criminal assault between two feuding gangs in the history of London, sandwiches wrapped up in a copy of Tara's obituary from The Times and a cut out of a picture of Tara and Jemima laying stuck to a wheel.'

He passed the picture to Amisha.

'Oh my God guv, do you think Dragusha and his firm targeted them? Why? It doesn't make sense. There's no connection, no motive.'

'Not at the moment Ames, no,' H said thoughtfully, 'not at the moment.'

40

H and Amisha pulled up outside Scotland Yard. H braked the car to an abrupt halt and leapt out. He was agitated and itching to get up to speed on the Tara case, and to speak to Hilary about the discoveries in Camberwell. The queue at the lift irritated him further. H barged past the crowd, made his way to the stairwell and started the climb to the seventh floor. He was knackered by the time they got to the third, but his agitation drove him on. Amisha's smooth and regular breathing, as she bounded up behind, stood in stark contrast to H's heavy panting.

H reached the seventh. Ignoring the faces surprised to see him turning up at work, he steered a path through the open plan office and burst his way into the incident room, where an update on the Tara case was in progress.

'Inspector Hawkins, how nice of you to drop in,' said Hilary. 'This is not your case - please leave immediately and make your way to my office. When I'm finished here you can update me on your case and explain where the hell you have been these last few days.'

H believed in the chain of command when he felt it was necessary. At this moment he didn't. He stared hard at the officer in charge of the Tara case and went straight to the crux of the matter.

'Marchant, you got anything yet?'

Miller-Marchant remained silent. H knew what that meant.

Hilary said, 'Inspector, I just gave you an order. In case you hadn't noticed, orders are still followed in this Police Service. You have a full debrief on what your team have on the Soho Massacre in thirty minutes. I suggest you go and prepare for that.'

122

His dislike of Miller-Marchant allowed his pride to get the better of him, and he exaggerated the progress made on the massacre.

'We have a highly reliable eye witness who can pinpoint the gang member who led the raid on the Russians and, oh yeah, I have evidence that links the two cases.'

H had gained their full attention. He was in control of the room. The massed ranks of detectives looked on, eager and impatient for more information.

'I'll see you in your office guv, when you're ready,' he said, and exited the incident room.

The outburst had had the desired effect and a few minutes later Hilary and Miller-Marchant entered Hilary's office.

'Now Inspector, where the hell have you been while your team has been working hard on this? The media have been all over us and upstairs are a hair's breadth away from hanging you out to dry. I've had to put some effort on keeping you on the case. H, the truth, please.'

H considered his response. He could say he had been underground working the case and he knew Amisha would back him up. But it wasn't part of his makeup to steal someone else's thunder, and he wanted the bosses to start realising just how good she was getting at the job. He went for the truth.

'Well Hilary, after the Tara murder I was in bits. I was having a drink with Ronnie when all the shooting started… The truth is the whole last few days have really got to me. I needed to let off steam. I met a few mates for a drink.'

Hilary was not amused.

'So, in the midst of two of the biggest cases The Met have ever had to deal with you decide to go on a three day bender while your partner and the whole team flounder around in chaos. There are a lot of powerful forces inside and outside the police that want you out Harry. I don't know if I can protect you much longer. You better have something good.'

Hilary had been aware that Amisha had found the CCTV of the transit vans following an anonymous tip off, but was unaware that the informant had identified the ringleader.

H filled her in. He explained that Amisha had worked the patch under the radar, found an eye witness and this was the lead that allowed her to trace back the vans to the location from which their deadly journey that night had commenced.

Hilary said 'And who, pray tell, did he identify?'

'Basim Dragusha, the leader of the Albanian firm on The Island. We have no direct proof he has been involved in anything, but the informant positively identified our top suspect,' said Amisha.

'That's enough for a full scale raid, I'll arrange the warrants,' said H.

'Hang on Inspector. Is this informant willing to testify?'

'No way,' said H.

'I promised to keep him out of it' said Amisha.

'I'm not sure that will be enough. We'll have to wait. With luck we'll find some forensics in the lock up in Camberwell,' said Hilary. 'Well done Amisha, great work.'

'And,' Miller-Marchant said, 'what about this link between the cases?'

H looked at Miller-Marchant with his usual contempt as he took out the plastic bag that contained the evidence and explained how he had found the obituary wrapped in a bag of sandwiches and the cut-out of the two sisters stuck to the wheel of one of the vans.

Miller-Marchant was, after his last experience of being in Hilary's office with H, slightly more cordial. But his nature was to try and take the moral high ground whenever the opportunity presented itself.

'Harry,' - unusual, thought H, he's never called me that before - 'are you suggesting that Dragusha had Tara killed so he could read about her life story?'

'No, soppy bollocks. I...'

'H!' shouted Hilary.

H flashed a wry smile and changed his tone.

'No, Inspector Miller-Marchant. What I am saying is that I have a hunch. Gangsters don't read obituaries in The Times. In fact they don't usually read The Times at all. It's just not a paper they would have lying about when one of their henchmen wraps up some cheese and ham on white. Someone was reading this and my hunch is that someone knows something. That's all. Hilary, let's bring Dragusha and the whole fucking lot of them in for questioning. We have the vans and an eye witness that has fingered this bastard. I realise the obituary is just a hunch but bring the fucker in and I'll get it out of him.'

'Calm down inspector. If the witness won't testify it might not be enough but I'll put the evidence before a judge and see if we can do a full search of "The Island", and get a warrant to arrest him. Given the profile of this case we should have enough, even before the forensics on the van come through.'

'One other thing,' said H. 'I saw him. As he was pulling his firm away, just as I arrived in Peter Street. He looked at me. He was balaclava'd up, but those eyes... I know it was him.'

41

2am the following morning. The streets of Bermondsey were deadly silent. Hilary had been true to her word and got the warrant in double quick time.

Fifty officers sat in unmarked vehicles, scattered throughout the large car park in Surrey Quays - or Surrey Docks, as H still called it. The essence of the plan was to drive unobtrusively to the site, block the three exits from The Island, encircle the camp and then go in hard and fast.

H was on the blower to Miller-Marchant going through, once more, the final details of the raid. Graham had managed to get involved after discussion of H's suspicions that the Soho Massacre might be linked to the Murders in St James' Park, and was leading one of the three teams. H ended the conversation and Amisha heard him mutter something about a one legged man at a turkey-kicking contest.

'Guv,' she said, 'you really do have to find a way to manage your anger. Everyone is getting to you. Miller-Marchant, Sir Basil, Joey Jupiter. I know you've been to hell and back the last few weeks but if you don't calm down you'll be of no use to anybody.'

'Don't talk to me about that dumb bastard Jupiter Ames, for God's sake.'

'Ok, if he were any dumber we would have to water him twice a week and prune him once a year, but all I'm saying is stop taking so much to heart.'

H laughed out loud, something he hadn't done for some time. Seemed like Amisha was continuing her quest to go native, so he joined in the fun.

'Yeah,' said H, 'the wheel's still spinning but the hamster's fucking dead.'

'He's so fucking dense the light bends around him,' continued Amisha.

'The fucking marbles I had as a kid were sharper than him' continued H.

They had a few more rounds classic dumb and dumber metaphors before the laughter subsided.

Amisha took a deep breath and steeled herself for the fray. H collected his thoughts, got on the intercom and gave the command.

'Operation Point Blank is affirmative. Repeat Operation Point Blank is affirmative. Go, go, go.'

At first all was calm as the cars drove quietly to their appointed destinations. No sirens, no screeching, no exceeding the speed limit. Two minutes later the three groups of cars had snaked their way around the one way system and cut off The Island. No one was getting in or out.

H shattered the calm as he leapt out of the car. He was first in. He preferred to control raids from the front. It was the only way he knew. The surveillance of the last few weeks meant he knew the site backwards.

With a select firm of handpicked officers he stampeded past the outer caravans and hit the door of Dragusha's little palace-on-wheels with all the force he could muster. The door burst open and he found himself inside the caravan with his gun pointing directly at the Albanian's forehead.

To H's surprise Dragusha sat at his table and smiled. He was all calm and self-assurance as he played patience with an old deck of cards. Almost as if he was expecting his visitors.

'Inspector Hawkins. I see you in papers. Pleased to meet.'

H considered his adversary as he sat looking confident, relaxed. He looked him in the eye and the same chill he'd felt that night in Soho went down his spine. H couldn't wait to get him into custody.

I'm gonna break your fucking world wide open.

'You famous, Inspector. I also read blog of Joey Jupiter. How can I help?'

127

H barked orders at his accompanying officers as he looked around the caravan. It was neat, tidy and compact. A copy of today's Times lay on the table.

'Cuff the cunt. And turn this fucking shithole upside down.'

'Nothing here to find, Inspector' Dragusha said.

42

Kyril Kuznetsov entered the plush foyer of The Savoy, London's most glamorous hotel, on the north bank of the River Thames. For generations the hotel had attracted the elite of British society, royalty, Lords and Ladies of the realm attending elegant functions, film stars and 'A' list celebrities enjoying discreet and sometimes not-so-discreet liaisons. The ideal location for the newer members of the super-rich to rub shoulders with the time-honoured members of the old establishment.

Kuznetsov passed confidently through the foyer and entered the Grand Ballroom. He was impressed, as ever, by the beauty of the vast chandelier that dominated the central space. Its thousands of hand crafted crystals refracted a near magical light across the ballroom, a symbol of opulence and wealth. He felt like he belonged here, in this self-congratulating melee of the great and the good. He arrived at his table and, after shaking hands with the male guests and kissing the hands of the ladies, pulled out a chair for his glamorous blonde wife, adjusted his expensively tailored Saville Row suit and sat down.

As he sat he considered the other guests at his table. There was Sir Peregrine Blunt the High Court judge, peer of the realm Lord Timothy Skyhill and high-powered lawyer Oswald Carruthers QC. All of these were well known to Kuznetsov.

The event was a glitzy charity ball to raise money for the needy and abused children of London. At two thousand pounds a pop the tickets, for Kuznetsov, were less than small change. He had just broken into the Sunday Times Rich list at number 762, his worth estimated at 876 million pounds sterling - a calculation made on the basis of his declared, above-the-radar interests. He smiled at his friend, Lord Skyhill, and exchanged some pleasantries.

Skyhill was a mountain of a man, so fat that even Kuznetsov might have struggled to afford the liposuction. His double chins rested uneasily on his cravat and his multiple stomachs wedged him firmly into his chair. He was also a true pillar of the establishment, who sat on a range of important government committees and was a constant presence on the TV, where his wit, wisdom, charm and eloquence were always in demand. He was the key speaker at today's event and, after a glass of wine or three and some jovialities around the table, the master of ceremonies called him up to the stage to make his speech.

'Ladies and gentlemen, may I introduce to you our keynote speaker. He has been a member of our charity for over ten years and in that time has been tireless in raising money for several other charities, concentrating on the young and homeless of our great city...please show your appreciation for Lord Timothy Skyhill.'

His Lordship rose like a bull walrus and somehow defied the laws of physics as he shuffled his mass forward. He had become expert in managing his bulk and it bothered him not one jot that his physical inelegance was the centre of attention. He enjoyed the applause as he made his way to the stage.

'My Lords, Ladies and Gentlemen,' he began, 'firstly may I say how pleased and delighted I am that so many of you have seen fit to attend tonight's event, to raise money and support our much needed charity work. Furthermore ...'

But Kuznetsov had switched off from the sideshow, as the words floated outside his consciousness, like so much flotsam and jetsam washed up on a beach. He had many other issues on his mind, not least of which was the recent trouble in Soho. He had spent an unscrupulous lifetime building his vast financial empire, and had always stayed at more than arms-length from its seamier sides, ensuring that several layers of management existed between him and his street-level interests.

But the massacre inflicted on his underlings by the Albanians had crossed a line that even his organisation had never gone near; not, at least, in the West. It was a level of violence that had alerted the whole world and he needed to get a grip, personally, before the level of police activity and news investigation started to get anywhere near him.

So secretive and cunning had he been in establishing his organisation's power structures that nobody on earth, except him, understood how information flowed around it. He wanted, needed to understand why the massacre had happened. What was the chain of events that led to it? How had his hand-picked senior managers not seen it coming? He wanted information now, direct from the horse's mouth.

He had one thing in common with Harry Hawkins in that he believed in the chain of command. Except when he didn't. He clicked his fingers and a henchman emerged from the shadows.

'Where is Agapov now?'

'Sir, we have him. He is secured in safe house, just other side of Waterloo Bridge.'

'Perfect,' said Kuznetsov, 'we will visit him after the event concludes.'

131

43

Kuznetsov, accompanied by a phalanx of brawny thugs in evening dress, turned left past the Old Vic theatre and then left again, before pulling to a halt outside a small block of flats no more than a stone's throw from Waterloo station.

Fired up but firmly in control of his emotions, Kuznetsov looked about him as he exited the car. The night wind howled through the empty concrete streets. One of his stone-faced lieutenants put the key into the lock of a small ground floor flat and opened the door.

The heavies checked the flat and ushered Kuznetsov into the living room. A doctor was removing a bullet from a bloodied man who lay sedated, drifting in and out of consciousness. Kuznetsov approached him and administered a firm slap to the cheek.

'Vladimir, tell me what the fuck happened? How could you allow this to happen?'

Agapov sprang to attention as the adrenalin rushed through his body and overpowered the sedative. He knew who Kuznetsov was, of course, but had always thought he was too far down the food chain to ever meet him face to face.

And here he was. The numero uno. The top honcho. Taking time out to come and see him on a one-to -one basis in a pokey little flat on the wrong side of the river.

Kuznetsov did not usually concern himself with the day-to-day activities of what he euphemistically referred to as his delivery units. Street violence, a murder here and there he expected - part of the general strategy to ensure his delivery units stayed on top. His financiers set them cash targets and if they didn't deliver they replaced the local leadership. Agapov knew this and he had always delivered. Until now.

He was aware of the organisation's penalty for failure. Situations didn't get more serious than this. He calculated the odds of getting out of the flat alive.

Absolute fucking zero.

He flinched as the quack pulled the last of the bullets embedded in his right calf muscle.

'Sir,' the doctor said to Kuznetsov, 'should I seal wounds now?'

'No.'

Kuznetsov took a seat.

'Explain, now. Include all the details of this feud.'

Agapov's breaths become short and sharp. His eyelids were getting heavy. He wasn't sure how long he'd spent in hiding before Kuznetsov's men had picked him up. He'd lost a lot of blood. He felt he couldn't last much longer.

The top man administered another slap.

'Talk, Vladimir. Now.'

Agapov came around once more and did his best to recount the details of the last few months. Just a few fist fights over control of a couple of clubs south of the river at first. Then a murder, then another in retribution. The cycle of revenge had got out of control faster than the anger of a spoilt brat who doesn't get the right toy.

Agapov gave him everything he knew about their enemy, which was actually very little. He knew where they lived; he knew, or thought he knew, what their capabilities were. But he had to confess, he had no idea they were capable of pulling off so devastating an attack.

'You lost control, my friend,' said Kuznetsov. 'Too much arrogance, I think. The organisation does not work well with too much arrogance. And now we have half of the fucking world crawling all over us.'

Agapov's breathing stopped. This sounded like a death sentence.

'I take care of business boss?' Said the lead henchman.

'Not yet. We have two choices. Bring in a small army from the mother country to destroy the opposition, or negotiate a settlement. I prefer to negotiate. Vladimir here may have some use as a sacrificial lamb; these peasants would love to torture him. But bring our men in anyway, in case the negotiations fail.'

Kuznetsov turned to the doctor.

'Give him a blood transfusion and fix his wounds. Keep him alive. For now.'

44

'He's in interview room three guv,' said the desk sergeant.

'How's he performing?,' asked H.

'Keeping schtum. We haven't had a peep out of him.'

H barrelled into the room, alone at his own insistence and in contravention of all the rules, blustering hard to prevent Dragusha sensing his unease. He was more nervous than he'd ever been going into an interview with a villain. He wasn't afraid of Dragusha as such - he felt confident that in an old school straightener, one on one, no weapons, he'd be able to handle him. It wasn't that; it was that he feared what this sort of man might be capable of, and what that would mean for the metropolis if he and his kind really gained a foothold.

'These gangsters don't follow any rules at all H,' Confident John had told him a few days before, halfway through their second day on the scotch All they care about is getting hold of money, getting control any way they can and going mental, really mental, if anyone fucks with one of their own. "An eye-for-an-eye" don't come into it mate. They'll chop your bollocks off and feed them to you. Then they'll go out and do the same to your brother, or your son, or anyone else they can find. These are the worst nutters I've ever seen. I am absolutely fucked if I know what you're going to do with them.'

'Alright, silly bollocks,' H began with gusto, 'let's not fuck about.

Dragusha raised his head from where it had been resting on his forearms and looked H in the eye; his own were cold and blank as a shark's. He said nothing, communicated nothing but mute indifference.

'Well I know who you are son. I know who you are and I know what you've been up to.'

Nothing. And then nothing. And then more nothing. This guy was giving him nothing squared.

On and on it went. H gave it all he had, from all angles, for an hour. He understood, finally, that he would get nowhere with this, and changed tack.

'What do you know about Tara Ruddock? Why were you reading about her?'

At last Dragusha stirred. His demeanour changed; he swivelled and shimmied in his chair; he was transformed, from dead-eyed shark to leering wolf.

'You mean this posh pussy? Very nice, very nice indeed. Where I come from we know what to do with pussy like this. She too good for this Russian scum.'

'What are you talking about? What Russian scum? Tell me now, or sitting in this nick will be the least of your fucking problems.'

'This Agapov' said Dragusha, spitting onto the floor, 'she his whore. She was his whore - scum is in his Russian hell now. Too bad she dead, I would show her good time. I give her good Albanian sausage.'

H went blank, and lost a few seconds; when he came to he found himself behind Dragusha's chair, with the Albanian's head in a lock and going hard at his windpipe, running now on pure, instinctive, vengeful hate, when the door burst open. The desk Sergeant, backed up by a posse of London's finest, immobilized his arms and shouted into his ear 'H! H! he's not worth it. Let him go, H!'

45

H drove back to Scotland Yard way past the speed limit. His head was spinning. He needed to get into the surveillance stuff they had on the Russians as soon as possible.

What is this Dragusha fucker on about? He's got to be winding me up. How could Tara possibly have known, let alone been involved with, a piece of shit like Agapov?

These thoughts were scrambling around the inside of H's head like lobotomised rats chasing their tails in a laboratory. None of it made any sense. Tara and Agapov lived their lives in different social circles, different parts of town, different worlds. Didn't they? What was this Albanian up to?

Amisha met him in the car park. She was shocked at how dishevelled, how disordered he looked. He had a look in his eye she hadn't seen in him before. Pushed to describe it, she might have said he was 'manically confused' or somesuch; she was concerned that he might be on the verge of dissociating again.

How can he go on like this? Sooner or later he's got to snap. Snap completely, in a way that would mean we might never get him back.

'What's happening guv? I…'

But the big man was not in listening mode. He swarmed past her, breathless and unsteady, with 'Upstairs Ames, now! Incident room. Get me everything we've got on the Russian firm - CCTV, photos, phone records, the fucking lot. All of it. Get it all set out. Now!'

'What are we looking for guv?'

But H still wasn't listening. He headed for the lift, jaw working, eyes glazed over, fizzing like a Catherine Wheel, like a man possessed… but with what? He burst out of the lift at speed, Amisha struggling to keep up with him. She had seen this before, of course, but it never ceased to surprise her.

How can a lump like this move so fast?

137

She was beginning even to think in the argot she'd learned from him and his Bermondsey cronies, she reflected. Was she becoming more like them, more like H himself? Was she crossing a line? Had she crossed it already, by covering for him so doggedly while he was out on the piss? She was beginning to understand him better now, beginning even to feel his pain.

How much pressure can one make take? How does he manage to deal with it all?

She snapped out of here mini-reverie as they reached the incident room: 'What do you want to start with then guv?'

'CCTV. From the beginning.'

The surveillance unit monitoring the comings and goings in Peter Street, Berwick Street and Wardour Street had been up and running now for weeks. That meant a lot of footage to wade through. But it was no good telling H that. He was clearly on a mission that he would not be diverted from, and with which he required no assistance.

He got himself a coffee from the machine and settled down into the chair in front of the monitor.

'Alright Ames, I can deal with this. Get yourself home now, if you like.'

She knew better than to argue with him in this mood. Whatever this mood was.

46

Alone now, the big man surveyed the list of files Amisha had set up for him and clicked on the first. Like the others he was to watch that evening, and through the long night, it showed what seemed like an infinity of murky images of people walking in and out of doors and getting in and out of cars.

He recognized some of the men, mostly gone now from this world. Dispatched to their 'Russian Hell' by the man whose windpipe he'd tried to crush earlier. They got in and out, and came and went, with their molls. Their endless strings of molls, their property. *Poor girls.* Coming and going. Going and coming.

By 2 am H's brain was as numb as his backside, and he broke for a hot dog from the stall by St James' Park. He washed it down with a snifter of scotch on the walk back to the Yard. Bleary eyed, he entered the building, rode up in the lift, slumped back into position and started clicking.

He moved down the list. Vladimir Agapov himself was beginning to feature more prominently, getting singled out for more and more attention by his watchers; standing around in the street like he owned it, barking commands at his guys, sharing jokes with his guys. Taking his ladies by the arm. H began to count them: 1, 2, 3, 4, 5, 6…7. There was something about 7. But he was struggling to stay awake.

He went to the bathroom and sluiced his face with cold water. He made a note of the file he'd seen moll 7 in and kept looking. There she was again a little later on, her face concealed as before by a wide brimmed hat. And again, on a windswept Berwick Street. And then the moment he'd been waiting for, but hoped would never come: the wind lifted the brim of her hat. H recognized her at once. It was Tara, being led along the street by Agapov. They were laughing like teenagers in love; she was practically skipping along.

Boom! Looks like it's time for another rollercoaster ride through another fucking shitstorm.

What does this mean? What on earth could it mean? His head began to spin, again - he was starting to get used to this now, these last few weeks. His heart was pounding and he couldn't think straight. He was filled with murderous rage, desperate sadness and utter confusion. He wanted to kill someone; he wanted to cry.

How the fuck did she get mixed up with these bastards?

What does this mean? What on God's fucking earth does this mean?

What'll I tell Ronnie?

47

Graham sat in his car and geared himself up for his approach to *Brown's*. One of those iconic gentlemen's clubs with its roots in the eighteenth century, in which his own grandmother would have struggled to get a job as a cleaner. The fact was, his double-barrelled name was a product of his wife's refusal to simply take his name, and not high breeding. Graham Miller's father had been the owner of a hardware shop in Peterborough. What Hawkins called his 'poncey Oxbridge drawl' had been picked up at Cambridge, where as a provincial scholarship boy he had been desperate to fit in.

And now here he was, at, or very near, the top of the tree, among some of the most condescendingly superior people on the face of the earth. Coming to this place had triggered all his old class insecurities, and they were threatening to suffocate him; he was literally struggling for breath as he moved past the mock-imposing comedy doorman, up the stairs and through the club's gilded doorway. He took a deep breath and hit the reception desk.

'Detective Inspector Graham Miller-Marchant, to see Sir Basil Fortescue-Smythe.'

He was led into the dining room. Sir Basil, he saw, was seated at a large mahogany table with half a dozen other old buffers, tucking heartily into the kind of full English breakfast that Graham himself might take on once or twice a year, if that. He was looking at the 'kippers and custard' syndrome he'd first encountered among the older Dons at Cambridge; the tendency of the sons of the old establishment to stick, for all their lives, with the dishes they'd learned to love as public school boys. Back in the days when an Englishman was proud of his disinterest in fine food. That could be left to the French.

Never come between a man and his full English. Best leave him to it.

'On second thoughts, please let Sir Basil know I'll be waiting for him in the lounge,' he said to the underling who was leading him in.

So he waited in the big leather chair in the lounge, with its rows of leather-bound but largely unread books and tables stacked with the Daily Telegraph. He rustled through a copy of one of these without interest, and waited some more.

Finally Sir Basil processed into the lounge. Graham rose to meet him, but was motioned to stay seated, and Sir Basil took up position in an adjoining chair.

'I am very sorry for your loss, sir,' said Graham.

Sir Basil did not reply, but stared at him stonily.

'Sir, as you are aware I am in charge of the investigation into the death of your daughters. I would like to speak to you about this at a time of your convenience. Is it convenient now?'

'No, it is not.'

A pregnant pause.

'I am grieving for the death of my children. I keep to my routines, but I am grieving for the death of my children. And you have the presumption to come here, tell me you are "sorry for my loss", and want to ask me questions about them? No, it is not convenient. Remind me, who is your commanding officer?'

'Chief Inspector Hilary Stone, sir.'

'Please inform her she will be hearing from me in due course. Good day to you, Detective Inspector.'

And that was that. Sir Basil had stood, turned crisply and was moving away from Graham before he'd fully registered what had happened. Dismissed like a schoolboy, by a man he could barely look in the eye and certainly couldn't bring himself to argue with.

He slouched disconsolately down the stairs and into the street, feeling very much the Little Manbot and, surprisingly, felt also a slight twinge of sympathy and regard for Hawkins.

Back to the Yard then. Hilary's going to rip my balls off.

48

As Graham exited the club with his tail firmly between his legs he was startled to see H standing before him. He could see he was no longer in control of himself. It seemed as if murder was in his eyes.

'Harry, you shouldn't be following me.'

'Update me. Now.'

'Nothing. I just cannot get through to these people. None of them will tell me anything about Tara's private life. They won't even talk to me. As soon as I try to escalate things I get told to back off. I'm getting nowhere.'

H had had enough. He swarmed up the stairs and headed for reception. Confronting Sir Basil Fortescue-Smythe held few terrors for him. They had history. Military history first, and after that personal history - H had, after all, been Ronnie's best man, and Sir Basil (or Old Shitbreath, as his men had always called him) had been forced, much to his obvious distaste, to socialise with him at the wedding.

Both had got heavily, aggressively drunk at the reception - a weakness for the scotch being just about the only thing the two of them had in common - and had treated one another to 'plenty of verbals,' as H would later have it. It had become one of his favourite stories:

'You were a bolshie bastard in the Army, Hawkins, and you're a bolshie bastard now,' Sir Basil had told him.

'Have me put in the tower, then,' was H's reply.

'You people…' Sir Basil, H liked to say, was at this point absolutely apoplectic, '…you people. If you were still under my command you'd be taught some manners, damn you.'

'Well we ain't in the army any more, are we, you old cunt? But you can take me outside and teach me some manners now if you like.'

At this point Jemima had stepped in and separated them. H had not met Sir Basil again - or Jemima, if it came to that - until the current sorry mess began.

'Detective Inspector Harry Hawkins' H told the receptionist. 'Is Sir Basil about?'

'Sir Basil is in the lounge, sir. If you would wait a moment...'

But H was way ahead of him, and was already breasting the door of the club's inner sanctum. As seen in a thousand and one old-school movies and TV shows. His man was seated in a circle with five or six others - H recognised Lord Timothy Skyhill, Oswald Carruthers, Sir Peregrine Blunt - engaged in hushed but apparently intense discussion.

'A few words, if I may, Sir Basil,' shouted H, bearing down fast on the circle.

'Hawkins? What in God's name are you doing here?' exclaimed Sir Basil, rising from his chair. 'If you wish to talk to me - though frankly I have no idea what we might have to say to one another - make an appointment with my secretary.'

'Nope. Now Sir Basil. Now.'

'Is this police business, Hawkins? My understanding is that the little fellow...Detective Inspector Miller-Marchant, is leading the investigation. Or has he been suddenly removed and it is now you' - this with a flourish, Sir Basil playing to the gallery - 'who is in charge?'

A gale of laughter from the cronies.

'Well, he's not going to conduct much of an investigation with you blocking his path, is he?'

The room was buzzing with the electric antipathy between the two men. H was working hard to control himself, to control his language, to control his hands, which were starting to itch. Uh oh. He was filled with loathing for this old bastard, but he knew he would have to ramp it down now, before it was too late.

145

'No, Sir Basil, I am not in charge of the investigation. But I am putting you on notice: I will not stand by and let you and your chums impede it. For whatever reasons you might have.'

At this Sir Basil let go a barrage of expletives and threats...but H was tuning out before they hit him. He was in the zone. His senses, his nose and skin, his copper's intuition, were kicking in. His flesh was crawling. Something was not right here. He did not know what it was, but he could smell a rat; and when Harry Hawkins smelled a rat, nine times out of ten there was a rat to be found.

This lot are up to something.

'Porter, have this man removed from the premises,' Sir Basil was barking. 'Now!'

'Alright, I'm off. But I'll be back,' said H.

49

H jumped in the car and slammed the door shut. He knew these full bloodied hereditary types were difficult to deal with. Everything was always done on their terms. But this was different. They were wilfully impeding the investigation.

Did they know about Tara and Agapov and wanted to keep it out of the papers? He doubted it. Their types had been through worse scandals than that and come up smelling of roses.

Now satisfied that Miller-Marchant really was as useless as he thought and knew absolutely nothing, H's mind turned to his only lead, and he made a call to Confident John.

'H, hello mate.'

'Alright John. That geezer I told you about, any news?'

'No firm sightings H. But it's hard to tell gossip from fact. The rumour mill's been working overtime. I've heard a top level Russian contingent has him holed up somewhere in London but also rumours that he's been killed. There's talk of a full scale war but also a reliable source is certain that the Russians and Albanians are setting up a meet. I ain't got anything concrete though.'

'Ok. Keep 'em peeled son. Anything. Anything at all, however small or insignificant, I wanna hear it asap.'

'Right you are H.'

H hung up, started the car and lit up the siren.

He called Amisha.

'Hello Guv, where are you? Find anything on the CCTV?'

'Yeah, just on my way in. Ten minutes. I'll give you a full update when I arrive. Get the whole team together. We'll divide up London and work every fucking patch of grass until we find Agapov, whether he's alive or dead.'

'OK guv, see you in a quarter of an hour.'

Ten minutes later H was pulling up by Scotland Yard when the phone went.

'Hilary,' he said, 'I've got a lead, I'm coming in to update everyone.'

'H...' ...Hilary paused.

It was only a single syllable but H could tell all was not well.

'Yeah, go on.'

'H, I warned you to keep well out of the Tara case, if you had anything to report it, but not get personally involved.'

'Yeah, but the case is connected somehow to the gangland murder wave, I've got clear proof.'

'H, two pieces of paper in a lock up are proof of nothing.'

H decided now was the time to tell her about the evidence on the CCTV, and was just about to talk when she cut him short, and came directly to the reason she had called.

'Detective Inspector Hawkins, I've called to tell you that as of this moment you are officially suspended from duty pending a full investigation of your conduct and psychological assessment. Do not come to the Yard, do not talk to any police officers and take no further part whatsoever in the investigations into the murder of Tara Ruddock and Jemima Fortescue-Smythe, the massacre in Soho, or any other ongoing police investigation.'

Part 3

50

Little Ronnie sat in his cell, lonely, distraught and in pain. How had it ever come to this? He'd taken a couple of vicious beatings and no doubt was going to take a few more; his old man had put half the convicts in this nick away at some point.

They could hardly believe their luck when Little Ronnie Hawkins turned up. The son of the great H, scourge of villains all over London, banged up on remand in Parkhurst high security prison. Young, innocent, naive. Ripe for the taking.

The opportunity for such easy, sweet revenge on the offspring of Hawkins of the Yard was about the best thing they could hope for in the hellhole in which they now lived their lives. Many of the villains H had put away were here long term, banged up until they were too old to be a danger on the streets. Forgiveness and redemption was not part of their makeup.

Time and time again the events that led to his arrest went through his mind. How could he have been so stupid?

He'd flown out alone to the Bulgarian coast, just to get away for a week or so. Have a break from London and forget about the dead end life he was living. This was the cheapest way there was now for young Europeans to get stuck into the no-holds-barred sun, sea, sex and booze madness. Ronnie had heard that in Bulgaria you could get buckets - actual, literal buckets - of booze for next to nothing.

I think I'll have some of that.

He could hardly believe his luck when, on the third day, the beautiful Elena sat down and started to talk to him at a beach bar.

'Where is from you?,' she asked, her accent so other, attractive and exotic. He was bowled over in seconds.

A little later, with a couple of buckets of he knew not what under his belt, he was introduced to her friend, Irajlo. The pair of them seemed so genuine as they showed him around, buying him drinks and taking a keen interest in his life back in London. He was high, he was happy. Never in a million years would it have occurred to him that he was being groomed.

It was on the day before his flight back, by which time he had tasted Elena's action and they had all become firm friends, that the beautiful Bulgarian girl and friendly Bulgarian boy asked him to deliver a package.

'Nothing to it, Ronnie. They not search good looking boys like you. Very easy money.'

But search him they had; and found six kilos of heroin. He hadn't even known what was in the package, although he suspected, of course. But he had made himself blind to the contents - Elena promised to join him in London as soon as she could - and to the consequences.

The lights on his block came on and the cell's locks clanked open. Once again he'd had no sleep, thoughts of suicide never far from his mind. But he'd made it, made it through another long, dark night. And now another day was about to start. Another day he didn't know if he could get through.

He was meant to be in a protected unit. But twice they'd got through. He didn't know who 'they' were, exactly. The beatings he'd taken had happened so quickly. Everything was a blur. They could have killed him if they'd wanted to but, it seemed, they wanted to keep him alive, to torment him, like killer whales toying with their prey before moving in for the final kill.

He knew it was coming; it was just a question of when, or whether he broke and finished the job for them. That was the only thing stopping him from ending his life: the thought that it was what they wanted.

As the cell door slid open he put his head in his hands, utterly despondent. He winced in pain as it reminded him the bruising around his puffed up eyes had not abated. He thought about the day ahead. A deep dark well of despair enveloped him.

First breakfast. The jeering, the insults, the spitting, the cuntings-off. Sure, he would be at a separate table with plenty of screws in attendance, but the constant hatred was almost as bad as a beating. It wore away at his nerves, knotted his guts up with dread.

Then more cell time - where he was alone and safe, for a while at least.

And then the worst part of the day. The exercise yard, fear stalking his every step. Shaking like a leaf; waiting - and at times praying - for the knife in the back that would end it all. True, he was separated from the majority of inmates (though he had to walk with the nonces, which made it even worse), but they could get anywhere, whenever they wanted. Whoever they were.

Then lock up time - another night of a despair so deep he had no idea where the bottom was, or if he would ever reach it.

The day, as days always do, made its inexorable way forward. Ronnie made his way to breakfast, accompanied by the voices of his many admirers: 'You cunt Hawkins,' 'You're dead, you fucking little wanker, do you hear me boy? I said do you fucking hear me?,' 'Any day now, you horrible little shitcunt. Get ready; you first, then your old man.'

Ronnie kept his own counsel. He tried to keep down a mouthful of porridge, but even that was more than his insides could manage.

Back to the cells. Then the day changed. When a screw next opened the cell it was at an unexpected hour.

'You're moving to 'A' wing.'

Ronnie was almost speechless as the implications rushed through his mind.

'What?'

'You heard. Get your stuff together. Five minutes.'

'But, but that has to be a mistake. I'm on a protected unit. I won't last five minutes out there. That's as good as fucking murder.'

'Look son, I don't make the rules. Either get your stuff together and go quietly or I'll come back with a firm and we can move you the hard way. Then I'll have you on the liquid cosh until you're dribbling like a little fucking baby. Your choice.'

Ronnie snapped. He'd been turned over twice by the inmates; if he was going to go down he would go down fighting.

'Go and fuck yourself.'

'Ok son, the hard way it is.'

51

Five minutes passed. Ronnie was almost past caring but prepared himself for the worst, trying to psych himself up to go mental. He had nothing to lose now; he wasn't going down without a fight. But things did not go according to plan; four tooled-up officers burst into his cell. He barely released a punch before the first truncheon crashed into his skull, and a split second later the end of the second thrust into his guts with the force of a battering ram.

As Ronnie curled in pain another blow smashed into his head. He lost consciousness.

He didn't know how long it had been - maybe five minutes, maybe five hours - when he started to regain awareness of his surroundings.

Bunk beds. He was in a different cell. He was on 'A' wing, completely at the mercy of the ruthless bastards who would break him now and kill him whenever they saw fit. He heard cruel laughter and banter outside his new cell.

No more. Can't take no more. Must end it now.

He looked around for a way out. His shoelaces had been taken when he'd arrived but the bed above had a sheet. He sprang up, grabbed it and quickly ripped it into long pieces. He wanted to act quickly but his fingers and thumbs shook, made clumsy by the panic that had gripped him.

Make speed not haste Ronnie, speed not haste.

He focused hard. His dad had taught him every type of knot in the book as a young boy. He remembered the lessons. He knew what he was doing. He didn't have time to consider the irony; the lessons his dad had given him so he could save lives now being used to end his own.

He tied two pieces of sheet together. Long enough now. He readied the noose.

Ronnie moved the lone chair to the window, stood on it and tied the sheet securely to the bars. An odd sense of serenity came over him as he tightened the noose around his neck and kicked the chair away.

But he'd made haste, not speed. He'd neglected to shut himself in. Alerted by the noise, a prisoner entered the cell, lifted his gasping body as if it was lighter than a scarecrow, undid the noose and tossed him onto the lower bunk.

Ronnie lay there frightened to look, frightened to think. What lay in store for him now? Multiple rape, beatings, torture. What more arrows of outrageous fucking fortune would he have to suffer now, before he would be released from this world?

He had learned that bravado and terror were uneasy bedfellows, as the derring-do of the suicide attempt collapsed into fear. He was utterly terrified as he lay on the bed, waiting for the dreadful fate he thought was about to be unleashed upon him. Fear had crawled inside his head, had burrowed its way into his subconscious and was now consuming every fibre of his being, like maggots devouring every single scrap of a piece of rotted fruit.

Then the prisoner spoke.

'Every prison is like separate kingdom. Has own rules, own kings, Ronnie.'

Ronnie turned round, startled by the reassuring reference to his name, and looked into the eyes of his new cell mate, eyes that were as deep, dark and impenetrable as his own despair.

'Who are you?'

'This wing now my kingdom. I protect you.'

'Why. Who are you? Why would you protect me? Why was I moved here? What's going on?'

The prisoner vaulted to the top of his bunk, sat back and wrestled with a broadsheet newspaper.

'My name is Basim. Basim Dragusha. Please to meet you, Ronnie.'

52

John was feeling not at all confident as he entered the Queen's Head pub in Waterloo. He'd heard from Podge, a small time crook and close friend, about some dodgy goings on in the area and had decided to take a look. John was a creature of habit and his days usually consisted of the same pubs, same bookies, same cafe. His confidence always plummeted when he was off his own manor. He needed his routines like a junkie needs a fix.

This particular pub was situated opposite a small estate just off the main drag that led up to Waterloo Bridge. It wasn't his type of pub. It was clean, modern and plush leather chairs adorned its spotless dark oak floors and crisp magnolia walls. Beer was a fiver a pint. It was a transient kind of place, designed to draw in commuters for a drink or two before they made their way back to suburban south west London from the Waterloo mainline. But it did have one advantage, which was the clean windows through which you could watch the outside world go by. And Confident John was here to watch.

H had made it clear he wanted an extra, extra special effort to find the bastard who he'd seen fleeing along Berwick Street after the mayhem at the Russians' club, and who had been getting hold of the wife of his best mate. He wanted Agapov found, double sharpish, if he was still alive. So John had risen to the occasion and decided to check out Podge's lead.

'I'm telling you John, there's definitely something happening on that estate around the back of Waterloo. My mate lives there and says a flat that's been unoccupied for months is suddenly a hive of activity. Geezers with dark suits dropping in and out all hours of the day and night. He reckons they sound like Poles, or Russians or something.'

He'd heard plenty of rumours and thought of giving H a call but didn't want to send him all over London on a series of wild goose chases. So here he was, giving personal attention to the possibility that the bastard the big man was so desperate to track down might be here.

He sauntered up to the bar in his best non-confident confident manner and smiled at the barmaid

'Pint of lager please love.'

He took his pint, found a seat and sat down with a copy of the Racing Post. He sat, unusually, in the middle of the bar because it had the best views of the outside world. Confident John was usually more of a quiet corner kind of bloke.

He sipped his beer slowly, occasionally looking outside with as much nonchalance and disinterest as he could muster.

He ordered another pint, and another. He wasn't used to this surveillance lark. Time drifted by as slowly as the double-maths lessons at Scott Lidgett school had, when he was a boy. But he didn't mind how long he sat there - if there was one commodity Confident John Viney had in spades it was time. Time to drink. Time to study the racing form. Time to watch the world go by.

He'd arrived at 2 pm and it was now 7; London had passed from daylight to darkness.

An SUV with tinted windows pulled up outside the flats he was watching. His heart rate accelerated. A mother with two crying kids in tow got the shopping out of the back and went into a flat a few doors down. John ordered another beer.

A few more beers later it was close to closing time and he was ready to get a cab back to Bermondsey when a black Mercedes crawled up and came to a halt outside the pub. Four lumps in dark suits climbed out and looked about, checking out the landscape. He fought his compulsion to look at them directly but failed, and one of them clocked him staring. He became agitated and his breathing quickened.

'Who do these fuckers think there're looking at?,' he mumbled, as he quickly refocused on the racing form in his paper. He nervously looked on from the corner of his eye, as the men made their way over to the flats he had spent the whole day watching, and went inside.

Number 72. Fuck me, I think Podge has nailed it.

He downed his pint and walked out of the pub. His confidence was still in extremely short supply as he crossed the road and headed for the flat. He was shitting himself. He didn't normally do things like this but he wanted to be certain. Just a peep through the windows, see what he could see. Just a quick look.

He was halfway across the street, perspiring heavily, beer sweating through his pores, when the door opened. Panic set in. He couldn't act or think. The messaging system inside his brain shut down, unable to process the situation. He was like a hedgehog curling into a ball to protect itself from the oncoming path of a 20-ton tipper lorry.

A suit stepped out from the flat; the same one who had clocked him earlier. Their eyes met. John mustered every single bit of willpower he could find, commanded every sinew in his body to keep moving and act naturally. He wasn't a brave man.

Front it son, front it.

He kept walking, head down, straining to look like everything was normal. Just another day at the pub. Hiding his fear behind a friendly smile, he strolled past the imposing figure of the shadowy sentinel. Without looking back he turned into the first stairwell he came to. A massive sigh of relief released the tension.

He sprinted up to the first floor where, from the stairwell, he had a reasonable view of the flat in question. The sentinel went back into the flat.

Who are these fuckers? Look like KGB men from a Hollywood movie.

So what did he have? Four big fellas pull up in a Merc, go into a flat and make him feel nervous. He didn't want to call H. He didn't have enough.

160

With uncharacteristic decisiveness John settled on a plan of action. Back of the flats, he thought, ground floor flats usually have small gardens. He made his way round.

He found the gardens and considered scaling the six foot fence that surrounded them and seeing if he could take a look into the flat. At that point his decisiveness and courage deserted him.

But he couldn't let the big man down. Adjacent to the rear gardens was a small play area. A few swings, a roundabout, a slide. John tucked himself into the bushes that surrounded the play area and prepared for night watchman duties.

53

A proper Italian pizza restaurant in Dean Street. H arranged to meet Ronnie at nine; Ronnie was running late. H whiled away a few minutes, nursed a double scotch and reminisced. They had a lot of spots like this, sites of their adventures as young men. Boys, really.

Late one wet autumn night in…what was it, 1977? - Ronnie would know – they'd wound up here after a long session; they'd needed to take some carbs on board to soak up all the beer. The meal was hearty, washed down with a couple of bottles of red and a few glasses of grappa.

'What sort of money you holding, Ron?,' H said, picking his teeth and kicking back in his chair.

'Nish mate. I gave what I had left to that bird in Crackers, for a cab. I ain't got a tanner.'

'We'll have to do a runner then. I can't cover this lot. We've done nearly thirty quid here,' said H.

'I don't know H…We've had a few tonight.'

'Sort yourself out, you fucking tosspot. What are you, a man or a mouse? There's only one way out of here tonight,' said H, watching the waiters closely out of the corner of his eye. 'You first…on my count…one, two…'

Ronnie was up, his chair flying backwards, before H got to three, swarming through the door like a tramp tanked up on paint thinner. Not the surest on his feet he'd ever looked. H was going to have to back him up. He leapt out of his chair and joined Ronnie on the pavement outside, straightening him up and pulling him forward.

'Liven up Ron, let's fucking do one.'

And they were off, haring down Dean Street like there was no tomorrow.

The blood was running high; they were moving fast and got separated. The pavement was wet underfoot. The curses of irate and beefy Italian waiters could be heard behind them - this shit came out of their wages.

H kept going, gasping for breath, his ears pounding. Suddenly he heard 'Fuck!' and a cry of pain as Ronnie went down. H wheeled himself round and saw four men in white shirts closing in on his friend like a pack of hyenas.

Ronnie was curled up, trying to protect his head and already well into the first phase of a proper kicking by the time H got back to him. He was moving at speed, behind a giant blue wheelie bin. He skittled two of the waiters over with it and then, while Ronnie struggled to his feet, launched himself at the other two, flailing, kicking and shouting.

The two of them on the attack was too much for the older men to handle. Sixty seconds of old school south London street fighting and the waiters thought better of it; they retreated back along Dean Street, gesticulating wildly and uttering foul curses.

Have that, you fucking mugs.

H snapped out of it and found himself back in 2015.

'Penny for 'em H,' said Ronnie, looming large over the table.

'I was just thinking about the time we did a runner out of here. You went down like a sack of shit that night, mate. I had to get you out of trouble, as usual. Remember?'

'Course I do. Happy days,' said Ronnie, breaking into his first real smile in an age.

'Happier than these, mate. Happier than these. Sit down son,' H said with a sigh, 'there's something I've got to tell you. About Tara.'

163

54

Ronnie's head was down, and H was having trouble getting him to lift it again. The Ruddock marriage had seen a few rocky passages, and Ronnie had suspected from time to time that Tara might have been at it with someone. But this? Sex club-owning Russian gangsters? Walking round town with her like they owned the place? Owned her?

H had hit him the second worst hammer blow of his life. Not the big man's fault. Had to be done. H had always done what had to be done.

Ronnie sat still, his head down, saying nothing. He had never known such pain, such rage, such impotent confusion as he had in the short period since H had phoned him in New York. And now this. He was glued to the spot, outwardly calm, while volcanic turmoil raged inside him.

H knew the signs. Better than anybody. 'Fancy a livener, son? Drop of scotch?,' he ventured.

Nothing.

Fuck me, he's lost it. He's worse than I was in the park. What did Amisha call it?...Poor bastard.

The long, horrible, pregnant pause stayed pregnant. H was starting to get the nasty sinking feeling he'd become too familiar with lately, like it wouldn't be long before he'd lose control of his emotions, and then his actions. He glugged his scotch and ordered two more doubles. He'd take care of Ronnie's if he didn't want it.

Ronnie raised his head; slowly, slowly. He was holding onto the sides of his chair; his face looked like a bag of wet cement. He fixed his eyes on H's.

'She was fucked up, H. Totally fucked up. I never told you about it…He nonced her. The old cunt nonced her, when she was a kid. He was interfering with her for years, on and off.'

Boom! Another boneshaking hammer blow, another horrible, gut-churning wrench. H processed it quickly; he'd had plenty of practice lately, and it was not, after all, the most unlikely story he'd ever heard. He made as if to speak. Ronnie held up his hand to stop him, and spoke wearily, with infinite sadness.

'Don't say anything H. There's no need to say anything...there's nothing you can say.'

Ronnie hung his head again and lapsed back into silence.

H thought back to the funeral. Ronnie hadn't talked to Old Shitbreath, hadn't shaken his hand, hadn't so much as looked in his direction. His instincts told him then that something was wrong - badly wrong.

H let Ronnie be for ten minutes, then said 'Listen, Ron, I want you to come and stay with us for a bit. I'll take you back to ours now. Olivia's about, she'll look after you. She'll tuck you in, you can get some kip. I've got to go out for a bit, so I'll drop you off and see you a bit later, alright?'

Sir Basil Fortescue-Fucking-Smythe - wrong 'un. I always knew he was a fucking wrong 'un.

He's going to pay for this.

55

Ninety minutes and three strong black coffees later, Ronnie having been safely deposited with Olivia, H pulled into Belgravia. He parked around the corner from his destination. He didn't have a plan as such: if Sir Basil was at home he'd play it by ear. He'd calmed down enough on the drive up from Eltham to see that going hammer and tongs at the old buffer in his own drum would get nobody anywhere, practically speaking; if there was no one at home he'd spin the place and see what he could find.

He snapped on a pair of gloves, stuck his hands in his pockets and sauntered around to Sir Basil's ground floor flat in a mansion block currently worth, he had read with interest, £18 million. No one about. He crept up the stairs. He held his breath as he pulled out his keys and jigglers and picked the lock. No burglar had much to teach him about making an entry - not even here, in what for years had been one of the burglary capitals of the Western world.

Inside, the hallway was quiet; getting through Sir Basil's door was a doddle. He was in.

No sign of a safe, so first things first: *nine times out of ten these old blokes think sticking things under the floor is the way to go.* H paced up and down, testing for hollows; he found a sweet spot, rolled up the Persian rug and loosened a floorboard. Bingo! A metal box. He jiggled the lock and pulled out an A4 brown paper envelope.

Here we go. God give me strength.

Photos. Disgusting pictures of children – small boys mostly - being got at. Breathing deeply and clenching his teeth, he stuffed the envelope into the back of his trousers and stood still for a moment to collect his thoughts. He found himself praying that Sir Basil would return home, now, and discover him.

166

If the old cunt comes in now I'll rip his bollocks straight off and feed them to him.

His eyes were accustomed now to the semi-darkness. He looked around, considering his options. A collection of framed photographs on a bookcase caught his attention. He sorted through them and one made his flesh start to crawl, a split second before he'd properly registered who was in it.

It was a group photograph taken at a fancy dinner. A group of eight men sitting around a huge table heaving with caviar and lobster, wine and vodka. H scanned the picture with ferocious intensity. He recognized four of the faces: Old Shitbreath himself, Sir Peregrine Blunt, and another face he had come up against plenty of times in his thirty year career, human rights lawyer Oswald Carruthers QC, and fat know-all around town Lord Timothy Skyhill.

At the centre of the picture was another face, one he didn't like the look of; a moody, foreign looking big shot he didn't recognize, or vaguely half-recognised but couldn't put a name to.

H was perplexed. What did all these paragons of virtue have in common, from such different sides of the political spectrum? This was no official function; this was a bunch of chums on a night out.

Fuck me. This lot are right at it. Sir Nonce and his noncey pals. Who else is on board? How far up does it go? And who's this moody looking bastard in the middle?

Questions, questions, questions. It was time to get some answers. He studied the photo again, looking for the weakest link in the chain…

Carruthers. Carruthers first. He could dish it out, when he was giving it large in the courtroom; but could he take it?

Let's see him try and talk his way out of this one.

H left the flat quietly, looking outwardly composed. But inside he could feel his moorings slipping. It took all his strength to keep himself from screaming. He'd had enough.

167

Of this hidden, never ending evil, of this sickening ruination of young lives. Of old Basil and his disgusting ilk, arrogant and untouchable, year after year.

Well someone was going to touch them now, and put the fear of God into them.

56

H had crossed swords on a number of occasions with Oswald Carruthers, QC; usually either being cross examined by him in the witness box or sitting mute while he talked a jury out of administering proper justice to some horrible villain. Carruthers had got more scoundrels off on technicalities than H had had hot dinners. H considered that this might be an appropriate point in their relationship for their roles to be reversed.

Time for me to ask the fucking questions.

Back in his car the big man called Amisha, the phone shaking in his hand, and began to channel his rage.

'Hello guv, how are you doing?'

'Ames, Oswald Carruthers QC. Address.'

'I'll have to go into classified records...'

'Now Ames, NOW.'

It was past midnight but it didn't take Amisha long to login into the police network and bypass the security protocols. In fact breaking the protocols of the Metropolitan Police was becoming something of a habit since she'd been teamed up with H. She felt she had the strength to resist his demands, if she wanted to. But she didn't want to. By the tone of his voice she knew he was onto something important. She gave him the address.

'So guv, what you got, what's happening?'

But H had already hung up.

Twenty minutes later he found himself sitting outside the gate of a large detached house in a private road in leafy Richmond, home to rock stars, media types and superstar lawyers.

He felt like a volcano moments before its eruption, ready to blow and bring its vengeance down upon an unsuspecting populace, but collected his thoughts and stayed calm for a few moments. He realised he'd just performed an act of breaking and entering, but had still only gone so far. Nobody knew. As he considered the immense implications of what he was about to do even H felt the need for a few moments' reflection. A last minute review before he went past the point of no return, before he himself became an outlaw.

Two absolutely mental firms were waging all-out war on the streets of London. One of the murderous bastards was getting hold of his best mate's wife, who then gets slaughtered in St James Park by someone nobody on planet earth has ever seen before.

Did Dragusha have her killed for revenge, or out of simple spite to undermine his foe? Having met Dragusha H knew it wouldn't be beyond him.

Did Agapov have her killed? Why? Fucking around with posh birds was one of his things.

Amidst this welter of chaos and uncertainty he discovers Tara was badly nonced by the old man. And as soon as he'd gone anywhere near Old Shitbreath and his chums he'd been suspended within ten minutes. Those guys had power, real power; they'd had various police enquiries shut down over the years. An old friend in MI6 had told him that.

Now, as he sat outside Carruthers' house his coppers intuition was zinging overtime. Something was wrong, something was very wrong.

The more H considered it the more apparent, in his own mind, his course of action became. His path was clear, as clear as an open road with no exits. If he stayed this side of the fence this fucking mess was never going to be cleared up. These people had already shown their power, their reach. He didn't doubt they had the ability to close down whole lines of investigation - and get him kicked off the force.

H's moment of calm, if not his confusion, was passing. He had always played it close to the line but he was about to throw away a lifetime of coppering. It was an illegal choice but, in his world at least, the only choice. Good was good and evil was evil, whatever the legalities.

H was about to go rogue. The calm before the storm was over. Time for the volcano to erupt.

57

H stepped out of the car, opened the boot and had a look at his tools. He always kept a crowbar and a 14lb sledgehammer in the back. You never know when they might come in handy. He tucked the crowbar inside his jacket, took out the hammer and walked purposefully over to the wrought iron gates. He lifted the heavy hammer, slung it behind his shoulders and brought it down with all the power and accuracy he could muster. Crash! The lock on the gate managed to resist the first blow. The second was more powerful, and more accurate. Bang! Still the gate resisted. But H had got his eye in. Wallop! The third blow was decisive.

The gate flew open and H marched up Oswald Carruthers' driveway with a crowbar in his jacket, a 14lb hammer in his hands and hatred in his eyes.

Inside the house Carruthers stirred. He'd fallen asleep, as usual, on his luxurious leather sofa whilst watching late night TV. He was a lonely man, his wife having divorced him some four years ago, since when he'd never searched for another partner. For years his habit had been to fall asleep on the sofa with a bottle of wine in hand.

He half registered the noise of hammer on iron. Was that coming from some late night horror film or was someone making a racket outside? Not here, he reassured himself, not in Richmond. His peace of mind was instantly destroyed, though, when H smashed through the lock on his front door. H's accuracy, timing and power were improving with each blow; the lock shattered instantly and the door burst open.

Carruthers sprang to his feet, scared and confused, and tried to grasp what has happening. As he pulled open the heavy oak door of his reception room a hand grasped him around the neck, lifted him a foot off the floor and let him go.

He fell to the floor, clutching his throat and looked timidly into the face of his attacker.

'Inspector Hawkins. May I ask what on earth you think you're doing? You are suspended as an officer of the law and...'

H's fist moved with the speed and accuracy of Mohammed Ali in his prime as he brought it down on the lawyer's s nose. He felt the nose break as a mixture of bone and blood gushed outwards and splattered against the embossed floral wallpaper that adorned the walls.

H took the picture of Old Shitbreath and his chums from his back pocket and opened it.

He pointed to the man in the centre of the picture.

'Name?'

'It's Kyril Kuznetsov. What's this all about, Detective Inspector?'

'Fuck,' said H, realising he had seen the Russian several times in the papers. He should have been able to recall that.

'And what is he to do with you?'

'Nothing. It was just a social event, I meet all types of people.'

H wasn't in the mood. He really wasn't. He brought his fist down in the same spot of Carruthers' face as before. Carruthers passed out.

Oh shit.

H made his way to the kitchen, found and filled a bucket with cold water, returned and threw it over his prone victim's face . The lawyer came to.

H took out the other pictures he had found at Sir Basil's.

'Do you know anything about these?'

'Oh God,' said Carruthers.

If H had expertise in anything it was in reading people. He was in no doubt about Carruthers' involuntary facial spasms, the gasping in his throat, the closing up of his body. He'd revealed himself.

173

'You sick little bastard. Who else in this group is involved with you and Sir Basil Fortescue-Fucking-Smythe. Where do you get these kids from?'

Carruthers was scared and in pain but his thirty years in the legal profession steered him into auto-lawyer mode. 'Detective Inspector Hawkins, you have no evidence … Do you really think it's appropriate to come to my house without a warrant. In a court of law...'

H couldn't stand it. He'd been cross-examined and outfoxed by Carruthers one time too many. He knew he'd lose in a court of law, no question.

But this was no court of law. He took the crowbar out from the inside of his jacket, extended his arm to its limit and smashed the crowbar into Carruthers' face with maximum force. It was a face that was never going to look the same again, as Carruthers' cheeks split open, his skull fractured and his jawline splintered in multiple locations. For the second time that evening the distinguished Queen's Counsel passed out.

Cunt.

58

It was 3 am by the time H pulled up outside Amisha's place in Greenwich. The adrenalin that had been surging since he'd made the entry into Sir Basil's place, and that had peaked during his hammering of Carruthers, had ebbed and flowed away. Now he was exhausted - manic still, but exhausted.

Was the lawyer dead? If he was alive, how long would it be before he could speak and identify his attacker? Had there been any CCTV cameras he hadn't seen? As it stood, H did not know the answer to any of these questions. But he'd crossed the line. He'd been driven over the line. And now he would be a fugitive himself, and get a taste of his own medicine. The hunter would now be the hunted.

She's good as gold, this girl. She'll never grass me up. But they'll use her to try and get to me.

'People are so stupid,' Amisha had told him not long after she'd come on board with him, 'they put their whole life on their phones. They don't seem to know, or care, that we can get to almost all their data now, and often as not figure out where they are.'

She'd schooled him long and hard on all that stuff, and in the end the penny had dropped.

H switched his phone off, removed the battery and eased himself out of the car. The street was quiet. Nobody about. He crept, bulkily but skilfully, round the back and into Amisha's garden. He peered in through the ground floor window and saw a dark kitchen but a light on in a room, or a passage, beyond it. He tapped on the widow.

Amisha appeared within seconds, dressed in silk pyjamas and wielding a whopping great baseball bat. H liked her style, and for the first time the sight of her triggered a severe stirring in his trousers. He pressed his face to the glass so she could see he was not some random burglar or sex monster. She recognized him with relief and motioned him towards the door.

H burst in. As she always did now, Amisha spent a few seconds carefully appraising his condition. Was he in control of himself? Where was his head at?

She assessed him as wired but rational. 'What the hell is going on H? Phone calls in the middle of the night, human rights lawyers, and now this? What the hell are you up to?'

'I need your help Ames. I'm onto something. Something big.'

'But you're suspended from duty guv.'

'Fuck that Ames. I haven't got time to fuck about. No time. I've got to go missing.'

'Again?'

'Again. But this is serious now. Something's coming together. In my head. Some sort of conspiracy. Nonces. Some big names involved. Very big names. I need you to help me join up the dots. The Dark Web, I remember you telling me about the Dark Web.'

'Guv... I don't know. You're suspended. We're not even supposed to talk. And you're creeping around finding conspiracies and asking me to help you? Have you lost the plot again? I...'

She's not up for it. She needs a persuader.

H held up his hand to slow her down before she could build up a head of steam, and fished the envelope containing Old Shitbreath's photos out of the back of his trousers. He handed it to her. She got as far as the second one before her eyes filled with tears, and she began to weep.

176

59

They sat at the kitchen table. Coffee for her, scotch for him. Amisha had regained her composure.

H brought her up to speed. He talked her through the sequence of events: his meeting with Ronnie, Ronnie's collapse, the search of Sir Basil's place. He showed her the group photo: Old Shitbreath and his pals, all merry and bright. The best he saved for last.

Amisha could not believe what she was hearing. 'What? You did what? Oswald Carruthers? Fucking hell H…is he even alive?' She shouted.

Fuck. I'm dragging her down into my world.

'Don't know. Don't care. You've seen the photos, Ames. I'm not having it. Not anymore. I'm going to bring this fucking lot down. If it's the last thing I do. That evil old bastard was abusing Tara when she was a little baby girl. And now he's got a whole bunch of these cunts round him, and they're doing whatever the fuck they like. All those kids…I'm not having it.'

'But guv…what are you now…judge, jury and executioner?'

H fixed her with the look. 'Ames, listen to me. These are the fucking judges and executioners. We're talking about the House of fucking Lords, the High fucking Court, and God knows what else. We can't even get an investigation into Tara's murder off the ground properly. They've shut the shop up. They've had me suspended. Look at the fucking picture.'

He dragged the group photo to the centre of the table.

'Look at them, Ames…Sir Basil Fortescue-Smythe, Lord Timothy Skyhill, Sir Peregrine Blunt, Oswald Carruthers QC, and the rest of them. And this moody looking fucker, Kyril Kuznetsov, one of the richest men in the world,' he said, pointing at the face at the centre of the group. 'If this ain't some sort of massive nonce conspiracy…they never hung Crippen.'

Amisha took it all in. She updated her assessment of the big man's condition.

He's finally lost it. It's all been too much. He's surged off the cliff edge, and he's hurtling towards the rocks like a character from the old cartoons.

And yet…everything he's saying makes sense.

'I don't know, guv. If Carruthers is alive you're a fugitive now. Being thrown off the force will be the least of your problems. You haven't just crossed the line - you've shat all over it so badly you can't even see where it is anymore. And what about me, my career. My life?'

Uh oh. I'll have to let her sleep on this one.

'OK Ames. Got it. Fair enough. I hear what you're saying. But I need information on their connections, all the stuff they hide. I won't be able to do it without you. And there's no one else I can trust. Look at those pictures of the kids again. Have a little think.'

He rose from his chair and headed for the door.

'Guv,' Amisha said, 'don't come here again. They're going to be all over me like flies on a Richard the Third.'

He smiled at her use of his kind of talk. She was still onside.

Good girl. Fucking good girl.

'And if you need to contact me - I mean really need to - don't use your phone. Use a burner. And don't email me.'

178

60

Graham, just back from his morning run, showered and set himself up at the breakfast bar. In a change to his former morning routine, these days he sparked up the tablet first and went straight to Joey Jupiter before he hit the decaff and grapefruit. He had developed a morbid fascination with the torrents of ridicule and abuse now being regularly swept over him by Jupiter; and he liked to try and guess beforehand, on any given day, whether it was to be himself or Hawkins who would bear the brunt of Jupiter's vicious sarcasm.

The page came up; it was headed by a new graphic, which showed Miller-Marchant and Hawkins comically entwined, gurning and drooling for all they were worth like an utterly deranged Punch and Judy. Graham scanned the screen quickly and breathed a sigh of relief: it was, on balance, an H day, as it had been for the last week or so:

'BIG MAN' AND 'LITTLE MANBOT': THE CHAOS CONTINUES

London's descent into chaos continues. Not content with allowing a murderous gang war to run the streets of the metropolis ankle-deep in blood, the Metropolitan Police now seem incapable of securing the safety of even the most respectable and highly regarded members of the city's elite. This morning Oswald Carruthers QC, whom as far as we know has never harmed a fly, lies in intensive care in the Richmond Royal Hospital, after being beaten to within an inch of his life during a home invasion.

We do not yet know which of the Met's titans will be leading the investigation into this deeply unsettling crime. For how long, in the continuing absence of Harry 'H' Hawkins, 'London's Top Copper,' are we to be left without a defender? Are the streets of our great city going to be allowed to melt down while this noble sleuth kicks his heels in Eltham, hammering the scotch and dribbling over his puzzle book? We should be told.

Meanwhile Detective Inspector Graham Miller-Marchant, of whom little more needs to be said – indeed, about whom there was not much to be said in the first place – remains in charge of the 'investigation' into the carnage in St James' Park. Can it be long, given this, before public demand begins to grow for a reinstatement of the mighty 'H'? Might it be, after all, since we appear to be restricted to the shallow end of the gene pool when it comes to the recruitment of our defenders of law and order, that a dinosaur with a brain the size of a walnut is preferable to a sleek but utterly useless invertebrate?

61

Kyril Kuznetsov walked into the plush surroundings of his offices in Knightsbridge with his regular bodyguards in tow. The Kuznetsov Corporation didn't have any external neon signs nor corporate logo pronouncing its power and grandeur to the outside world. Kuznetsov had learned to use his power quietly, from behind the scenes.

A small plaque saying 'Kuznetsov Industries Incorporated' embossed in gold hung discreetly on the wall behind the reception desk, the only visible sign that one had entered the London HQ of one of the largest energy companies in the world.

Kuznetsov crossed the marble entrance, smiled pleasantly at the receptionist as he passed by into a restricted access corridor and took the private lift to the top floor. He maintained the pleasant smile and air of cordiality as he greeted various employees on his way to his office. A quiet, serious looking man was waiting for him outside; Kuznetsov beckoned him.

The serious looking man was one of Kuznetsov's most trusted and was a man who could keep a secret, which was just as well as he knew more secrets about Kuznetsov than anyone else alive.

With the office door firmly closed behind them Kuznetsov's mask slipped to reveal the fury and anger that was waiting to burst out into the open. He was a man who liked his illegal businesses to tick over nice and easy, bringing in a little cash flow but, far more importantly, affording him access to those members of the great and the good of the British establishment who had an ingrained, uncontrollable predilection for young boys, a predilection he had exploited to great advantage for many years.

'How fuck has this happened? A war breaks out on streets of London. Threatens everything I have built. The police investigations will be wide and deep, and may drag high profile clients in. This stops now.'

The other man spoke in soft tones, calmly and without fuss.

'What are negotiation parameters?'

Kuznetsov subdued his anger and spoke in a more businesslike manner. This was just business, after all.

'Offer the Albanians ten million pounds. Agapov they can have to torture and kill and they can control business south of the river. I don't care what happens there. If they accept these conditions, all violence stops.'

'If they not accept?'

'Bring in a small army. A hundred men.'

The inscrutable one nodded his understanding and turned to leave. As he opened the office door Kuznetsov gave a final instruction:

'Make it very clear to them that they can accept my terms, or they can all be killed. They will all die: men, women, children. All of them.'

62

Ronnie felt physically and emotionally exhausted after the ordeal in the pizza place. He'd gone down like a sack of spuds; he was asleep as soon as his head hit the pillow. The last few weeks had been the worst of his life. When he woke up it took him a while to get his bearings. He recalled the night before and remembered he was at H's.

The revelation of Tara's deepest secret had unlocked half a lifetime of lies, evasions and repressed emotion. For years he had tried to keep it locked securely away, at the back of his mind, in the part of the brain labelled 'Pandora's Box,' the part that needed to be kept locked to contain the demons that could burst forth and destroy his world. At Tara's insistence he had kept the secret all his life.

He recalled the shock when she had first told him the gory details, when she'd first found the courage to trust him. The news shattered him, made him murderously angry.

'I'm going to confront him. I'm going round to his house and God help me if I don't kill him.'

'Ronnie, no. Please. I asked you to stay calm. For my sake. I've held this in all my life. I've never told a soul. It's taken me years to find the courage to tell you. You have to keep the secret with me. You have to help me live with this - just you and me Ronnie. Nobody else.'

After he'd calmed down he'd stuck to his promise and kept quiet. He knew he could never heal the pain Tara carried with her. He thought about it often, as the years went by, and he wished she'd never told him. The secret hadn't unified them. Over time it had opened a gap between them and, as much as he loved her, he found it difficult to live with. He wanted to protect her, to avenge her. But he had been sworn to secrecy, and to inaction.

And when he'd suspected she had started to have affairs he turned a blind eye. Keep things under wraps. Keep Pandora's Box locked tight.

But the shock of her involvement with savage gangsters had hit him hard, made him confront the truth. The box had been opened and could never be locked again.

He trundled downstairs, head bowed, and entered the kitchen where Olivia was making tea. It was as if a tidal wave of sadness and regret had flooded the room. Her heart went out to him and she gave him a big hug and tenderly kissed his cheeks.

But as good a listener as Olivia was she was not quite ready to hear the full story, and Ronnie was not quite ready to tell it. So they skipped around it.

'Tea?'

'Thanks love. Any news from H?'

'No, nothing. God knows what he got up to last night. I've known him a long time and seen his rages and moods over the years. But last night was something different. The rage was there, but mixed with a kind of abandon. Like he just didn't care about anything, or maybe he cared so much about something that he didn't care what he did. I'm worried sick Ron.'

'Don't worry Liv, whatever he's up to he'll come through. He always has. He always will.'

63

H came to in an unfamiliar bed, alone. It was 1pm, and there was a two-thirds empty bottle of scotch on the bedside table. He felt as if some great animal, maybe a big brown bear, had sliced the top of his head off, scooped out what was left of his brain, and shat into the hole. Same old same old. He had some trouble figuring out where he was, but focused hard and recalled that he was in one of Ronnie's high-end apartments, which were dotted around Rotherhithe, close to the river.

Not the best spot in the world to go to ground in, but beggars can't be choosers.

He still had no idea if he'd killed old Oswald, put him into a coma or merely given him a proper old-school pasting. He fumbled for a remote and switched the TV on. It was wall-to-wall Carruthers. The Royal Richmond Hospital. The great man in intensive care. A home invasion. Hilary doing the honours at the press conference, talking a lot but saying nothing. No news on the culprit or culprits.

He moved to the kitchen and pottered about, in ultra-slow motion, until he managed to put a cup of coffee together. Now he was ready to focus. Yesterday's highlights: Ronnie in bits; Old Shitbreath's paedo club; Carruthers on the deck, twitching in a pool of blood; the summit meeting with Amisha.

He was in the shit now; bang in it. He reviewed his position: suspended from the only thing he knew how to do, a public laughing stock, soon to be a public enemy. His boy in the nick. Hiding out in Ronnie's flat, unable to go and see Olivia. Up to his bollocks in the grief being caused by the Russians and the Albanians. And now, to top it all off, he was on the scent, as a completely rogue element, of a nonce conspiracy involving a bunch of the most high-profile and powerful men in the country. His psychological and emotional state he left out of the reckoning.

Focus on the details. Figure out a way through the maze.

He threw on his clothes, snapped the battery back into his phone and sparked it up. Just a quick look to see if there was anything, any message, he could use. He scanned his inbox: nothing but aggravation there, except for a message from Olivia. He didn't read it.

First thing: get a few burners. Got to call Olivia, she'll be worried sick.

He turned the phone over to take the battery out, but heard a Ping! as he slid the back off. Number unknown. He opened the message, and read:

HAVE SEARCHED DARK WEB. WE NEED TO TALK. URGENT. MEET AT EGG AND BACON BARRY'S. 2PM.

Amisha. She's on board. Fucking good girl! I've got half a chance now.

The big man was out of the flat in a flash, pocketing the phone and pulling on his jacket as he swarmed down the stairs. He jumped into his car, lit up the blue light and gunned towards the Walworth Road for all he was worth.

It was 1.40.

64

Confident John had stayed awake at his post all night, fuelled by the charlie he always kept round him for emergencies and by his commitment to helping the big man. He'd surprised himself at his staying power; 99 times out of 100 he'd have normally given up.

He'd watched the four KGB lookalikes patrol the area in turns throughout the night, and as dark turned to light he'd watch the sunrise slowly shine its rays onto the dawning of a new day. It was something he hadn't seen for a number of years given his normal routine: bed around 2am, up by midday, maybe a little later.

He'd taken the liberty of nipping off for a quick breakfast but was soon back at his post at the rear of the flats. A few more hours, a few more lines of cocaine to iron out.

He continued his vigil. The sun reached its zenith. One of the sentinels did another round. He'd worked out they were creatures of habit and that it would be at least half an hour before another one came by.

Fuck it - enough hanging about. Time for action

John did another line to boost his confidence and went for it. He cut a comic figure as he scaled the fence that secured the rear of the flats. Anyone watching would have creased up in laughter as he tumbled down the other side. The eight or nine pints from the day before hadn't done much to help his co-ordination and spatial awareness, but the marching powder drove him on and numbed the pain as he landed on a broken bottle.

Fuck it!

He collected himself together and, with as much stealth as he could manage, inched his way to the rear window and knelt down below it.

He sat for five minutes, as once again fear gripped him and tried its best to determine his behaviour. Once again he overcame it.

The things I fucking do for H. Next time he can do this his fucking self

Slowly, ever so slowly, he lifted his head. He had a sense of what it might feel like going over the top of a trench and was half expecting to be met by a volley of automatic gunfire. Through the net curtains he saw two men watching TV, and a third reading a paper. The fourth, the one who had now clocked him twice, was nowhere to be seen. On patrol somewhere in the locality, no doubt.

But asleep on the sofa, with a drip of something or other feeding his veins, was Agapov. No doubt about it.

Bingo!

He got out his mobile. Even he had a mobile now, and he'd learnt how to use it. He quietly tapped the phone icon, then contacts, and pressed on H. Straight to voicemail.

Fuck it - the fucker's never about when you really need him.

He'd only ever sent a few texts in his life but the recent lessons from his niece were standing him in good stead. He got control of his quivering hands and started stabbing at the tiny keys.

H. FOUND YOUR MAN. FLAT 72, HUXLEY HOUSE, FARADAY STREET, WATERLOO. 4 GUARDS. THEY LOOK TASTY. BE CAREFULL.

He hit the send button.

Time to do the off.

65

H was bang on time. He said his hellos to Egg and Bacon Barry, ordered a full-scale heart attack on-a-plate and settled back into his plastic moulded chair to wait. His hangover needed feeding and Olivia was not around to restrain him. He felt free; a man on a mission, out in the world on his own, taking orders or advice from no one.

No Amisha yet. He surveyed the scene and waited for her to walk in. His food arrived and he gorged on it like a hungry dog, hunched low over the plate.

'Any good H?' asked Barry, after the show was over.

'Blinding. Top notch. Another cup of tea please mate,' said H, leaning back in his chair. But where there should have been contentment there was only unease. It was ten past two. H had never known Amisha to be so much as a minute late. For anything. Ever.

I'll give it 'til half past.

He gulped down a third cup of tea and hit the street at twenty five past. His guts were churning; he was electric with anxiety. High anxiety. He rushed into an all-purpose Nigerian shop - 'International money transfer. Cheapest rates' - and bought the cheapest dumbphone he could find, pay-as-you-go. He punched Amisha's number into it. Nothing.

He was certain now; something was up. There was nothing else for it - he would have to risk going to her place. There was no other option. He jumped back into the car and, for the second time in less than a day, set a course for Greenwich.

H pulled into her street slowly. No sign of her flat being watched. He parked up and crept round the back and into the garden, as he had in the early hours. Straight away he saw, with alarm, that the back door was open. It had been forced, by someone who knew what they were doing. He reached inside his jacket, pulled out his cosh - the good old spring-loaded he'd been cracking heads with for donkey's years - and eased himself inside.

All was quiet. His heart pounding, he moved to the living room and sized up the scene immediately: overturned chairs, bits and pieces strewn all across the room and, in the middle of the floor, a baseball bat, flecked with blood.

That's my girl, didn't go without a fight... fuck me, she's got some bottle...but who's taken her? And why? What the fuck is going on?

His head span and his blood surged. He sat down; he needed to breathe, to think. He needed a plan - but he was out on a limb now, winging it, almost alone. *Almost.* He still had Ronnie. And John. But how could they help him with his next move? And what was that going to be, exactly?

Fact was, he was out of ideas, or directions to move in. He'd go out, get another dumbphone, and let Olivia know he was OK. And then...? Without thinking, he slid the battery back into his proper phone. Scrolling down his inbox, he again saw an endless list of messages that could only drive him nuts, text after text he would never read, until he came to:

H. FOUND YOUR MAN. FLAT 72, HUXLEY HOUSE, FARADAY STREET, WATERLOO. 4 GUARDS. THEY LOOK TASTY. BE CAREFULL.

Bingo! Gotcha, you cunt!

H had no idea how, or if, Agapov was connected to Amisha's disappearance. But he was sure as hell connected with Tara's death. This was the break he'd been waiting for. He drove into Greenwich and bought a handful of second hand dumbphones. They were getting harder to find. With one of them he let Olivia know he was safe and well.

That was as much as he could do for now.

66

John's text had advised caution. But it was too late for careful. Far too late.

H had sent Amisha into the Dark Web, recruited her to his lone wolf campaign against a high level conspiracy, and now she was gone. This was on him. He had no idea if the bastards who had taken her would keep her alive. What had she found? How had they found her?

If she was still alive, though, he would find her. And if she was dead he would find everyone, absolutely everyone involved, and he would take no prisoners.

In war he had always acted under the constraints of the Geneva Convention; in Civvy Street he had, for the most part at least, acted within the constraints of the legal system. Now he was outside, outside of everything he had spent his life defending. All bets were off.

Time was of the essence. He needed to act and act quickly. He'd never memorized many phone numbers but Confident John's was one that had stuck in his mind along the way. He thought about texting but it took too long. He needed proper communication so he punched the number into one of the dumbphones and pressed call.

In normal times Confident John didn't usually accept calls from unknown numbers. But these were not normal times.

'John, it's H.'

'H, fucking hell mate. Have you read my text?'

'Yeah, thanks. Nice work mate. I need a shooter, now. Something proper. Automatic.'

'Thought you would ask that; it'll take some time.'

'No time mate. No fucking time whatsoever. What can you get hold of now?'

'An old revolver. Six rounds. But I shouldn't think this mob want to play cowboys.'

'On my way.'

H was on autopilot. He unthinkingly navigated the route to John's as he considered the situation and constructed a plan. He thought the Russians might move Agapov to a new location and he didn't want to turn up and find him gone. He knew they didn't know anything about the kidnapping, didn't, in all likelihood, know anything whatsoever about Amisha. But he knew Tara, knew Tara well, and if the kidnapping was related in any way to Amisha investigating Old Shitbreath and his chums...well, it was the only possible link he had.

He arrived at John's third floor flat, gulping in air after his breakneck sprint up the stairs, and hammered on the door.

'John, lively mate.'

John opened the door. He looked like shit, exhausted from more than twenty four hours of non-stop surveillance. H could see he'd pushed the boat out to help him but this was no time for niceties.

'Thank fuck I'm not a copper,' said John as he passed the gun to H. H checked it was fully loaded; all six bullets were present and correct.

'Don't suppose there are any more bullets about?'

'Afraid not H,' said John, 'that's your whack. Tell me you're not going it alone? You'll need more than that with this firm.'

H made no reply. Just eye contact, a faint smile and a nod of friendship. He turned and bolted down the stairs as fast as his girth and joints would allow. Which was actually very fast. He was inside his car and heading for Waterloo before John knew it.

Less than fifteen minutes later the big man came to a juddering halt in Faraday Street, jumped out of his car and ran at number 72 like a crazed rhino. Fast and direct had always been his preferred option, once he'd discounted all the others.

To a casual observer it would have appeared as if a man pulled up outside a flat and ran at the door without thinking. But the casual observer would have been wrong. H was in the zone and had assessed his options at lightning speed the moment he turned into the street. He had a mental map of the landscape and every individual; the traffic situation and options on a getaway were clear, and he'd stopped bang in the middle of the road to make sure they stayed that way. He'd flipped the switch to open the car boot, left the engine running and left the driver's door wide open. Now to use the best weapon he had - surprise.

He ran at the door, assessing it as he moved. He reckoned it was light enough to knock through at first contact if he hit it with everything he had.

Tasty are they John? We'll fucking see about that.

The door gave way as if it were a plywood prop, like a flimsy saloon door in an old Western. H stormed into the flat with pistol in hand.

Bang! The first of the sentinels went down in the kitchen.

John said four. One down three to go.

H kicked the living room door in.

His actions had been so fast that the two thugs guarding Agapov were still removing their guns from their holsters. As he burst into the room H delivered a shot to the right knee of the first, disabling him. The second guard needed two shots, one in each leg, to slow him down.

Tough bastard. Only two shots left now

He turned his attention to Agapov, who stared in astonishment at the speed, accuracy and sheer balls of Inspector Harry 'H' Hawkins.

'Right sunshine, you're coming with me.'

H cut loose the drips that were providing their slow burn sustenance, threw Agapov over his shoulder and was back at the front door within seconds.

67

Yevgeny Kondrashin, the guard who had clocked Confident John the previous evening, watched on amazed as a lone nutter pulled up, attacked the safe house and came out with the booty in less than a minute.

As he kneeled behind the boot of Harry's car, pistol in hand, he thought it was almost a shame he had to kill such an impressive guy. He would have liked to have met him for a vodka or two, learned about what made him tick.

Who is he? What fuck is he on?

Kondrashin raised his pistol and took aim as H, with his parcel secured on his shoulder, charged out of the flat.

But the Russian really had no idea just how extraordinary H was when he was in the zone. H knew these firms always posted a sentry outside and had already clocked Kondrashin on the way in. A tall no-nonsense type in a dark suit and tie and what was obviously a gun holster crinkling an otherwise impeccably tailored suit.

Gotcha - I'll deal with you on the way out my son.

H would have bet his mortgage the guard would take up position by the boot of his car. Good cover, clear direct shot as soon as H exited the flat. Close enough not to miss, almost guaranteed a kill on the first shot. In truth H had bet more than his mortgage on it, much more. H had bet his life on it.

And every time in his life H had made a wager this large he had backed himself with utter conviction. It was the reason he was still alive.

As he charged out of the flat he kept low and at an angle, ensuring Agapov covered nearly all of his body, if viewed from the angle he expected his assailant to be seeing things from.

H had positioned his valuable merchandise perfectly. The human shield was enough to make Kondrashin hesitate for a split second, still confident his anonymity ensured the upper hand. This moment's hesitation was all H needed.

He who hesitates is lost.

H fired off one round with pinpoint accuracy, putting a hole through the palm of Kondrashin's hand. More than enough to disable him and send his gun juddering backwards across the street.

H made his way to the car.

The wounded Kondrashin piped up: 'Whoever you are, wherever you go hide, we find you. We hunt you down. You dead man.'

'Bollocks' said H as he threw Agapov into the back seat of the car. 'You got it the wrong way round pal. Tell your bosses they have absolutely no fucking idea whatsoever who they're dealing with. And tell them to look over their shoulders because I'll be the one coming for them.'

H jumped into the front seat and sped off like lightening, driven by the hurricane of emotions raging within him. It had taken him less than two minutes to bring Waterloo to a standstill, but the storm hadn't blown itself out yet, not by a long stretch.

Right fuckface, we'll take you somewhere nice and cosy and then you and me can have a little chat.

68

Confident John was reclining on his battered old sofa. The smell of three days unwashed dinner plates permeated the air, mingling with the aroma of the finest skunk his variable income could buy. After the excitements of the previous day he needed to block himself up and calm himself down.

He was in the middle of a long draw, trying to relax after his earlier encounter with the big man. He was racked by guilt for letting H take on a serious Russian firm single-handed, but the level of bottle and violence needed for such a mission just wasn't in him. *H knows that*, he kept repeating to himself, trying to assuage his deep sense of shame at letting the big man go it alone.

God help him...what if?

His phone went; with a surge of relief he saw that it was the same number H had called him on earlier. He pressed ACCEPT.

'H, you at Waterloo yet mate?'

'The merchandise is secured. Need a favour.'

Fucking hell, how has he managed that?

'Anything H, anything at all mate.'

'You still any good at the old taking-and-driving-away?'

'Yeah, when do you need it?'

'Fifteen minutes, I'll meet you in the car park behind your flats. Get something roomy: this Russian's a right lump.'

Twenty minutes later H was bundling Agapov into the back of a spacious estate whilst barking orders.

'I'm off. Make that other motor disappear John, quick as you can; half the coppers in London will be looking for it in ten minutes.'

'Right you are H.'

H jumped into the newly stolen car and unwound the window.

'John, I've asked a lot of you these past few days. Thanks mate, I owe you.'

John smiled, his earlier sense of guilt fading from his mind.

'No problem H, go and do what you gotta do.'

H now kept to the speed limit - nice and easy does it - as he cruised through the south east London streets. The area around his lockup, one of a series of arches underneath the railway station at Elephant and Castle, was relatively quiet. It had been in the family since the days his grandfather had run a rag and bone business and, later, had been used by his kid brother to store the kind of back-of-a-lorry stuff H didn't want or need to know about.

H pulled the car to a halt inside the lockup, jumped out and sealed the metal doors tight with the heavy bolts. He returned to the car, flipped the boot open, dragged out his load, dropped him onto the floor and administered a well-aimed kick to the bollocks for starters.

Agapov was still writhing in agony as H placed his hands in the police issue handcuffs he always kept on him, found an old chain, threaded it through his victim's bound hands and secured him to a metal post.

Right then soppy bollocks, let's to get down to business.

69

H considered the Glasgow Smile, Waterboarding, skin flaying and various other forms of exotic torture he had come across on his travels, but not for long; at the end of the day he was old-school Bermondsey boy. He decided to just beat the fuck out of his prisoner with his bare fists.

Agapov looked on, mute and sullen, as H stripped to the waist. As far as he could tell it was a case of out of the frying pan and into the raging inferno. He knew his masters would either kill him or use him as a bargaining chip to make peace with the Albanians, which amounted to more or less the same thing. He considered giving up what he knew but he had never collaborated with the authorities before, either in Russia or in the UK, and he wasn't about to start helping the police with their inquiries just yet. He was committed to his code.

Agapov knew his captor by reputation. He knew he was a no-nonsense kind of guy, and expected the famous 'H' might rough him up a bit. But he was still a member of the UK Police Force and policemen in the UK didn't, as a general rule, go around torturing and killing people.

But the events of the last few weeks had put H through whirlwinds of pain and confusion and now, with Amisha missing, he was losing his bearings. His inner savage, never that far beneath the surface, was now gaining the upper hand.

The two adversaries eyed each other; like prehistoric monkey men at the dawn of time staring across a watering hole, neither of them was prepared to give an inch. No quarter would be given, and none asked for.

H opened with a simple line of questioning

'Why did you have Tara killed?'

'Fuck you,' came the reply, followed by a mouthful of spit.

The beating began. After five minutes of what was shaping up to be the most savage walloping H had ever dished out, he stopped for a breather. The only constraint on H's behaviour was the fear overdoing it, of dishing out too much too soon. He didn't want his prisoner passing out, or having a heart attack, or being reduced to vegetable status. But this was turning out to be easier said - or thought - than done: Agapov was clearly capable of soaking up tremendous punishment.

H had broken the Russian's nose and jaw, and had bruised a good few ribs. But Agapov, whose face now no longer looked like a face but like a death mask, was no Oswald Carruthers.

Fuck me, this is one hard bastard.

The beating continued. It had to. H's face and body were covered in the dark red blood of his adversary. From Agapov's perspective he looked, through red-misted and almost-closed eyes, crazed, demented, merciless. Exasperation was pouring out of H like a torrent of shit from a ruptured sewage main as the blows rained down.

Another pause.

'Listen, cunt, we don't have a lot of time. Either you start talking to me or I kill you here and now. Why did you have Tara killed?'

Agapov laughed a laugh of deep irony and arrogance. H had never heard a British villain make a sound like it; he realized, for the first time, that he had no real understanding of who these people were.

'You know nothing. You stupid fucking pig, you so fucking stupid. You more stupid than your stupid fucking whore mother.'

H watched this response with intense concentration. Not a trace of guilt about the murder, he surmised. But this guy knew something...H knew when somebody knew something.

At last he's started to talk - the beating's getting to him.

H lashed his fist hard across Agapov's face and continued with the questioning.

'Why would your bosses kidnap my partner?'

H saw the surprise register through the puffed up eyes of the death mask.

He's not aware of it, but he knows something.

'Why did you have Tara killed?'

'Why would I kill posh girl? I like her. We have good time. She like big Russian sausage.'

A laconic smile spread across Agapov's bloated features. H couldn't stand it. Seeing Tara cut to pieces in the park, learning about the abuse she suffered as a child and then having her memory defiled by a gangster talking about her fellatio skills tipped him over the edge.

'You cunt!'

H put his arms around Agapov's neck and leveraged his position for a clean break. His victim understood what was coming; he realized now that H was prepared to go all the way, and that he was not in control of himself.

Fuck, he ready to kill me.

He could take any amount of beating, but he was not prepared to die. He signalled this with a nod. H relaxed his grip.

'You want to know why posh lady killed? You want to know why your partner taken? Find phone. Find fucking phone of posh lady.'

BOOM!

The words were like a mortar shell exploding in H's mind. H fell to his knees.

In the melee and mix ups and fuck ups and killings of the last few weeks he'd somehow forgotten all about it. Tara's phone. Tara's fucking phone.... had the answers to this mystery been in his hands right from the beginning?

H went to the car and retrieved the gun he'd done the business with in Waterloo. He'd kept a close count of the shots fired.

One shot left.

Part 4

70

H had been broken down into bits before: after the Falklands, after his marriage to Julie broke up, after his dad died. But this was something new. His focus was fragmenting; he'd been running on instinct and intuition for a long time now, but whenever he'd tried to sit calmly and join up all the dots it was never long before he hit the wall. And now this Russian had dumped and extra bucket of confusion onto his throbbing, steaming head: 'Find fucking phone of posh lady.'

The phone. Tara's phone. How on God's earth did I manage to forget about that?

Squatting down low, holding his head in his hands and rocking gently back and forth, H surveyed his handiwork: Agapov would not be chasing the daughters of the British aristocracy around hotel rooms again any time soon. For the second time in days Harry Hawkins, the famous law and order avenger and protector of proper values, wondered if he'd killed a man with his bare hands, in an uncontrollable fit of rage. Of pure, animal rage.

Amisha had been right: he'd obliterated the line with blood, and now he was well on the other side of it. All bets were off. There was no going back until he'd seen what was on the phone and dealt with the consequences. And if Carruthers, or Agapov, or both, were dead…there was no going back at all.

Think. Think about the phone. Where is it?

He thought hard… Bermondsey. Him and Amisha in the pub with Confident John. The phone had been left in the car; some little wanksock had driven away with it. That was it. He'd have to start there, on the old plot. Again. It seemed to be dragging him back. He pulled out a dumbphone and punched John's number in.

'John, it's me.'

John picked up, half awake at best; his speech was slurred, his voice shaky: 'H! You alright? In one piece? What about that Russian? I've been shitting myself. I…'

H took a deep breath: 'Slow down, son, slow down. He's been dealt with. Everything's under control. But I need one more thing, one more thing to clinch it. And I need it asap.'

''course. What time is it?'

'Don't worry about the time son. I need to find a phone. Remember the day me and Amisha came to see you and someone had our car away? There was a phone in it. I've got to have it. I don't give a fuck about the car, I just want the phone. Put yourself about, quick as you can, talk to everyone you know. And everyone you don't. This is a matter of life and death mate. Top priority. I don't care what it takes. Bell me on this number when you've got something for me.'

H, exhausted now that the adrenalin rush he'd got while he was hammering the Russian had faded, slumped and keeled over. He stretched out on the concrete floor, working his arms and legs.

Think. Don't sleep, think. What happens next?

The phone was out there. John would find it, if anyone could. Amisha was out there, going through…what? She was his to find. But how was he going to track her down, tiny little thing that she was, in the largeness of London? He'd need help, and plenty of it. He'd have to risk it and talk to someone at the Yard.

Time to catch up with Little Miss Drama Pants.

Agapov wasn't breathing; H threw an oily rag over his shattered face, locked up, and found himself, blinking hard, in a gloomy London dawn. He clambered wearily into the car John had got for him and gunned it towards Clapham.

71

Graham, fresh from his morning's humiliation at the hands of Joey Jupiter, had cleared away his breakfast and was just about to get dressed when he heard a tap on the door. It was 6am. He looked through the peephole and saw with a start that it was Hawkins, of all people, looking like he'd just been dug up and released from his grave.

The shambling hulk formerly known as London's Top Copper mimed to Graham that he would like to be let in. Graham opened the door.

'Good morning, Detective Inspector Hawkins. This is a pleasant surprise. I trust you are well?'

'Morning Graham. Any danger of a cup of coffee? I've had a hard night.'

And not for the first time. Well, I suppose being suspended from duty has its benefits. But Jesus, he looks rough.

'Coffee. Of course, come in. We'll have to be quick though, I leave in half an hour. To what do I owe the pleasure of this morning visitation?'

'We need to talk, Graham. About the investigation. How far have you got? I need to know what's going on,' said H.

'Well, to be honest I'm not really at liberty to discuss the investigation. What with you being suspended and…'

H shot him the look, and growled. Graham fingered his throat, gently, and thought better of it.

'Nothing. Nothing's going on H. I'm still not getting anywhere. Nobody on God's green earth has ever heard of, or seen, this guy in the park. He may as well be Martian. The Murderer from Mars. No change with Sir Basil Fortescue-Smythe; he is not exactly chomping at the bit in his efforts to assist the investigation. If you ask me, he's impeding it. I know not why. I'm being jerked around like a puppet, and getting nowhere. Here endeth the report.'

No surprises there then.

H changed tack:

'What about this other thing, with Sir Basil's chum Carruthers? The home invasion. Is he brown bread, or what? Is anyone in the frame for that?'

'No, he's still in a coma. Could be worse, he's not in a persistent vegetative state or anything. They say he has a chance of coming out of it, with a bit of luck. We've got very little on this one either. No witnesses, Carruthers lives alone. His CCTV was down. They're working on DNA and all the rest of it, obviously.'

H tried not to breathe a sigh of relief.

Thank fuck for that. They're not on me. I've still got time.

H gulped his coffee and thought for a bit while Graham busied himself with his clothes and hair. Yes, he had some time, but how much? There was the phone, but would John find it? Most importantly, there was a brave and beautiful young copper out there in severe danger. At best. What were the chances of him finding her under his own steam, even with the help of John, and maybe Ronnie? He would have to put Miller-Marchant, useless as he was, in the picture. It was his only option, and it was better than nothing.

'Graham, listen. I'm being serious now. I've been doing a bit of rooting about on my own. Amisha's been taken. I don't know who's got her, or why, but I think she's in terrible danger. I can't talk to Hilary, so I'm telling you. We've got to get her back, and I shouldn't think she's got much time.'

Time. One way or another, it's all about time now.

72

On his train into Victoria Graham sparked up the tablet. He had almost no choice now; his old love of surfing of the digital waves had been wrecked by the compulsion to check in on Joey Jupiter's blog on an hourly basis, just in case he and Hawkins were once again under the cosh. He needed to keep up with the latest instalments in his public humiliation - everyone else did.

Looking at the shattered, hulking figure slumped on his sofa before he'd left for the station he'd felt a twinge of…what was it?…not affection, exactly, but fellowship in suffering. That was it. He and Hawkins were in this together, whether they liked it or not. And, though he knew that the big man was not exactly a keen follower of Jupiter's blog, or of any blog if it came to that, he felt that he'd been treated with a little more respect than usual during their surprise morning get together.

Up came the page, the dreaded page. Graham saw with relief that, for this post at least, Jupiter had found a new theme:

THAILAND TRICKS

It is with alarm that this blog has learned of the recent, shameful shenanigans of Lord Timothy Skyhill, that bastion of the establishment and our public life. Until now there has been barely a blemish on the great man's record, making him an unusually upstanding public figure in this day and age. Not for him the excesses or perversions - be they financial, sexual or otherwise – of other lords of the realm, politicians and banksters.

But His Lordship's recent 'business' trip to Thailand, though it appears to have involved neither the provision of backhanders to corrupt officials nor a spree with the ladyboys, has cast him in an altogether darker light. It turns out that Lord Timothy is, to use the parlance of the criminal fraternity, a 'nonce case.' Though reports of his adventures in the tropics have been carefully handled by the authorities in both Thailand and the UK, we have it on good authority that Lord Timothy was caught, on more than one occasion, going at it hammer and tongs with the young 'uns.

This regrettable episode raises a number of important questions: Is His Lordship to be allowed to get away scot-free with these crimes? Are we to see a full and transparent investigation into the facts of the case? Are there more where Lord Timothy came from? Are there no depths to which the powerful men who govern our country will not sink?

We have become accustomed to the fraud, the shady deals, the tax loopholes, the screwing of us all for every penny they can get, the orgies in the corridors of power. Must we also become accustomed to this? Are our schoolchildren even safe on their tours of the mother of parliaments? We should be told.

73

The masked assassin understood his orders clearly. Find and execute Harry Hawkins immediately, and with extreme prejudice. The order meant there was no need for secrecy, or fake accidents, in fact no need for any kind of sophistication. Just find and kill, job done. The orders had come through at 5am. It was now 7.

Ronnie and Olivia were chatting in the kitchen when the assassin made his entry, via the drainpipes, into the bedroom Ronnie had been sleeping in.

Olivia passed Ronnie a piping hot cup of builder's tea and two slices of generously buttered toast.

'Thanks love. Anything from H?

'He's sent me a couple of texts, each time from different phones, letting me know he is ok. Other than that I have no idea what he's up to.'

'Well, he'll be in touch when he's ready, when he needs us. I have no doubt about that,' Ronnie said.

The masked assassin was good at his job and had memorized the picture of his intended victim. He enjoyed his work and had never missed a target. He crept along the corridor and made his way towards the voices, the silencer already secured to the gun in his right hand.

The cup fell from Oliva's hand and smashed to pieces on the floor as he entered the kitchen. Ronnie swivelled on his kitchen stall, and stared straight down the barrel of a gun. The assassin surveyed Ronnie's face and knew he wasn't the target. He would have to kill them both, of course, but he needed information.

His voice had the measured, neutral tone of an old-school BBC newsreader.

'Where is Hawkins? You have ten seconds to tell me before I kill you both.' He didn't waste time in commencing the count.

'9…8…7'

Olivia was in shock. H's work had never been brought home like this before. Being in the line of fire was a new experience for her.

'We have no idea where he is,' said Olivia.

'6…5…'

Ronnie thought quickly.

Have to stop the clock - give us a chance.

'4…3….'

'Wait,' said Ronnie. 'If we knew we'd tell you, but we don't. He'll be calling us in ten minutes. We'll talk to him. Find out where he is. It's the only way you'll find him.'

The assassin considered the option. Almost certainly lying, he thought, but he had the time.

Ronnie had turned ten seconds into ten minutes.

The assassin held his gun up.

'Do not speak. If the phone does not ring in ten minutes I will kill you both.'

Inexorably the minutes started totting up. Five, six, seven.

Ronnie concentrated on the intruder, hoping for a moment's lapse, a turn of the head. No one could stay 100% focused for 10 minutes. Except, perhaps, a trained assassin with a 100% success rate.

But Ronnie stayed focused.

One moment, just one moment.

Sometimes, in life, there are moments of coincidence, and Olivia and Ronnie would later reflect on them. Some people call them fate, or providence, or maybe even destiny. Or perhaps sometimes you just get damn lucky.

The phone rang. It was Olivia's mother calling for an early morning chat. At the split second the assassin turned his attention to the phone Ronnie was on him. With the gun knocked out of his hand he didn't add up to much.

Ronnie secured a vice-like grip and smashed the assassin's head into the wall, swung him round with maximum force and smashed his head onto the edge of the sink. He'd forgotten nothing of his army training. He repositioned his hold and watched Olivia wince as he applied the coup de grace. As neck snaps go this one was pretty straightforward. Ronnie released his grip and the dead assassin slumped to the floor.

Olivia answered the phone.

'Hi mum…er, can I call you back in half an hour?' She said.

74

Amisha's stomach reflexes forced the water from her body. The coarse brown bag was lifted from her head and she flickered back to life as the light penetrated her eyes.

'Let me ask you once more,' said her interrogator, exuding a gentle charm, 'how did you manage to find and access those files, and who have you passed the information on to?'

Amisha coughed and gasped for more air, some of the water still seeping out from her eyes and ears, her chest heaving in its desperate search for oxygen.

She was close to talking. To saying almost anything her captor wanted. But after only five breaths the sack was once more placed over her face and once more the water poured forth. As it entered her respiratory system the panic gripped her as she became unable to breathe. Her brain triggered its primal, powerful, irresistible response, a response of pure dread, the "God help me I'm drowning" response. It was as if she was being submerged at the foot of Niagara Falls, unable to fight its awesome powers and reach the surface.

The process had been in play now for 15 minutes.

Sack on. Twenty seconds of water. Sack off. Questions asked to which she could not respond whilst she gulped five or six life giving intakes of precious air. Sack on. Twenty seconds of water. Sack off. More questions…

God help me, when will it end?

The voice of her tormentor had started to sound oddly reassuring. She was at breaking point.

'Take your time, my dear. We have plenty of it,' he said as he lifted the sack once more. Again the reflex vomiting, the return to full consciousness and her body's desperate intake of the maximum amount of oxygen in the minimum amount of time.

'What do you want?...' she managed to force out before the sack was replaced, suffocating, overpowering all her senses. The water poured in as Amisha again lost consciousness. Her tormentor was not ready, just yet, to allow the young girl her moment of release. He was enjoying himself far too much for that.

The process continued for a few more minutes, enough for a further 4 rounds.

'Now, my sweet, where were we?'

Amisha had been made aware of waterboarding during her training. Its effects on human physiology and psychology, its ability to panic the brain into saying almost anything the torturer wanted to hear. She now understood the difference between theory and practice.

'Oh, yes. How did you manage to access those files? Who helped you?'

'Nobody... helped... me. It... wasn't... that difficult,' she said.

'Come come now, you managed to access some of the most secure files in existence. You really managed to do that all by yourself?'

'Yes,' said Amisha.

'My my, you are a smart young lady. Smart and beautiful. We're going to have such fun, you and I.'

Her tormentor's loins had been stirring for some time. He couldn't help but notice the contours of her fine figure as the water had soaked through her shirt. But that was for later. The first order of business for today was to find out who her accomplices were, and what they knew.

'Suppose I believe that you are a very bright young lady and managed to access all those files on your own. The next question is why, and have you passed what you found on to anyone else?'

Amisha doubted she could withstand another round of near drowning but something deep within her refused to give. She found an ounce of courage, the very last ounce she had.

'Nobody. I sent them to nobody.'

'Oh dear. Then why did you find it necessary to completely wipe your hard drive. I've checked the whole thing. All traces of your access gone. Very clever, not many people, including officers of the law, actually know how to do that so effectively.'

The torturer's phone rang and he answered the call. She heard some mumbling but couldn't make out anything distinct. She looked about her. A small, windowless room. Could be anywhere, anywhere at all. The balding man with the soothing voice was fiftyish, short, plump and very sweaty. The fact he was making no effort to conceal his identity told her all she needed to know about her future prospects - torture, rape, death. Not exactly the career path she'd signed up for when she joined the Met as a bright eyed, eager young graduate.

'Oh it seems I'm going to have to leave you for a little while. I'll be back soon to conclude our conversation.'

Her tormentor left Amisha alone to consider her plight. But her torments didn't leave with him. The lights in the small, windowless room flashed on and off with punishing regularity - pitch black, bright lights, pitch black, bright lights - whilst white noise smashed into her brain like two particles obliterating one another in an atom collider. She was being mentally broken down.

How long had she been here? Five hours? Five days? How quickly she had lost track of time.

She understood the torture techniques being applied, but understanding did nothing to soften their impact. She would break. She knew she would break. The question that reverberated through her mind was not whether but when; would she break before H found her, would she give H up before she was killed?

She knew H would be looking, frantically tearing up the streets of London in a way only he knew how. If anyone could find her in time it was her partner. As the lights flashed and the chaotic, formless noise assaulted her senses she tried to cling to that hope. It was the only hope she had.

75

Amisha was nothing if not resourceful. As she lay tightly strapped on the inclined board, the only piece of furniture in the small room that was her prison, and would most probably be the place of her death, she knew there was nothing she could do physically.

But mentally was a different matter. She made a huge effort to block out the noise and think back, across the sequence of events that had led her to where she was now. From the deep dive into the Dark Web to the moment she realised she'd been tumbled; from the desperate race against time to garner as much information as possible to the wiping of her hard drive; from the second they'd broken into her flat to the struggle; from being bundled into the waiting car to the journey and her imprisonment.

If she got a moment's opportunity, a fleeting half chance, she would be prepared. As aware as she could be of where she was and why and how she'd got here. As desperate as things looked, Amisha was still holding out for life.

She recalled the moment H had arrived with news of his hunches. At first she wasn't sure, although she'd come to appreciate the fact that H's hunches were usually spot on. She thought there may have been one or two people involved, but a child abuse conspiracy at the heart of the establishment, involving the House of Lords, one of the most venerable and upstanding institutions in the world? It just wasn't credible. Was it?

There was no way, no way a group of powerful people in the UK could get away with such a thing. Her parents had always told her what a wonderful, civilized place Britain was. Its institutions were incorruptible, matured over centuries to limit naked power and protect its citizens. Things like this happened in third world countries, in corruption filled post-communist hell holes, in countries run by tin-pot dictators. But not here, not in the mother of all democratic parliaments, not in Great Britain.

Amisha had studied Computer Science at Cambridge and joined the Met to work in their specialist IT security division. But she had been bored and asked for a transfer so she could work in the real world of gangsters, where people still spoke to each other. Reluctantly the Met agreed. As a consequence, over the last year or two, everyone had forgotten just how advanced and skilful she was in matters of technology and online security.

And then H had turned up, urging her to go deep in the darkest recesses of the web.

Time to put those skills back to use.

She started with the police IT systems she already had access to. Within half an hour she knew H was really onto something. She checked and cross-checked multiple references to all those in the picture H provided, and soon knew who they all were. She was surprised to find that at some time they had all been questioned by someone in authority or other but all the interviews were marked 'Top Secret' and she didn't have access. A pattern was emerging - every time one of them had been in contact with police the investigation had been closed down. Quickly. She made multiple attempts to access the top secret files. She knew every attempt was logged and monitored but was confident it would be days before the cumbersome plods of the Met had the wherewithal to investigate the failed attempts further.

She resurrected the old user IDs she used when working for the Met security division, where her main job was to locate and entrap terrorists, paedophiles and the like, and she quickly started to make contact with the scum of the earth.

As she typed, her brain cross-referenced every name, every comment she found that connected to the information on the police systems. She had written some unique pattern-matching software while at Cambridge and also had access to the Met's advanced software used to encrypt and de-encrypt software keys. She employed them to their maximum ability and marvelled at the high level of expertise she still had at her command.

She sat mesmerized, focused, rigid with attention as she put out fake messages to draw people into her world, ran responses on her software and went deeper into the web. She accessed the most sickening images she had ever seen and held her disgust in check.

She had reached a website with a chat room that she was now certain was used by many of the co-conspirators in the photo. Maybe she was even talking to one of them.

Think Amisha, think. However clever these people think they are they are creatures of habit. They make mistakes.

She found a highly secure messaging porthole, and the secret database that stored its messages, a database that would be filled with incriminating emails.

That's it. Have to access that database.

For three hours she worked using every tool at her disposal, and ran an automated script that collated all the information she had and generated thousands of passwords. She drew on her knowledge of the conspirators, police software, her own software, her keen intelligence and her intuition. After several thousand attempts to gain direct access via the administrator password she almost screamed with joy when the message flashed on her screen: ACCESS GRANTED

I'm in.

76

Amisha gritted her teeth and forced herself to concentrate, to block out the noise and the flashing light.

Think back girl, think back.

She had worked quickly and methodically, going through the torrent of repugnant data, so vile, so repulsive. How did the minds of these people work? How had they become so corrupted, so shameless, so evil? She didn't think too deeply about the answers, answers nobody really had. Their numbers were growing, growing all over the world, like a plague of demons swarming over innocence and beauty.

Some of H's eye-for-an-eye values had rubbed off on her.

Castration's too fucking good for them.

As she went through each email she printed them off, one by one, for another hour or so. And then horror struck her. In the midst of her excitement she'd forgotten to do the obvious, namely ensure she herself was secured. A piece of Trojan software had accessed her computer, almost definitely triggered by her access into the secret database. And it had been operating for some time, reading everything directly from her disk and sending the information to God knows where.

Oh my God, they'll know where I am.

Amisha disconnected her computer from the internet and set in train a specialist programme, developed by a friend of hers at Cambridge, that would wipe clean her entire drive. It would leave no trace whatsoever of what she had accessed.

She was struggling to recount what she did next when her environment abruptly changed. The noise stopped in the windowless room. The lights stayed on. The door opened and the small plump man returned.

'Hello my dear, have you missed me?'

She forced her mind back to the events of her capture, but bits of it were already hazy. She recalled the sound of her back door being forced open. She remembered the fight with the three assailants and being dumped into the boot of their car. The journey. What had it been - thirty minutes?

While in the boot of the car she noted that radio reception was interrupted. She was in a tunnel, a long one. Must be heading under the river. Rotherhithe tunnel, maybe Dartford?

And when they'd taken her out of the boot she'd had a glimpse of a huge bridge. She recognised it - the Queen Elizabeth II Bridge. It was all coming back to her now: she'd been driven through the Dartford tunnel, and then first exit off the motorway as the car slowed down.

She was somewhere in or near Grays, Essex, on the fringe of the great metropolis. She was sure of it.

The small plump man retrieved the coarse brown sack and placed it gently over her head.

'Now, where were we?' □

77

H lay, slumped and exhausted, in the twilight zone between wakefulness and sleep. He hadn't had a proper night's sleep in weeks. He wanted to wake up and get going but was struggling to keep his eyes open; he drifted back in the direction of sleep.

A multitude of images from the last few weeks vied for dominance inside his head. He saw the brightly coloured remains of Tara and Jemima. He could feel the texture of the severed heads in Bermondsey as if they were in his hands. He could smell the charred remnants of the dead in Soho.

And now he was back in the Falklands, launching himself into a ditch and savagely ending the lives of two young men. He physically shuddered as he felt the force of his rifle butt smash through their skulls. Young men like him, young men who had died so he could live. He was suffocating. Hemmed in. His breathing become short. He started gasping for air.

Mortar shells were exploding all about him. He looked around. Ronnie lay still and crumpled on the floor as the men of 2 Para descended on the sniper who had shot him.

'Please be alive Ronnie, for fuck's sake, please be alive,' he screamed out loud. He was sweating and shaking as he came out of his nightmare and his senses readjusted to the here and now.

He was startled by the pinging of a dumbphone, and found himself back in Ronnie's place in Rotherhithe. He wasn't ready yet to go home to Olivia. He didn't want her to see him like this, unravelled and animal-like. He was in pure hunter mode now, and H in hunter mode was no fun for any woman. The best he'd been able to do was send her texts assuring her he was in one piece.

The message was from John. Bingo!: HAVE FOUND PHONE. YOU'LL NEED A NICE FEW QUID OR A SMALL ARMY TO GET IT BACK THOUGH.

221

H was in no position, or mood, to speak to anyone just yet. HOW MUCH?, he texted back.

I'VE GOT THEM DOWN TO 50K. THEY WON'T GO ANY LOWER, John replied.

WHO ARE 'THEY,' H asked.

OUR FRIENDS ON THE CARAVAN SITE, came the reply.

OK. MONEY NO OBJECT. BE AT HOME.

50K? For a stolen phone? What the hell is on the fucking thing?

H washed his morning painkillers down with a mouthful of scotch and called Ronnie, who arrived an hour later with a brown paper bag containing the cash. He was a bit more like his old self now, chipper and ready to go. A couple of days rest and a little tender loving care from Olivia had done the trick; God knows she'd had plenty of practice.

But there was something else that had put a spring in Ronnie's step. He told H about the dead man in his kitchen. He hadn't wanted to tell him over the phone; but he knew now that H was a loose cannon, capable of almost anything. It would have to be face to face.

H was apoplectic with rage.

'They came into my house and threatened Olivia…I'm going to fucking murder…'

'H,' said Ronnie, 'slow down. She's safe in one of my flats, where no one can touch her. I've taken care of it. Let's move on: tell me about the phone.'

H contained his rage. There would be a reckoning for this violation. A terrible reckoning. But Ronnie was right, he needed to stay focused.

'I got hold of that Russian, the one she was involved with. I put it on him. He didn't have a lot to say but he swore that it had something on it that would clarify the picture. It was nicked from our car the other week. John's tracked it down, says the Albanians have got it.'

'Where's the Russian now?,' asked Ronnie.

'Having a little lie down. Don't worry about him. If we can get our hands on the phone we'll have the full picture. Then we can cut our cloth accordingly, if you're in. This is not going to be a walk in the park son. Whatever's going on, we're going to be dealing with some proper bastards, and someone is going to get hurt. No way round that.'

'H, when have I not been in when it's come to the crunch? When we get to whoever killed Tara I'm going to send them straight to hell with these bare hands. I will not be fucking about, or seeking a warrant, or asking for your opinion. I can assure you of that. Are you sure you can handle it?'

Sweet. Ronnie's on it. His run in with my would-be assassin has done him the power of good. This is music to my fucking ears.

'Give me two minutes son. I'll just get my strides on.'

Five minutes later they were barrelling along, side by side, for the short walk to Silwood Road. It felt good, just like the old days. But, as they turned a corner and approached John's block, H looked at Ronnie's profile and began to think a little bit harder about just what, exactly, he was about to unleash.

78

Confident John had lived on his estate for donkey's years. He'd watched quietly over the years as everything changed, and his neighbours these days were Nigerians, Poles, Algerians, Columbians and Iranians. He'd found it hard in the early days of the noughties, when things really sped up. But he'd come to see, now, that they were mostly decent people, raising their families and trying to do the right thing. He'd learned to live and let live, and keep the peace.

Where he drew the line was with the latest arrivals, the gangsters who had taken over on the caravan site. These he did not need – they interfered with business. The business of ducking and diving. They had their fingers in everything now, and John and his mates were not amused.

And now I'm going to have to hand fifty grand over to the bastards.

His musings were interrupted by the doorbell. It was the dynamic duo, back on the plot.

John nodded to H, and said 'Hello Ron. Fuck me, you look well. How you been?'

'Terrific,' said Ron, scanning the condition of the flat and deciding not to return the question. John ushered them to their seats and poured three tumblers of scotch.

'Bring us up to speed on the phone, John,' said H.

'Well, it took some finding, I'll tell you that. Like I said before, this mob don't talk to outsiders, and most of them don't speak English anyway. I…'

'Can we fast forward to the crux of the matter please John?,' said Ronnie. 'Have you seen this phone? Are you sure it's the right one?'

'Yep. Well…I finally got into negotiations with a character from the site. I get the impression he's the number two on the firm, after the one H just banged up. It was all a bit heavy. He brought half a dozen evil looking lumps to the pub with him.

He said he wanted two hundred large for the phone. I laughed out loud - which I shouldn't have done - and he started hollering and hooting. He said something about "your posh English lady and her fucking Russian" and "porno clips", that sort of thing. So he knew he had something, but he didn't really know what to do with it. But he mentioned your wife by name Ron…Well, this geezer is not in any danger of winning University Challenge, to put it mildly, and to cut a long story short in the end I got him down to fifty. He told me to ring him today to confirm I've got the money. These people scare the shit out of me, boys, to be honest.'

Ronnie poured three more scotches, and he and H talked John down. He had never really been a man of action. They walked him through setting up the meet, told him they would be waiting across the road with the bag and that nothing would happen to him, and that he should ask to see some confirmation it was the right phone before he came and got the money from them.

After the deal was done and John had finally emerged, white as a sheet, with the phone, Ronnie thanked him and palmed him a wad of notes.

'I don't need that Ron, I…'

'Don't worry about it John. That took a lot of bottle. I appreciate it. Treat yourself…and don't insult me by trying to give it back.'

'Alright, got it. Thanks Ron. What happens now? Shall we plot up somewhere and have a look at the phone then?'

'No mate, me and H are going to shoot off and do that now. What you don't know can't hurt you. We've got a lot to think about. We'll give you a bell in a day or two. Before then see if you can lay your hands on a few bits and pieces, will you mate? Couple of assault rifles, grenades, smoke bombs, that sort of thing,' said Ronnie.

This was good enough for John. More than good enough: 'Alright boys, see you soon. Be lucky.'

79

H and Ronnie were three minutes into their walk back to the Rotherhithe riverside when they heard someone calling out to them. Wheeling around, they saw that it was John. He was running furiously and waving something about. He arrived at speed, panting hard.

'Sorry H, I completely forgot about this. Came this morning,' said John.

It was a thick A4 manila envelope, addressed to 'Harry Hawkins, c/o John Viney.' Yesterday's date, postmarked Greenwich.

'What the fuck's this, H?,' said Ronnie.

H steadied his breathing. 'Not sure mate,' he said, 'let's get back to yours and have a look at it. See you later John.'

Amisha. It's from Amisha.

Now we're getting somewhere.

They stepped up the pace. Back at Ronnie's flat, they put the phone and envelope on the coffee table, got the scotch on the go, sat down, and took deep breaths.

'Read your letter H. I'll take the phone,' said Ronnie.

'I thought we'd…,' H started.

Ronnie interrupted him: 'H, I've just spent fifty large on this fucking thing. From what we've been told it's got bad stuff about Tara on it, very bad stuff, and pointers towards whichever cunt killed her. I want to look at it first. I'm going to the other room with it. You read your letter.'

There was only one person in the world who could get away with talking to Harry Hawkins like this. The big man let it slide; he watched his blood brother leave the room, opened the envelope, and trained his weary eyes on the cover note:

> H, I don't have much time. Just about to leave my
> place. I think they're coming for me. No time to

summarise everything. Read the email transcripts - they took a lot of effort to decrypt.

Nutshell version: You were right. There's a high level paedophile ring. It's been going on for years. Very well protected and their activities have been very skilfully organized and concealed. Big names involved. And they've been getting help from Kuznetsov. I strongly suspect that the Tara case and your suspicions about Sir Basil and his chums may be connected somehow - the establishment types and the Russian are connected.

I've triggered an alarm in the Dark Web; they know now that someone knows. They've got real expertise on board, so they'll be able to find me. I'll be in touch when I can. Get these bastards, H. Bring them down.

Amisha.

H gulped a mouthful of scotch, and began to leaf through the sheaf of documents. Email transcripts mostly, a few financial statements, some of them in Russian. They'd been super-encrypted and deeply buried in the parts of the web most people don't even know about, the hiding place of the terrorists, the paedophiles, the freelance drug and arms dealers, and the other shining examples of humanity at its worst. Amisha had hit the jackpot. But who, in this pile of filth, had most to lose? Who had come for her?

H began to read. He figured Amisha would have put them in descending order of importance for him, so he started at the top and worked his way down. Messages from Lord Timothy Skyhill to Sir Basil about upcoming 'parties.' Sir Basil passes this on to Carruthers and Blunt. Skyhill and Kuznetsov discuss locations, arrangements, security. Skyhill peppers the Russian with technical questions and requests. Agapov gets the odd mention. Links to folders containing movies and pictures. What looked like movements of large sums of money in and out of Moscow bank accounts. Carruthers, Blunt and Sir Basil gushing to one another in excited anticipation, like schoolgirls looking forward to a pop concert… Again, Skyhill and Kuznetsov discussing, planning, arranging things in measured tones, all business… These two again, talking about a 'wrinkle'; whose men shall we put on this, Skyhill asks, yours or mine?

On it went, page after page. It would all need to be gone through with a fine tooth comb - but that was for later. For now H skimmed through the pile looking for references to Amisha, or any other name or event he was familiar with. But there was nothing further down other than unspecific discussions; and nobody other than Sir Basil Fortescue-Smythe, Lord Peregrine Blunt, Oswald Carruthers QC and, clearly pulling the strings, Lord Timothy Skyhill and Mr Kyril Kuznetsov.

Well, I was right. Bang on. Horrible bunch of cunts.

I'm going to rip their fucking bollocks off for them.

But who among them would have the wherewithal and resources to kidnap a police officer? Sir Basil? Blunt? Carruthers? Hardly; bullying small children would be the limit of their capabilities. Skyhill? Highly unlikely.

H's money was on the Russian.

80

'Mate, I've got some shit here you will not believe,' said H, walking into the bedroom. Ronnie was sitting on the bed with Tara's phone beside him. Tears were streaming silently down his face. Otherwise, he was not moving. He seemed to be deep within himself.

Fuck it! He's in bits. It's like the pizza place all over again. Bollocks!

There's no time for this now.

'Ron, snap out of it son. Liven up. You need to see what Amisha's come up with…What's on the phone? Tell me what's on the phone.'

Ronnie gestured for him to take it.

He's blanking me. Not good.

H rushed out and was back thirty seconds later with two tumblers, each one half full of scotch. He put one into Ronnie's hand, and forced it up into his face. Ronnie gulped.

H saw that he'd have to take it up half a dozen notches. He shouted 'No, I don't want the phone. I want you to tell me. Sort your fucking self out and talk to me. You can have your breakdown later, after we've done what we've got to do. What's on the phone? Ron! What's on the phone?'

Ronnie turned his head - slowly, slowly - and met the big man's eye.

'They we're using her like a whore, H. Like a filthy whore. They had her doing all sorts. Pictures, films, the lot. Her and that Agapov, mostly.'

'Sorry to hear that mate. We knew about that already though. What else is on there?,' said H, easing more scotch down Ronnie's gullet.

'There's a film…it's horrible. Old Shitbreath and his mates, at it with young boys. It's like a full scale fucking orgy.' He was coming out of himself now, getting angrier.

'OK, good. We've got them,' said H, '…but what the fuck is that doing on Tara's phone?…What else?'

'There's something funny about the calls she made, the last calls she made. Just after she uploaded that clip she phoned… what's his name?…that fat ponce from the House of Lords?…Timothy Skyhill.'

The gears in H's head were beginning to grind in earnest: 'Is he in the clip?'

'Oh yes. Big time. He's all over it. He seems to be the daddy,' said Ronnie.

'OK, what else…what else?'

'The last call she made, right after Skyhill, was to her sister Jemima. That's the last thing on there. It's the last call she made before she died. Before they died. Here, take it. Have a look…my head is fucking spinning. What does it all mean?'

H's head was spinning furiously as well, and beginning to form all the bits and pieces of information, from Tara's phone and Amisha's package, and from the last few weeks, into a pattern. His golden girl was right: this stuff was all somehow connected: Tara's death, the conspiracy of nonces, Amisha's disappearance, the blood flowing through the streets of London…it was all connected.

'What it means, Ron, is that we are going to have a word with this fucking "oligarch". Get your coat on.'

81

Before setting off for Knightsbridge they swung by the Walworth Road, to fortify themselves with double portions of pie and mash. As they reviewed the situation over their heaped plates Ronnie told H that Kuznetsov was known to him, and had been for years.

'Fucking hell, Ron, you could of told me you know the geezer,' said H.

'I didn't know who you were talking about - all your "oligarch" this and "honcho" that. I just know him through business.'

'What business?'

'Oh, nothing major. A few bits and pieces. Property, mostly,' said Ronnie.

'You mean you help him and his money-laundering mates sell London off to the highest bidders, while proper Londoners…'

'Let's not get into the politics of it mate. We're all just getting a living. Business is business. Do you want me to set up a meet with him or what?'

H gave Ronnie the look, but nodded yes. Ronnie made the call.

'We're on. Four o'clock. But…where exactly does he fit in? I mean, what exactly are we going to accuse him of?'

'Losing your bottle, Ron?,' said H.

'No, I am not losing my fucking bottle. If it turns out he was involved in Tara's death I'll rip his fucking throat out myself. I'm just a bit confused. Lay it out for me again will you, all of it, before we go barging in there.'

'Well, here's how I see it,' said H. 'Tara and Jemima were executed, by a professional hit man. We don't know who he was, but he was obviously a top-notch professional. We know she was involved, or dragged into involvement with, Agapov, a big man in the Russian firm. I'm guessing she saw or heard something, or was getting in the way, or was wobbling and trying to cut loose, and...I don't know, Ron. But I know one thing: thugs like Agapov never run the show. Someone further up will have been pulling his strings, and we know from Amisha's package that he and Kuznetsov were connected in all sorts of ways. And on top of all that, we know he was setting things up for and protecting Old Shitbreath and the other nonces. We've got him bang to rights on that...I haven't even mentioned that pop someone just had at me. Who do you suppose was behind that? And what if you hadn't been there? If they'd hurt Liv?... I'm going to have him.'

'OK, but how are you going to have him? You're suspended from duty, we've got no backup, and he's practically untouchable. These types always seal themselves off completely from the naughty stuff, you know that. Not to mention he's probably got a small army to call on. Probably all former Spetzsnaz nutters, ruthless as fuck and armed to the teeth,' said Ronnie.

'They don't scare me mate. I've dealt with them before. Kuznetsov is going to help us with what we need to know, on both fronts, or I am going to put it on him. Severely.'

'I hope you've got this right mate,' said Ronnie, 'if he's what you think he is, this is one man we do not want to piss off.'

'Hold your bottle, Ron. Eyes on the prize. We'll know what happened to Tara soon. Very soon. Just get me in there.'

82

Beauchamp Place, Knightsbridge. H's mum had once had a cleaning job here, when he was a kid. That was the closest anyone in his family had ever got to the place. Ronnie, much more at ease in these surroundings, nodded to a few familiar faces but saw that H's jaw was working, and working hard; he was building himself up for a big blast.

'A few things before we go in, H. I've good pretty good idea of how these blokes work. You won't be able to wind him up, or put the frighteners on him. You can go in all guns blazing, but all you'll get back is the super-successful legitimate businessman, the smooth gentleman with establishment connections, civilised and confident as you please. He won't play ball with us unless there's something in it for him, or he thinks he has to cover his own arse.'

H looked him in the eye, steadied his breathing and nodded: 'Alright mate. You do the pleasantries. I'll give you five minutes.'

It was 4pm. The building was all plush and good taste, but nothing too fancy. They were ushered into Kuznetsov's inner sanctum. He rose from his desk, gushing with charm, and in accented but otherwise perfect English said:

'Ronald, how good to see you my friend. It's been too long. And Detective Inspector Hawkins, such a pleasure to meet you at last. Your reputation precedes you.'

Fuck me, Ronnie wasn't kidding. This bastard's oilier than a giant slick in the Gulf of Mexico.

'Something to drink gentleman? No? May I assume this is not a social call?'

'You may, Kyril,' said Ronnie. H had his mouth clamped shut but was exuding waves of manic, aggressive energy, like invisible solar flares bursting out into the space around him. Ronnie felt the blast, and knew he didn't have much time. He composed himself and, in the measured tones of someone who knew how to negotiate with ruthless and unyielding competitors, laid everything out. Step-by-step and piece-by-piece: the evidence contained in Amisha's package… the contents of Tara's phone… H's assessment of the situation and of Kuznetsov's position.

Ronnie's presentation came to an end. A long, pregnant pause followed. Kuznetsov looked at each of them in turn, composed and unruffled, and considered his options.

Eyes like a shark. He's got eyes like a fucking shark.

'Gentlemen,' the oligarch said eventually, 'I propose a deal. I will tell you everything I know about everything I know, and provide you with detailed information that will aid you greatly in your investigation. In return my name will never be mentioned, documented or appear on anybody's radar in this matter. I understand that the evidence of which you speak is solid and is in safe hands, and might be used against me at any time in the future; I will therefore take no further action, and we will never meet again. Is this arrangement agreeable to you?'

H nodded, and said 'Alright son, start talking.'

83

'First of all, I assure you that I know absolutely nothing about the abduction of your colleague, Detective Inspector Hawkins. None of my people are involved in that, and I don't know who is. I can, however, shed more light on the activities of Sir Basil Fortescue-Smythe and his friends, though I must make it clear that I myself am not a sexual predator, or any kind of "nonce case." I simply provided infrastructure and security for the paedophile ring. I took no part in their "meetings." Over the years I have worked hard to earn the trust of these people, whom I cultivated as part of my strategy for gaining influence and position in this country. I sometimes secretly filmed their activities as insurance. They are very sick people, and I despise them. But they have been very useful to me.'

'What about the kids? Did you provide those as well?,' said H.

Ronnie's heart began to beat faster: H was about to blow.

'Yes and no,' continued Kuznetsov. 'Agapov had - I assume he is no longer with us, Detective Inspector? - targets to meet. Financial targets. He employed the usual means: drug smuggling and distribution, people trafficking, prostitution etc. Some of the children were, I believe, supplied by him.'

'You mean supplied by you, you horrible cunt!,' shouted H.

'Only indirectly,' said Kuznetsov, calm as ever. 'I don't deal directly with any of those things. That was Agapov's job. His replacement is now doing the same. Business is business.'

H exploded out of his chair and moved at speed towards Kuznetsov's desk. Ronnie got his body in between the two of them just in time.

'Sit down H. We need more. Keep to the deal!,' barked Ronnie. He turned to Kuznetsov: 'Tell us about Tara. Who killed my wife, and why did she die?'

The Russian fixed his eye on him; he was unwavering: 'Ronald, of this I know very little. Your wife's tragic death was not connected in any way to my activities, or those of any of my people. Of this I can also assure you.'

'He's lying Ron,' H screamed, 'give me five minutes with him. Cover the door and give me five minutes.'

'There really is no need for these histrionics, Detective Inspector,' said Kuznetsov. Ronnie almost admired his cool. 'No need at all. You must look elsewhere for your culprit.'

'Where? Tell me now,' said Ronnie, himself now on the verge of exploding. 'I'm running out of patience with this bollocks. Who killed Tara? And why?'

'Look again to our nonce friends, Ronald. As to the whys and wherefores of her death, for those you would have to ask Lord Timothy Skyhill, that great peer of your realm: my guess would be that it was he who commissioned her murder.'

84

'It all makes sense if you think about it, Ron,' said H, back in the car. 'Tara comes across the clip of Old Shitbreath and his pals, bang at it. She must have got it from Agapov somehow. She watches it in horror and uploads it to her phone. Five minutes later she phones Skyhill, in a terrible rage. Maybe she threatens him, maybe she just needs to let it out. But she shows her hand. The next morning she's murdered.'

Ronnie was on fire.

'He's got to die, H. Skyhill. He's got to go. Help me find him. Just help me set it up. Then you can make yourself scarce.'

'There'll be none of that mate. We'll go after him. Together,' said H.

Ronnie called Skyhill's PA and was told that His Lordship was out of the country. Business. Singapore. Back tomorrow.

H was alarmed at this: the clock on Amisha's life was ticking loudly, and with Kuznetsov apparently out of the running Skyhill was now the odds-on favourite; if it was true he'd had Tara killed, he would certainly not be beyond a bit of kidnapping. He would need to know what she had discovered, and to whom she'd passed the information. And what about the attempt on H's life? Skyhill was now also the main candidate for that.

Time for some quick, and clear, thinking. 'Bollocks,' said H, 'But...Skyhill will just have to wait. So let's go and have a word with Sir Basil, and learn what we can learn from him. Let's not go at this half-cocked. Let's make sure we get the full picture, and think things through. Do it properly. A day's grace for Skyhill could work in our favour.'

'What if the old bastard won't cooperate?,' said Ronnie.

'Oh, he'll cooperate, don't worry about that. He's got no backbone, there's nothing underneath all that old- school bollocks he comes out with. He'll just want to try and save his arse once he knows it's all coming on top.'

Ronnie said nothing. He was trying to control his emotions; but he was near bursting point. His leg was pumping up and down like a steam piston, and H could hear his teeth grinding above the roar of the traffic.

Jesus, I haven't seen him this agitated since Goose Green.

We'd better just get this done. Too late to stop now.

'OK,' said H, 'round to Sir Basil's then. We'll get him to lay it all out for us, and gather some more evidence. Then we can take care of the others. Blunt and then Skyhill. Yes?'

'Check. But when you say "take care" of, what exactly do you mean?' asked Ronnie.

'I mean I want to nick Old Shitbreath and Blunt, or at least tuck them up and arrange to have them nicked. Skyhill, once we've got what we can out of him, I will leave to you.'

'Is that a guarantee, H?' Said Ronnie.

'Nailed on. That is nailed on son.'

I owe Ron that. Natural justice. An eye for an eye...Anyway, it's that or have the whole thing covered up again, and Skyhill gets to carry on following his cock around the world in pursuit of little boys.

At this Ronnie seemed to calm down a little; he began to focus his negative energy, channel his hatred, towards their goal: 'Alright H. It's five o'clock. He'll be at his place in Belgravia. He always has a kip at around this time, then goes back to his club for dinner.'

'Is anyone likely to be about? Does he have any staff?,' asked H.

'There's a cleaner, as far as I know, but I suppose she's finished by now.'

'Right. Buckle up Ron. We're going to bring the hammer down on the sick old bastard, and not before time.'

85

They found the old man swinging from the ceiling in his bedroom. Ronnie was exultant, and laughed out loud.

'Well, he's done the job properly,' said H, feeling for a pulse, 'he's definitely brown bread. I'm no pathologist, but I'd say he hasn't been here long.'

Good riddance to bad rubbish.

Couldn't have happened to a nicer bloke.

'Have a root about, Ron, see what you can find.'

Ronnie busied himself in the lounge while H rifled through the bedroom drawers and wardrobes. There was nothing to be found. Not that it seemed to matter much now.

'In here H,' shouted Ronnie. 'He's left a note.'

H went through. Ronnie picked up the letter from a desk, and read:

To Whom It May Concern

The net is closing in. I have decided, now that my crimes are about to be revealed, to dispatch myself to hell before somebody does it for me. I have been made aware that my lifelong friend and partner in crime Lord Timothy Skyhill is responsible for the murder of my daughters. This is a consequence of the way we have lived our lives. I can take no more. I have been a weak man, and a bad man. I am ready now to accept the judgement of God.

Sir Basil Fortescue-Smythe.

'Fuck it,' said H, 'Kuznetsov has put them all in the picture. They'll know we're coming for them. We've got to get to the others before they do anything stupid as well.'

'Skyhill won't top himself,' said Ronnie. 'Think about his performance in that clip. And all those times you've seen him on the telly, giving it. The cunt is so full of himself it's a wonder he can stand up straight. There's no way he's going to top himself.'

'I hope you're right mate. OK, let's go and deal with Blunt,' said H.

86

Sir Peregrine Blunt was at home - an old pile outside Tunbridge Wells - considering his situation. He had been instructed by Skyhill, in the aftermath of Joey Jupiter's expose of the shenanigans in Thailand, to work with his friends at the War Office and the Press Association and get a D-notice issued. There was to be no uptake of Jupiter's findings in the news media, and his blog had mysteriously disappeared. Anyone who wanted to run with the story would risk being buried under a ton of hot bricks in the name of national security. Another cover up was now in full swing; the method was tried and trusted.

But they had not counted on H coming after them. He and Ronnie had now blown the usual order of business out of the water and Blunt, like the others, was dreadfully exposed. The message from Kuznetsov had shaken Blunt to the core. The game was up. H, to whose own son he had shown no mercy, would be on his way, soon.

Blunt had always lived alone. He had known little love or genuine companionship in his life. But he had spent a distinguished career dishing out severe justice to wrongdoers, and for that had at least earned respect in some quarters. But Kuznetsov had sold them all out, and now that would be gone. Gone. Along with everything else.

There was nothing else for it. He drained a bottle of brandy, took some rope chording from a curtain, made it into a noose, went into his conservatory and fitted the noose high, on the metal framework at the ceiling. He had seen enough botched jobs over the years - people making their problems worse in the long run by using doors, doorknobs, windows - to know you had to go high and solid. He stood on a chair. He had been depressed - quietly, desperately depressed - all his life. No one would miss him. He felt strangely calm as he pushed the chair away.

Crunch! He found himself, with a rush, in mid-air. An agony of writhing, jerking and gagging. His head exploded with flashing lights and his ears rang like cathedral bells.

Not long now.

Ronnie was first in; he smashed through a glass pane, barrelled across the floor and grabbed Blunt's legs, taking up the slack.

H was right behind him: 'Is he alive?'

Blunt's attention came back to the room. To the mortal world. The ringing in his ears subsided; he heard voices. He wanted to live - to return to earth and live forever. He was overcome with relief.

'Sir Peregrine,' he heard someone say, 'I've got a few questions for you. Answer them nicely and we'll get you down. Don't mess us about now. Simple questions, simple answers. Play the game and we'll take you straight to the hospital. Understood?'

Blunt nodded: yes.

'Is it the case that Timothy Skyhill ordered the murder of Tara Ruddock?'

Blunt nodded: yes. He tried to speak, and in a low whisper said 'Yes. But I never knew...the Russian has only just told me.'

'OK,' said H, 'next question: a young policewoman has been abducted. We think also by Skyhill. Do you know about this? Do you know where she is?'

Blunt nodded: no. Fear and despair rose within him.

I've got to give them what they want, but...

'I know nothing about this,' Blunt whispered. 'No abduction, no. Skyhill in charge...the "tidying up" activities all between him and his people. He has a former MI6 man with his own team.'

'OK Sir Peregrine, last question' H said gently, 'think very carefully before you answer this one. Don't hide anything from us now: where do you think he would have her taken? You must have had some hideaways for your little parties? No?'

Blunt was getting weaker.

'Let me down, please. I need to sleep,' he whispered. He was becoming hard to hear.

'Absolutely. But where would he have taken her?'

Blunt searched his brain; it was not exactly fizzing with oxygen. 'We used…a place in Leysdown, on the Isle of Sheppey…a clubhouse on an old caravan site…and an old warehouse on a wharf, in Grays.'

'Grays in Essex, Sir Peregrine?'

'Yes.'

'OK, thank you for your cooperation Sir P. Let him down now Ron. I'll phone an ambulance,' said H, turning to go into the house.

Blunt breathed a sigh of relief. Ronnie lifted him high, high, higher…and with a mighty guttural roar threw him as high as he could. Blunt rose into the air, as if in slow motion, and came down much faster, with a massive stomach churning CRACK!

H heard it in the other room, and surged back into the conservatory.

'Ron!' he screamed, 'what have you done? What the fuck have you done?'

243

87

The information from Blunt had given Amisha a lifeline; a lifeline H intended to grasp and haul in with every ounce of energy inside him. Back at Ronnie's flat he laid out a large map of London and surrounding areas.

'Skyhill can wait. There's only one game in town now. If Amisha's still alive we'll find her tonight,' he said. Leysdown and Grays were both areas he knew well.

Leysdown, just far enough out of London to dupe south London kids arriving on holiday that they'd arrived at an exotic location by the sea, rather than a dead-end outpost on the south side of the Thames Estuary. Grays, 20 miles east of central London on the north side of the river, through the Dartford Tunnel and a couple of miles off the M25. It was said in repeated opinion surveys to be one of the unhappiest places in England, although H had no idea why. He'd always rather liked it there.

Ronnie said 'H we're going to need manpower. We can't cover everywhere.'

'Quiet Ron, I'm thinking.'

A plan of action crystallised in H's head. He called Confident John.

'John, do you know anyone in Medway, Sheppey, especially around Leysdown area?'

'I've got one or two old mates down there, yes. Why?'

'Call them. Ask them to have a root about on the old, disused caravan sites...Look for anything going on where there shouldn't be. Any dodgy looking types. Anything, anything at all. There's a 50/50 chance Amisha's there. Tell your mates there's a young woman's life at stake. This is very urgent John.'

'OK, will do H.'

'What about those bits and pieces me and Ronnie asked for?'

'I got hold of two semi-automatics, a few grenades - stun grenades, like Ronnie said - and some smoke bombs. I've also got a couple of long trench coats and some balaclavas. I got them on tick off the Albanians.'

What a fucking turn up.

'Blinding. On our way,' H said.

'Let's go Ron.'

H filled Ronnie in on the plan of action as they sped back to Bermondsey.

'Blunt gave us two locations. Amisha might be somewhere else completely - if that's the case then she's as good as dead. All we can do is assume it's a 50/50 she's either in Grays or Leysdown. Grays is nearer and I know it well, did a bit of work there not long ago. There's a couple of deserted warehouses. If she's there that's where she'll be. I'm sure of it. If not we move on to Sheppey. About another 45 mile.'

'H, this might be too much for us, have you considered that? They're probably mob handed and tooled-up. We're not spring chickens anymore mate. Amisha will stand more chance if you call this in.'

'Listen Ron, think it through mate. I'm suspended. Skyhill has his fingers everywhere. For all I know he's already having people build a case of trumped up charges against me. If I can manage to get someone to take this seriously, which is unlikely, it'll be a day before they act. If Amisha's still alive I'm pretty sure she doesn't have a fucking day left.'

They pulled up outside John's. H was in the zone, thinking clearly, quickly, crisply. After the dash up the stairs to John's flat he returned with the goodie bag. He and Ronnie checked the guns were fully loaded and in good order. The pistol John had got for him earlier was also in the car. H trousered it.

'Only one bullet left in this Ron, but every one counts,' he said as he jumped into the car and headed east towards the Dartford Tunnel.

Ronnie sat, pensive, as the bright lights of the London evening whirled past and his manic driver accelerated, broke, shifted gear and ducked in and out of the traffic with the fearlessness and unconditional focus of a kamikaze pilot on a mission.

'Woah, be careful or we'll never get to Grays alive,' said Ronnie as H jumped a red light and swerved out of the path of an oncoming lorry, broke sharply, slammed the car down a gear, regained control and pushed his foot back onto the accelerator.

But H wasn't listening, his whole being concentrated now on his destination, on a single objective. They'd arrived at the last chance saloon and this was the last throw of the dice for Amisha. Inside his guts were churning faster than a washing machine on top speed and his heart was pounding. But these feelings never controlled H, never slowed him down or held him back or made him fearful. Instead they spurred him on, drove him to action, zoned him into the present emergency.

The near miss had snapped Ronnie out of his pensive mood. He felt like he was going into battle, like it was 1982 revisited. But this was London in the here and now, not the south Atlantic in the dim and distant past. Here he was, all these years later, following the best friend he'd ever had into battle. Some things never change, he thought, as H jumped another red light, navigated a slip road and launched the car onto the motorway that led to the Dartford tunnel.

'Ten minutes Ron, ten more fucking minutes. Get your head straight.'

88

Amisha hadn't lost touch with reality entirely, but normal awareness of the world around her had faded. She wasn't entirely certain about anything, about where she was, what she was saying or how she had wounded up in the torture chamber of this repulsively sweaty sadist.

But they had come to a point past which she could not go and, after hours of relentless punishment, she gave up H and Confident John.

'I… sent the files to…H…Detective Inspector Harry Hawkins.'

Despite her tenuous links with life a profound remorse cut deep as soon as she uttered the words.

'Ah, our tough, no-nonsense "coppers' copper", no longer of the yard, I understand. I do hope you're not expecting him to come riding through the door at any moment on a white charger. We're already onto him, I'm fairly confident he will not be around much longer. But where, exactly, did you send the information? And how many copies did you make?'

'One copy. I sent it to…to… a friend of H's. John Viney.'

'I see. And where does this John Viney live?'

'Bermondsey.'

'Address, my dear, address and full name.'

'I can't remember …he's just John, Confident John…I copied everything from the address book on my computer.'

'I see. How convenient, given you have so expertly wiped your hard drive.'

He began to lower the sack again. Amisha screamed a scream of despair, deep and penetrating enough to wake the dead.

'No… please, please… if I knew I'd tell you.'

The plea fell on deaf ears; the plump man smiled, with the satisfaction of the Devil when another lost soul arrives at the gates of hell. He lowered the sack with sadistic glee. After another four rounds of drowning, screaming, gasping and lost consciousness, Amisha once again jerked back to life.

'Now, if you recall I asked you for the address of this John.'

Amisha genuinely couldn't remember the address. So she made one up, a number and a road she remembered somewhere in Bermondsey. Anything to make him stop.

The plump man took a note of the address, went over to and opened the door of his torture chamber and passed it to one of the goons posted outside. 'Go and check this address, see if you can find the files. Report back to me directly, no phone calls.'

He now refocused on his victim.

'Well, while we await the result of my associate's investigation I think it's about time you and I got a little better acquainted.'

He had never had anything that could be termed a relationship with a woman - healthy or otherwise - in his life. Despite his pleasant voice he'd always found it impossible to connect with individuals on a human level and had only ever had sex with two categories of people, prostitutes and victims. It was the latter that really got him going. There was something about inflicting pain, about watching a human suffer, about having absolute power. He wasn't really sure. He didn't really care. All he knew was he was as about as excited as he had ever been.

Amisha lay strapped down and helpless, physically exhausted and mentally broken; but she knew what was coming next. How much more could she take? She was filled with loathing and nausea as her torturer ran his hands over her body, ripped off her shirt and slobbered at her breasts. He loosened the straps that held her legs in place and climbed on top of her.

While the rape was in motion her mind shut down, as she tried to blank out what was happening.

To increase his enjoyment he lifted her head by the hair and slapped her face with venom. He wanted tears, to see her cry and beg. He slapped her again and a trickle of blood made its way from her mouth to her chin. But the tears and the begging didn't come.

After he'd finished he stood over her, merciless and triumphant.

'Don't worry my dear, as soon as we find the files you printed we can put you out of your misery.'

Amisha no longer cared. Her mind was empty, detached, oblivious of space and time. The plump man stood, fascinated by her suffering, observing her as if she were a specimen in some kind of diabolical experiment.

Eventually there was a knock on the door. The goon was back from Bermondsey: 'False information. Wrong address. A flat with an old lady and three cats. No files.'

'Oh, my poor dear,' said the plump man, and grinned from ear to ear as he retrieved his sack and watering can.

'Time for more fun.'

89

H and Ronnie were all focused concentration as they watched the blue car pull up outside the isolated and gated warehouse. A gangly, nefarious looking type with a gash across his face got out and made his way past the guards posted at the gate. He looked like he was on a mission as he walked swiftly through the warehouse door.

H followed and marked his movements. Through the door and left. Thirty seconds later H saw the ungainly silhouette pass several windows. A door opened at the far end; there was a conversation by the door with somebody he couldn't see. The door closed.

Through the door, left, up some stairs, door at the end.

H had got it right. After all the reconnaissance he'd done in the area he knew there were only a few places Amisha might be. He and Ronnie had pulled up half a mile down the road, scouted the area around the riverfront and found a bunch of moody looking types hanging about. H and Ronnie were now tucked in on the banks of the Thames watching the activities around the warehouse, seventy or so yards away.

With part one of the plan coming to fruition H's brain was moving as fast as it had done in that fateful moment in the south Atlantic.

Option 1: Wait it out. The sentries had no idea they were here. They could stay hidden, wait for the changing of the guards so they knew how many were inside, and then strike with a fuller knowledge of their enemy.

But there was no time.

Option 2: Scale the fences from the rear. Ronnie was a lifelong gym bunny and could maybe make it if he could avoid impaling himself on the railings. But H knew the chances were not great, and he didn't want them to split up; they needed to provide cover for one another.

Option 3: Full frontal assault. The option H preferred, once he'd discounted all the others.

'What's the plan then H?' whispered Ronnie.

Old Father Thames, murky and laden with sewage, rolled on behind them, H turned and stared at his friend. They'd been here before, the two of them: outnumbered, outgunned and alone. Falklands images flashed through his mind and he remembered the young men he had killed there. He'd spent a lifetime coming to terms with it. They were men like him, under orders and ready to die for their country, protecting and doing the bidding of their politicians. But Falklands images didn't incapacitate him this time round. He was too zoned-in to the present danger and the scum in front of them had made a choice. In H's world that made them fair game.

Ronnie's piercing blue eyes sparkled with life from inside his balaclava. He was all charged up and ready to go, fuelled by a burning hunger for revenge.

No fucking pep talk needed this time.

'We charge up out of here. You go left, I go right. I'll toss a grenade into the courtyard. You take care of the two on your side and I'll do the same on mine. Through the door, left, up the stairs. Whoever's inside gets the same treatment. Bob's your uncle.'

Some fucking plan.

The two blood brothers burst forth from the riverbank. The four sentries outside the warehouse could hardly believe their eyes as two oddballs dressed in trench coats and balaclavas came charging up at them, like two new life forms emerging from the primordial soup, raw and untamed.

'What the fuck is this?' Said one of them, unsure whether he should laugh or be afraid. He would have laughed, if not for the fact that a hand grenade exploded behind him and a bullet ripped through his throat. In the aftermath of the illuminating light thrown out by the explosion, rifle shots were being discharged with devastating accuracy, and the four men went down before they could put up a fight.

H and Ronnie entered the compound and rushed the warehouse door. But they'd missed a trick: behind them a fifth guard appeared from the shadows and started firing. They'd had no idea he was there and were now no more than target practice, like sitting ducks at a funfair. They hit the deck, but it looked like there was no way out of this one; they had pushed their luck too far. Ronnie started to say something…and there was a flash from a weapon being fired by someone coming up from the river.

H and Ronnie swivelled as the guard fell to the floor, and saw smoke emanating from the gun in Graham Miller-Marchant's hands.

Fuck me, saved by the Manbot. What a turn up.

'How the fuck did you get here?' Said Ronnie.

'You've been causing absolute havoc all over London; following you two is not exactly rocket science.'

90

'No time for niceties now, boys,' said H as he continued his surge towards the warehouse, rifle at the ready.

Through the doors turn left - No problem.

Up the stairs to the second floor - No problem.

Into the warehouse area - Big Problem. Very big problem.

H scanned the large, open warehouse area as he emerged at the top of the stairs, and was immediately aware of the positions of all remaining seven sentries; they were hunkered down behind overturned tables, weapons at the ready. He launched a grenade as he dived into the exposed area at the top of the stairs. Ronnie, close behind him, dived and rolled across the floor, spraying bullets left, right and centre. Their enemies, whoever they were, were stunned by the sheer audacity and speed of the attack.

Most were dead by the time Miller-Marchant stopped at the top of the stairs. He wasn't about to dive into the line of fire but made a useful and necessary third man as he took careful aim and picked off a shadowy figure coming back for more.

The warehouse went quiet. H and Ronnie lay on the floor, their eyes scanning for movement of any kind. All was silent and still. Then Ronnie looked at H, and realised the big man had been hit. He crawled to his friend's side.

'It's a flesh wound, H. Nothing to write home about. I'll stick a tourniquet on it, you'll be as right as rain.'

He started to tear strips off his shirt, but H shouted 'Door Ronnie, door at the end.'

Ronnie signalled to Graham to finish the tourniquet and checked the door. Locked from inside. He charged at it and gave it everything he had. It didn't budge.

'Stand back,' said Graham. He aimed his pistol and blew the lock. The door opened and H moved as if the bullet in his leg was no more than a splinter, leading the newly formed gang of three into the torture room.

91

H poured into the room like pent up water bursting through a dam, ripping off his balaclava as he took the situation in: waterboarding gear, a snivelling little plump man cowering in a corner and, in the middle of the room Amisha, naked, bound and bloodied.

She's alive, she's fucking alive.

He felt a rush of emotions he found impossible to process and control. Relief. Joy. Love. Hatred. An almost overpowering sense of guilt. He had got her involved and then failed to protect her. This was on him. No doubt about it.

Amisha came to and their eyes met. H felt like his heart was going to explode. H walked over to her, laid down his rifle and loosened her straps. He took off his coat and lay it over her. She wrapped it around herself and stood up; a single tear rolled down H's face as they embraced.

He didn't know what to say. Whereas danger spurred him to action, the kind of emotions he was feeling now left him speechless and frozen. He kissed Amisha's forehead tenderly and squeezed her tight, letting her know she was safe now, that they couldn't hurt her anymore.

She was weak and shaking and barely had the strength to talk, but she needed to say something, to get it out in the open straight away.

'Guv, I'm sorry. I'm so sorry. He broke me, I gave him your names. You and John.'

Later, whenever H thought back to this moment, it filled him with admiration and respect for her. After all she'd gone through the first thing she thought of was saying sorry, apologising because these bastards broke her, these experts in torture, this merciless fucking scum.

But for now her words turned a switch on in his brain. It was the switch marked KILL.

You're sorry. You're fucking sorry.

Despite his injured leg H now moved swiftly across the room, retrieved his rifle, surged towards the corner and smashed the butt of his weapon into the plump man's face. Teeth clattered from his gums as his cheek bones crumbled like chalk.

Fucking coward. Snivelling little fucking piece of shit.

H smashed at his face twice more with the butt and then pointed the business end of the rifle at his head.

'Harry, no, not in cold blood,' shouted Graham. H gave him the look, but Graham swallowed hard and stood his ground. The Little Manbot had come of age.

Fuck me, he really has grown a pair.

'Look H, I know you have a strange code that I don't purport to understand, but gunning a man down in cold blood, is that really part of it?'

H ignored him. He lifted his rifle and took aim.

'No' shouted Amisha.

But this was not another plea for clemency. 'Let me do it,' she said.

H and Ronnie looked at each other. They were both in a state of mind in which the old rules no longer applied. H pulled the revolver out of his belt and gave it to her.

'Only one bullet left Ames. An eye for an eye or the justice of the courts. Bear in mind it was Skyhill who put you here. It's down to you.'

H, Ronnie and Graham stood frozen to the spot. Amisha released the safety catch and pointed the gun at her defiler's head.

'What's your name?'

'Malcolm' said the snivelling sadist, shaking with fear and curling up into a ball. Blood oozed out of the wounds in his shattered, gurning face.

'Mercy, please, mercy,' he whimpered.

Mercy. Amisha was no longer sure she knew what that meant. What mercy had he shown her? He had tortured her to within an inch of her life. Raped her. Defiled her.

Yet she was an officer of the Metropolitan Police Force. The first of its kind in the modern world. She had sworn to uphold the law and to protect the people of this great city. She had taken the oath seriously; it meant something, something deep and necessary. She had sworn to help keep the law of the jungle at bay.

For a full 45 seconds she pointed the gun at her defiler's skull, trying to resolve the moral conflict raging inside her. She had always believed revenge should play no part in justice. But then she had never been raped or tortured.

She turned her gaze to H, looking for some kind of inspiration, some direction on which path to take, and realised the choice was hers.

'Down to you,' he'd said.

She returned her gaze to the grovelling lump on the ground before her.

He had no doubt what he would do, in the same situation, and his life flashed before his eyes; the prelude to his final moment on earth. But Amisha had already made a different call. She reset the safety catch and passed the pistol back to H without taking her eyes from 'Malcolm.'

'You're pathetic,' she said, 'fucking pathetic.'

She sat down. 'Malcolm' whimpered. Graham gave a sigh of relief. H stood brooding.

Ronnie was agitated. 'Still one more bit of business to conclude tonight H,' he said.

'Yep' said the big man, holding his leg.

'We have to sort this out,' Ronnie continued, 'before Skyhill hears about Old Shitbreath and Blunt and surrounds himself with what's left of his little army.'

H wanted to stay with Amisha, to take her home to Olivia. To care for her.

'Listen,' he said as he gave her another hug, 'things are going to be tough, really tough. I know that much. But you'll get through it. We'll get through it.'

Sirens wailed in the distance. H turned to Graham,

'Graham, will you look after Amisha, and clear this fucking mess up?'

'How am I going to explain all this away?'

'You'll think of something. You're a clever boy... a good man. Thanks.'

And with H and Ronnie turned, quickly, and disappeared into the night.

92

The reception began at eight o'clock sharp. One of the sexy, super-high, glittering skyscrapers dotted across London's new skyline. A star-studded charity event; penguin suits and evening dresses, big-name after dinner speakers.

The great and the good in attendance, among them Lord Timothy Skyhill; showered, shaved, suited and booted, fresh from the airport. It was business as usual for Lord T: the cover up was in motion, and it was now time to hide in plain sight, in the most public way possible. This was going to be a big night. A very big night.

The bullshit train began to roll: five lavish courses, and the world's best wines; the purring, preening hubbub of the global city's social and political elite; the self-congratulatory speeches, the competitive charity-donation pantomime; the climactic highlight of the great peer of the realm's speech.

His stomach full, Skyhill leaned back into his chair and scanned the room, nodding at familiar faces, searching for others. No Basil. No Peregrine. But other friends, new and old, were in attendance - from people he had known at school, and through every stage of his glittering career and public life, to the nouveau riche types from all over the world who had cultivated him more recently: his friends from the East, the Gulf; the bankers, the property developers, the oligarchs, the princelings, the money getters and launderers of the new global economy.

His sense of control, of achievement, of wellbeing, was complete. He was the daddy here - the sparkling room, filled with movers and shakers, waited expectantly for his after dinner turn. His routine was one of the most popular on the circuit. No one could touch him.

H and Ronnie pulled up and parked in a side turning off Borough High Street just before nine thirty. Ronnie checked the boot and readied the gear; he reloaded for both of them and got their bits and pieces together. He looked back inside the car. H was breathing hard and looking woozy. Ronnie tightened the tourniquet around the big man's leg and said: 'All set then H?'

'All set, son, all set. Don't you worry about that.'

Ronnie handed him a baseball cap and a pair of sunglasses: 'Alright…put these on now, we'll get balaclava'd up when we get a bit closer.' They both knew the score: London, CCTV surveillance capital of the world. And then some.

H was feeling terrific, the best he'd felt in years. The adrenalin from the battle in the warehouse, plus whatever body chemicals were dealing with the pain in his leg, were fizzing. More than that, Amisha was safe, Olivia was safe and, though Little Ronnie was in the shovel, bang in trouble, he'd deal with that later. The main thing, though, was that he and Ronnie had done the business; they had stood up, as proud, dignified warriors, and done what had needed to be done when nobody else would.

It was time now to finish the job.

Ronnie pulled his cap on, buttoned up his coat, helped H out of the car and said 'Right, let's go and deal with this bastard.'

93

They entered the building via the back way and set their plan in motion. Their luck was in; the porter on duty was an old-school looking local. H played him like a violin. At the sight of the two tooled up men in balaclavas bursting into the building the porter had instinctively reached for a button. But H got to him before he hit it.

'Stop! Slow down old son. We're SAS,' said H, flashing a shield, 'don't do anything. Get this door behind us locked - no one in or out. Stay calm. Stay away from all your buttons till I've put you in the picture.'

The porter did as he was told, and sat back in his chair.

'What's your name then captain?' asked H.

'Bill. I…'

'Shh, just listen. Did you serve Bill?'

'Yes.'

'Who with?'

'I was in the Navy, I…'

'OK, good,' said H, 'So we all know where we stand. You're going to have to work with us on this, Bill. There's a terrorist incident shaping up on the 40th floor. They've got hostages and they're threatening to blow the place to bits. We haven't got long. Our main blokes are going in the front way in five minutes. We're scouting ahead. I want you to knock out all the lifts except the one we go up in. Keep all the doors down here locked. Under no circumstances press any buttons or communicate with anybody until we get back down. There's a total communications lockdown in effect. And keep yourself out of sight. Any questions, old son?'

'No, I…'

'No time now mate. I'll buy you a pint later, after we've dealt with these bastards. Sound like a plan Bill?'

Bill nodded, and slid down behind his counter.

The lift began to swish them up to 40th floor; they looked one another in the eye, shook hands, hugged. No words. They came to a halt. 'Hard and fast mate, hard and fast!' roared Ronnie, as they burst into the corridor and ran to the Diamond Room.

They crashed in together, side by side. H administered a light slap to the security guard and lobbed a stun grenade into an empty corner. That did the trick, no need for shouted threats. Everyone went down immediately, and jostled for space under the tables. Ronnie had already scanned the room for Skyhill. 'Got him. Top table. The fat bastard's under the top table.'

A moment of eerie calm fell over the room, as the initial shock subsided.

'No one gets hurt except Skyhill Ron, not a scratch on anyone else,' H had said in the car.

' 'course,' Ron had replied.

But his blood was up now, and his hatred for Skyhill was in danger of running away with him. H hunkered down close to him and whispered 'Stick to the plan Ron, stick to the plan. I'll take care of the room - you grab the target.'

Ronnie was haring across the room before H finished speaking, locked onto his prey. H laid down three smoke bombs and chucked in another stunner for good measure. The sprinkler system kicked in and the alarm sounded. The room was a maelstrom of smoke, wailing, moaning, coughing and crying. H positioned himself at the lift and waited.

He didn't have to wait long. Ronnie reared up out of the chaos, hauling, pushing and kicking a panting, dishevelled, crawling Skyhill by his trouser belt.

'Going up?,' said H.

'Yep,' said Ronnie. 'Observation platform. I think His Lordship here wants to take in the view.'

94

Far, far below they could make out a crowd forming, and cars and vans arriving, sirens wailing. It wouldn't be long before the chopper arrived. No time to lose.

The day's efforts were catching up with H. But his friend was still on fire, all business. H bent over and caught his breath as Ronnie, saying nothing, pushed and kicked Skyhill towards the window. Ronnie had never been a man for speeches; and this was not a movie. Skyhill had killed Tara, and spent decades ruining the lives of innocent children. For these crimes he was now going to pay, before his protectors could save him and make it all go away.

Not this time, fat bollocks. This time justice will be done.

'He's going over, H' said Ronnie, coming to a halt. 'I'm launching this sack of shit over the edge. His Lordship is going to fly. He'll have plenty of time on the way down to say his prayers.'

For H, the room was starting to spin; he was weakening, and the enormity of what they'd done, and were about to do, blew through him like a gale: 'Ron, are you...?'

'No H. No need for any of that. No words. He's going over. End of. Get yourself into the corridor. These windows are shatterproof, they reckon. Things are going to get a bit lively in here.'

Ronnie pulled a limpet mine out of his trenchcoat and attached it to the glass. H hadn't seen a limpet mine in years; he sure as hell hadn't seen this one.

Where the fuck did John get hold of that?

Skyhill was on his knees, blubbering quietly to himself, otherwise silent. Where were his speeches, his know-it-all pronouncements, his-larger-than-life imperiousness now? Ronnie dragged him into the corridor and motioned for H to follow him. Ronnie seemed to have swelled up to twice his usual size. He was now larger than life, glowing, exultant.

'Remember how it goes H,' he said, 'head down, ears covered. Stay down till everything settles. Move a bit further along the corridor mate - better safe than sorry.' He went back into the observation area, attached the mine and returned to the almost unconscious H, now losing blood again out of his leg, and the whimpering Skyhill. Heads down. BOOM!

Ronnie dragged Skyhill back to the window, and with an almighty, vein-popping effort summoned all his strength and heaved him up, up, up and through the hole in the glass. 'Thank you and goodnight, you horrible, no good cunt,' he said, as Skyhill began, slowly at first it seemed, to cascade down the irregular side of the building, wailing and slobbering as he went. His Lordship had been a lump in life, and now he was a lump in death, hugging the building on his way down and bouncing off it three times as he hurtled towards the ground. God alone knew what kind of mess he was going to make down there.

The crowd gasped; the sirens wailed; the searchlights continued to sweep the night sky; the chopper arrived.

Ronnie was breathing hard - it had taken an enormous physical effort to send Skyhill to meet his maker - and now he sank to his knees, closed his eyes and said a silent prayer for his lost, beautiful wife.

95

H was feeling weak now. He crawled, through howling wind and roving searchlights, over to the shattered window. And he saw through narrowed, weary eyes the lights of London, stretching out in all directions as far as the eye could see. Huge, ancient, unknowable London, the city he loved and had hardly been out of in thirty years. He thought of its people, swarming and heaving night and day, of their troubles, their joys. The multitudes of poor and rich, low and high - it seemed like all the world was living here now, struggling to gain a foothold and get a living, to survive or flourish, to love and be loved; here, at the centre of things. The greatest city in the world.

He had done everything he could to protect the safety and dignity of its people, and to avenge the wrongdoings of evil men. But he was tired now and close to sleep, and only dimly aware of what was happening when Ronnie, strong and reliable as an ox, lifted him high onto his shoulder and said 'Right H, let's get the fuck out of here.'

Epilogue

Little Ronnie Hawkins was forced from the safety and security of his dreams by the clanging of the lock on the door of his cell. Dragusha was already awake, going through his usual morning press-ups and sit-ups.

'Take out slops. Make tea,' he ordered.

Ronnie had quickly learned that there were advantages in accepting Dragusha's protection. Firstly, he was still alive. Secondly, he hadn't had the fuck kicked out of him for over a month, and thirdly Dragusha could ensure they had a few luxuries like tea, chocolates and, most importantly, synthetic weed. The Black Mamba was not doing him a massive amount of good, but it got him off his head. And that was where he needed to be.

As Ronnie carried out his master's bidding he felt the eyes of hatred penetrate him. Despite this being an everyday occurrence he still couldn't get used to it. He found it difficult to understand the true hierarchy in the prison, given so few people spoke to him.

One of the few people willing to speak to him, Peter O'Reilly, was an aging Irishmen his father had put away many years ago. He didn't have the anger or the lust for vengeance many of the others had, and he didn't seem to be scared of anybody.

'Listen son,' he said in the exercise yard one wet Saturday afternoon, '…I hear it was your old man that put Dragusha away. So why this fucker is protecting you I have no idea. Be careful son, be very careful. You're just a pawn in his game.'

But with half the inmates baying for his blood there was nothing Ronnie could really do, except what Dragusha told him to. They didn't speak much, except when Dragusha gave him orders; he was never allowed to sit with or talk to his protector's inner circle. He sat alone at breakfast, walked alone at exercise time and did whatever little jobs he was given:

slopping out, making the tea, delivering Black Mamba and whatever else to Dragusha's customers.

So Ronnie knew he was a mere pawn in Dragusha's game. But every night, as he lay down and pulled the covers over his head, he remembered the advice his dad had given him many years ago, when he was teaching him how to play chess:

'Don't waste your pawns, son; they might seem powerless but at the end of the game the outcome often depends on them.'

Thank you for reading our book. If you enjoyed it, won't you please take a moment to leave us a review at your favourite online retailer or book review website?

Thanks!

Garry and Roy Robson

Other Titles in this Series

London Large: Bound by Blood

Mass murder stalks the land. A damaged, hurting cop at war with his son. One last shot at redemption.

Bound by Blood is the second book in the London Large crime thriller series, featuring the exploits of Detective Inspector Harry 'H' Hawkins, an old-school London copper in a new world. H is only just back at work after a mental and physical breakdown when pop superstar Bazza Wishbone is murdered in the dead of night in a top London hotel. As the whole world looks on in horror H investigates the crime in the only way he knows how; he embarks on a full-blooded, uncompromising search for the truth.

But the truth can be brutal. As the investigation gathers pace H discovers that his own neglected son has been sucked into the international crime ring responsible for one of the worst mass murders in British history, and has been turned against his father.

H's mission is now no longer merely a search for a killer but also a quest to save his boy and deal with the man who has corrupted him. As events move towards their climax H is faced with a trio of extraordinary challenges: can he find the killer of Bazza Wishbone, get to the truth about the twenty bodies discovered in a mass grave in Kent, and find and reconnect with his son before he is spirited out of the country – or worse?

If you like the hard-boiled, gritty and action packed novels of Martina Cole, Stephen Leather and Andy McNab you'll love Bound by Blood – let it take you through a thrilling, rollercoaster ride through the dark underbelly of criminal London.

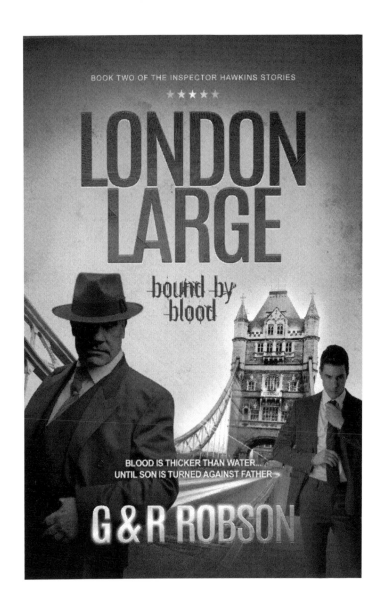

★★★★★

LONDON LARGE

bound by blood

BLOOD IS THICKER THAN WATER...
UNTIL SON IS TURNED AGAINST FATHER

G & R ROBSON

1

This was his time. At this moment in his life he could have anything he wanted; women, yachts, a mansion with a swimming pool in deepest Surrey. It was the women he wanted more than anything now- now he'd made it. After a short lifetime of dreaming and praying for success here he was, on the top floor of The Ritz, overlooking the London skyline. He felt like London was all his - like he really owned it. A world of endless possibilities lay before him.

'Sort another line out will you babes?' he said to this month's impossibly sleek, skinny and beautiful supermodel girlfriend. Jacynta Packington nodded yes and carried on getting set for another night of fun and games in the marbled bathroom. That was where Bazza liked to go large. They'd met a few months before, at a celebrity bash to celebrate another number one single. Their whirlwind romance was near perfect for the times, a celebrity journalist's ideal story delivering a stormy on/off affair of two beautiful young stars at the top of their game. Since they'd met the tabloids had been filled with lurid tales of the affair, of the arguments and bust-ups and reconciliations, of the sex and the drugs, of their infidelities.

Kicking back, he recalled the previous week's centre spread in one of the red tops that gorge on celebrity relationships like vultures on the corpse of a slaughtered animal, and a wry smile spread across his face: 'Bazza Beds a Brace of Bouncing Beauties.' Sex God, he thought, No. 1 Party Animal. His world was moving faster than a tornado tearing up a row of houses, and it was a world full of low-hanging fruit - he hadn't even bothered to ask the names of the bouncing brace of beauties but had just picked them out of the scrum that had been lying in wait for him as exited the back entrance of another gig in another provincial town, a town he'd forgotten about as soon as he'd left it.

He hadn't yet reached the point where all the media hype annoyed him. In fact he loved it. He craved the attention that he felt was his due, now that he was one of the world's most marketable superstars. Jacynta had read the article of course, like she'd read all the others since they'd hooked up. But she had a career to build and being associated with the new Prince of Pop was doing it no harm at all. So she kept quiet - she'd take what she could before the relationship blew up once and for all. Faithfulness was most definitely not on the agenda.

Bazza had never been the sharpest tool in the box, and had dropped out of school at 16 after failing his exams. But he was an angular, blonde and blue-eyed boy with a finely chiselled face, had a passable voice after auto-tuning and just the right amount of late-adolescent arrogance to make him irresistible to the kiddies. And his backstory was spot on: raised in an utter dump by a single mum after his father overdosed on barbiturates, in and out of trouble with the police as a boy, a proper little tearaway. Redeemed by his love of music. The British public ate it all up and begged for more, voting for him in their millions as he romped home as the winner of Britain Blazes Bright, the most watched talent show on T.V., the show that had propelled him to global stardom.

Within the space of a year Bazza Wishbone had gone from wannabe nobody to one of the biggest pop stars on the planet. He didn't know how long it would last but one thing was for sure - while it lasted he was going to gorge on success like a hungry wolf. He was going to gorge until he could gorge no more.

'Come on then babes, I'm ready for you,' he heard Jacynta call from the bathroom. The marbled bathroom. He bounded in to find her dressed in high heels, a dirty look and not much else. She bent down to get at the marching powder set out by the sink; Bazza followed suit.

The charlie hit the spot, and as the drug surged through his body he stretched out on the cool floor in a state of euphoria

276

and thought again of just how lucky he was. When Jacynta eased herself down to join him - lower, lower, as if in slow motion - he wondered if it was all a dream. Could he really be here, top of the charts, top floor of the Ritz, with one of the world's top supermodels getting on top of him? Her silky smooth blonde hair caressed his face; her lithely perfect body joined itself with his. His pulse raced, and as the blood pumped around his body he embraced her and proceeded to make the most of his good fortune. Yes, he could take whatever he wanted now - every minute of every day belonged to him, up here on top of the world

Much later, when they had finished, he curled up on the floor and Jacynta brought him a pillow and cover from the bedroom. Daylight was beginning to penetrate the gloom. He was tired now. 'If this is a dream I hope I never wake up,' he thought, as he closed his eyes in the hope that sleep would take him.

2

Outside the Ritz the killer stood behind a street light, head down low. It was cold and raining so he didn't look out of place wrapped up in his long trench coat, collar up, ensuring the hoodie he wore beneath his coat covered his face. He looked up at the top floor and considered his course of action. He knew without doubt his prey was in there. He wasn't sure of the room number, but he soon would be.

He'd been outside now for some time and had seen Bazza and Jacynta pull up in a limo, witnessed the army of photographers descend on him like a pack of braying hyenas, watched as the army of fans, all young girls, screamed with uncontrollable hysteria, with unquenchable desire. He wondered jealously what it was that fed such unthinking adoration. He watched as the celebrity boy-god of the moment, shielded by an phalanx of heavies, pushed his way through the crowd to the front of the hotel, stopped for a brief moment to wave and soak up the adoration and disappeared into a world of opulence the likes of which his adoring army would never see or know.

The killer decided to go for a walk, to let things settle down a bit. He set off up Piccadilly, took a stroll around Leicester Square and found one of the many pubs that adorned the side streets of London's West End, all the time keeping his head down low, hoodie on, shades pushed up on to the bridge of his nose. He ordered a pint of London Ale and supped slowly as he reflected on the task at hand.

He'd always been a small fish, and felt the resentment that small fish feel when they spend most of their lives swerving from the path of big fish. Tonight, however, would be different; tonight he was going to take down a big fish, and to hell with the consequences.

If Bazza wants to play in the big pond he better watch out for the fucking sharks.

Ping! He read the text that came through on his mobile and replied. The meet was on. The landlord called last orders so he went to the bar for a second pint. Just enough to steel his nerves but not too much to make him sloppy. He sat over it until the girl he'd been waiting for entered the pub. Svitlana Kovalenko caught his eye and moved across the room; she looked tired and drawn but was pretty with light auburn hair and a winning smile. She sat down next to him.

'Hello,' she said in one of those east European accents that had become so much a feature of the metropolis in recent years.

'Have you got it?'

'Yes,' she replied.

Svitlana worked on the desk at the Ritz. Like all the central London hotels it could only function now with employees from the far-flung corners of the world. So many employees started and finished their stint in the great global village each month that it was almost impossible for anyone in authority to keep up with the constant flux.

Finding a chancer who was just passing through to describe the layout and confirm Bazza's room had been easy. She had already provided the killer with a plan of the top floor suites. Two grand and a glass of wine was a small price to pay for the information he was about to receive. He had given her to believe he was a thief who'd like a chance to root about in some of the pricier rooms. What difference did it make to Svitlana? Where she came from, money talked. In any case she'd be heading out soon to take care of her ailing mother. She passed him an electronic key and a piece of paper with the name of a suite on it and walked her 'thief' through the plan. She would text when the coast was clear. In through the tradesmen's entrance, through the kitchen and up the lift reserved for staff. Turn left, 3rd door on the right, a quiet entry: game on.

He knew Bazza had the girl in tow, the one he'd seen him with in the papers. He didn't have a plan for her. He'd cross that bridge when he came to it. Then the retreat, back down in the same lift, lower ground floor, stroll out through the car park and melt into the London night. Head down, hoodie up, shades on tight. He knew he'd be on every CCTV in London, then on the TV and in the grainy pictures in every paper. He also knew the images would be useless as long as he kept his face under wraps.

Svitlana herself had no idea who he was. He looked at her with a mixture of desire and contempt, contempt for the unsuspecting, the weak and naive. She was pretty, no doubt about that, and in different circumstances he'd be all over her whether she liked it or not. But as the pretty girl left to return to her late night duties he had no regrets that the only thing he would be giving her tonight was an appointment with the grim reaper.

Time for the kill.

London Large: Bound by Blood is now available on Amazon.

London Large: Bloody Liberties

Book three of the Inspector Hawkins stories will be titled 'London Large: Bloody Liberties'. Details to be announced on the London Large website at: http://www.londonlarge.com
If you wish to be kept informed of the release date, please subscribe to the website.

London Large: Tipping Point

A father and son standing together. A brutal political conflict. Can they, and their bond, survive?

Tipping Point, set against the backdrop of the dark days of the 1974 three-day-week crisis and wildcat strikes, follows the fifteen-year-old Harry Hawkins through a crucial, formative week in his life. When his father persuades him to get involved in his strike-breaking activities Harry is launched onto a steep learning curve that will test both his ability to hold his own in a violent street-level struggle and his allegiance to his father.

Can, and should, the strike be broken? Will the son live up to the expectations of the father? Will they get out of the conflict in one piece?

Get your **FREE** copy of Tipping Point from the following link: **https://instafreebie.com/free/zLDJ3**

About the Authors

Roy and Garry Robson are, unsurprisingly, brothers from the Elephant and Castle, south east London.

Their father (variously a pig farmer, cab driver, haulage contractor and general ducker and diver) and mother (homemaker, cook and doctor's receptionist with a well-timed left hook) raised them and their siblings with some old fashioned south London working class values. These included hard work, respect for their elders, a willingness to duck and dive when required and a love of their city and their country.

One day, whilst enjoying a beer or two, they decided to write a Crime Thriller Series. They awoke the next day and were surprised to discover that they meant it.

Roy lives in Bromley and works as a Service Delivery Manager for an International IT Consultancy. Garry lives in Krakow and is now, of all things, a sociology professor. Both career choices served as a source of confusion and humour to their parents, who were born and raised in the days before computers and sociology professors existed.

Although Harry 'H' Hawkins, the protagonist of the London Large novels, shares some of their old-fashioned values, he is not based upon Garry or Roy, neither of whom would survive the first chapter of a Harry Hawkins novel.